CORNERSTONE

PHANTOM SQUAD SERIES

J.M. LEDUC

SUSPENSE PUBLISHING

CORNERSTONE
by
J.M. LeDuc

PAPERBACK EDITION
* * * * *
PUBLISHED BY:
Suspense Publishing

J.M. LeDuc
Copyright 2013 J.M. LeDuc

PUBLISHING HISTORY:
Suspense Publishing, Paperback and Digital Copy, June 2013

Cover Design: Shannon Raab
Cover Photographer: iStockphoto.com/Maica

ISBN-13: 978-1484188682
ISBN-10: 1484188683

ALSO BY J.M. LEDUC

Trilogy of the Chosen:
Cursed Blessing
Cursed Presence
Cursed Days

Novella:
Phantom Squad

Phantom Squad Series:
Cornerstone

Coming Winter 2013:
Sinclair O'Malley Series
Sin: Book One

DEDICATION

First and foremost, "Cornerstone" is dedicated to God, the cornerstone of my life, for never giving up on me even when I give up on Him.

I would like to further dedicate "Cornerstone" to the people who may not be in the epicenter of my life, but without them, my life would be empty. To my father, Arthur, whose life is the example I live by and the standard I strive to achieve. My mother-in-law, Birdie Tomlin, your love and acceptance means the world to me—I love you, Mom. My lifelong friends, Tom Woodford and John Shea, who were the foundation of my youth and are still the cornerstone on which I base all friendships.

And finally, to the two women who ground my life. My wife, Sherri, you are my inspiration. You give my life meaning—I love you more every day. To my daughter, Chelsea, you have taught me to *fly with my own wings.* I love you, Bella.

ACKNOWLEDGMENT

None of this would not be possible without the amazing team at Suspense Publishing.

John Raab, thank you for your expertise, your leadership, and your loyalty. I couldn't ask for a better publisher. Shannon Raab, thank you for . . . *everything*: your time, commitment, knowledge, skill, humor, and friendship. Starr Reina, my editor extraordinaire, thank you for your skill and for not killing me—figuratively or physically. Terri Ann Armstrong, you were and continue to be a light shining bright in all whom you touched. Thank you for sharing a tiny bit of your life with the Suspense family.

John D. Moore, thank you for your help in researching some rather obscure topics and for your and Mary Theresa's friendship.

PRAISE FOR J.M. LEDUC

"Stunning suspense. J.M. LeDuc's "Cornerstone" is the kind of book that will make you forget life's obligations and have you riveted to your chair flipping pages and making you believe you're actually an integral part of the Phantom Squad, the inner circle, protecting the President and loyal to the Ambassador to the power punched end."

—Sandra Brannan, author of the acclaimed *Liv Bergen Mystery Series*

"Perfect research as always; the in-depth facts regarding history and locations are right on the money. But the descriptions, the flow of this writer's work, allows readers to feel as if they are standing in the most revered locations on this planet. Not surprising, considering this is one of the most revered authors of our generation.

"What's the conclusion? "Cornerstone" is a TOP PICK for 2013 when it comes to action, emotion and pure entertainment!"

—Amy Lignor, author of the *Tallent & Lowery Series* & *The Angel Chronicles*

" "Cornerstone" is a tour-de-force political thriller and religious action-adventure steamroller, wrapped in all the fun of a TV espionage show like *24*, and all the mystique of pulp adventures like 'The Shadow.' On top of that, LeDuc has crafted a grippingly honest and raw emotional catharsis for several characters throughout, making this one a perfect addition to the Brent Venturi series, and an excellent jumping on point for new readers."

—Kane Gilmour, Bestselling author of "Ragnarok" and "Resurrect"

" "Cornerstone" by J.M. LeDuc brings us back to that ragtag group that you cannot help but affectionately consider family. Here we see the Phantom Squad after the Trilogy of the Chosen and watch Brent struggle with some of the worst pain he has had to deal with yet and thus go through another painful but necessary transformation.

"Just when Brent is ready to give up, he receives a message from the divine that gives him the push he needs to finish his mission. Although there is a religious base to this book (as with the previous trilogy) it is not so overpowering as to overtake it and definitely worth reading.

"Be prepared for tears with this heart wrenching story and an ending that leaves you wondering where this tale will go next."

—Carol "Pixie" Brearley author of *The Dark Angel Trilogy*

CORNERSTONE

PHANTOM SQUAD SERIES

J.M. LEDUC

PROLOGUE

One month ago

In one combustible moment, Brent's life became a tumultuous cascade of happiness and horror. He had witnessed the birth of his daughter and the death of his wife.

Two weeks ago

Eight years ago, after his first encounter with the Omega Butcher, a sadistic serial killer, Brent Venturi lost his identity. Emotional and physical scars forced a sabbatical from the team he led: The Phantom Squad. It was only through the peace he had found in God and in his hometown of Palm Cove that he was able to recover from his physical and psychological injuries.

He was once again sliding back down that slippery slope of despair into a deep, depressive abyss. The place he once ran to for tranquility no longer provided comfort. He spent his days alone and his nights wandering the streets.

The nightmares that once plagued his life, the nightmares he thought were in his past, once again tore a path through his subconscious mind. It was terrifying enough when his dreams brought visions of his own torture, but now, the visions and images were different. More vivid, more personal, more terrifying. The tortured was now Chloe. His nightmares were made worse by the images of blood: so much blood, pools of blood, on her, on him . . . everywhere.

When he did manage to fall asleep, Brent woke up in a pool of sweat and vomit, fearful that the wetness he felt was blood. Chloe's blood.

Agony was making him less of a man and more of a weapon of mass destruction.

CHAPTER 1

Present

Seven walked with a purposeful stride down the halls of SIA headquarters which made all other three-letter intelligence agencies seem like child's play. The sound of his footfalls as his heavy boots struck the tile floors reverberated in his ears like the base of a stereo. He heard it echo off the solid steel walls. As he walked deeper into the labyrinth, he looked up at the writing over the door that led to the inner sanctum.

We are called upon when others fail

He placed his hand on the black glass panel next to the steel door. Like all others in HQ, it worked by palmer recognition. A faint red line slid under his hand. The door's air lock disengaged. He repeated this maneuver multiple times as he descended further into the maze, finally arriving at his destination, the security office. Joan's lair.

Joan, an eclectic blend of bohemian and punk was Maddie Smith's personal assistant and a self-taught computer genius. Her office was nestled in the midst of SIA's security hub. A sea of computers and flat screen monitors filled every bit of desk and wall space. As he entered, she sat transfixed and stared at a video feed. The monitor she was glued to took up one entire wall and was embedded in three feet of concrete and steel.

"How long has he been there?" Seven asked.

Joan turned just long enough to acknowledge his arrival. "I arrived at o-eight hundred hours. The security clock shows he's been there since…"

"O-five hundred." Seven finished her sentence.

It had been the same pattern for the past ten days.

He stood behind her and watched Brent in the armory. Seven, like all of those close to Brent, was showing the signs of stress. In the past weeks, wrinkles from age crept into his face, like dried fissures on barren land.

He blinked the sleeplessness from his eyes. "Can you roll the tape back to when he arrived?"

"I can, but nothing has changed. Brent is still anal—a man of pattern."

Seven reached into the back pocket of his jeans and took out his tobacco tin. Watching the screen, he tapped the lid, shook loose the tobacco, and placed it between his lower lip and gums.

Joan looked at him, rolled her eyes and shook her head. "Much like yourself."

Seven smirked and spit in his empty coffee cup. "Oblige an old man," he drawled, "and run the tape."

"Yes, sir." Joan reached over with her left hand, nimbly fingered the keyboard, and brought up the tape.

"Finally, a woman who will listen to me."

"I hope that wasn't meant for me."

They both turned and saw Maddie standing in the doorway. Maddie Smith was the director of the SIA and Seven's wife. As always, everyone's eyes were glued to her—she was stunning. A voluptuous redhead who knew how to draw attention from both sexes. She embodied a 1950's movie starlet.

"Good morning, Darlin," Seven smiled.

"Good morning, Madam Director," Joan said.

Her piecing emerald green eyes focused on Joan. "Why so formal this morning?"

Joan shrugged. "Everything seems so formal since . . ." her eyes moistened, "you know."

Maddie's voice took on a saddened tone. She stood behind Joan, lightly rubbed her shoulders, and kissed the top of her head. "Yeah, I know, but I would feel better if you went back to calling me Maddie, or Mom, or the 'B' word that you mumble under your breath from time to time."

Joan wiped her tears and sniffed. "And what word would that be?"

"Beautiful," Maddie joked.

A partial smile surfaced on Joan's lips. "Oh, that 'B' word. Right."

"That's the first time I've seen you smile in weeks. It feels good." She looked at Seven expecting a sarcastic comeback, but he was glued to the screen. The look in her husband's eyes made her shiver. "What is it?"

"It's Brent's eyes. They're blank. Emotionless. It's as if he were on a squad mission."

"Is that so bad?" Joan said. "Isn't that the way you all look when you're engaged in training?"

Pointing to the monitor, Seven said, "This is different. Look at his jugular veins. His eyes may be expressionless, but the rest of him is about to snap."

Maddie drew in a deep breath as she watched the monitor. Blowing it out, she knew what she had to do. "We can't put the inevitable off any longer. Call the directorate and the Phantom Squad to a meeting at thirteen hundred hours and Seven," she waited for him to acknowledge her. "Get him there."

CHAPTER 2

Seven continued to stand next to Joan and watch what was happening on the screen. Brent Venturi was not only his best friend but also his superior. He was the leader of the Phantom Squad, a group made up of the five best soldiers regardless of which branch of the armed forces they were assigned or whether they were even in the U.S. military.

Seven sucked hard on his lower lip. He pulled as much nicotine as possible from the tobacco as he thought back over the past four weeks.

Brent had been through hell over the past twenty-eight days.

Seven squinted and pulled in his lower lip with more force, tasted the mint-flavored tobacco and spit in the empty cup. With a deep cleansing breath, he turned and exited the room. He couldn't put off the inevitable any longer.

Brent heard the footsteps in the hall outside the armory as he reloaded his Spring Armory 1911-A1 handgun. He knew it was Seven by the sound of his footfalls, just like he knew every other SIA employee by the sound of their steps. He also knew them by their breathing pattern, the sounds they made when they chewed, and any of their other 'tells.'

Brent's eyes, hollow from a lack of sleep, made the slightest glance towards the door. "Are you coming in or are you just going to stand there and watch?"

Seven walked forward and held a cup of black coffee at arm's length. Brent hesitated to take it.

After a few seconds, he put his gun and ammo clip down and reached for the cup, making eye contact for the first time. "You didn't brew this, did you? I don't think I could make it to the closest bathroom."

Seven's laugh was phlegm filled. He didn't answer, just maintained his position. Brent's body language didn't change. His words may have been light and sarcastic, but the rest of him said, 'go time.'

"Are you sure you didn't spit in this one?"

Seven smiled a tobacco-filled smile. "That's what makes it fun. You want to believe, but you never know." He spit in his ever-present cup. "It's like second hand smoke, only a little different."

A smile tried to make its way to Brent's face. It crept up like a slow rolling wave about to crest dry sand, but then it was gone. It was as if a smile or a momentary second of happiness would blaspheme the mourning he felt for his wife.

Seven released the clip from his own gun, checked the ammo, replaced it and pulled back the slide chambering a bullet. "Game on?" he asked.

Brent nodded. "Head or heart?"

Seven spit. "Let's make it interesting. I'll take the left shoulder, you take the right."

Brent put on his safety glasses and ear protection. Seven did the same.

Brent flashed back to his squad training.

Seven, the squad's training officer was a man of few words, so when he spoke you had better be listening. He wasn't one to repeat himself and he didn't take kindly to his men screwing up. The trainees had just been whittled down from four to three. Private Jensen, a muscle-bound, anger-filled 'roid' head had just been dismissed from training for not keeping his emotions in check.

Seven paced the lone airplane hangar at the base of the Teton Mountains. "As I was saying before I was rudely interrupted, emotions will get you killed on the battlefield." His words were garbled due to a mouth full of tobacco juice. His spit cup was missing from his left hand. "Soldier," he said, staring at Lieutenant Venturi, "pass me the cup by the wall."

Brent looked around and saw an old metal, military issued coffee mug about twenty feet away. "Yes, sir," he answered. He was about to take a step when Seven stopped him.

"Fetch it from where you're standing," he smirked.

Assessing the situation, Brent saw a three to four inch gap between the wall and the cup. He closed his eyes and went into a deep squat. As he meditated, he cleared his mind. He quickly went over each scenario until he decided on the best one. He stood up, withdrew his smallest knife from its sheath and threw it, much like a boomerang. It hit the far wall and deflected back towards the cup. The knife clipped the cup and pushed it about five feet forward. Without hesitation, he instinctively grabbed the largest, heaviest knife from its sheath and did the same. With its weight and size, it bounced off the wall with more force. It struck the cup with more speed, causing it to roll all the way to where Seven stood.

Seven bent down and picked it up. "Nice job, Professor." Eyeing the other two recruits, he said, "The difference between what Venturi did now and what Jensen did an hour ago is simple." He spit into the cup and pointed to Brent. "One acted on instinct and knowledge and one ..." he pointed to Private Jensen who was lurking outside the facility, "acted on emotion."

Seven paced the hangar, stopping to pick up Brent's knives along the way. He walked back to the group, stopped in front of 'the professor' and handed them back. He stared at each of the three men. "Burn this on your soul," he said. "Emotion will get you killed." He walked toward the door, turned toward the men and finished his thought. "Not some of the time ... all of the time."

Brent nodded toward Seven who stepped on a small toggle switch causing the paper human target, fifty yards down range, to start to move.

He and Seven faced the target and took a classic shooter's stance. A green light flashed which signaled them to begin. As the target moved, twisted, dipped and jumped, they emptied their guns in less than ten seconds. The target stopped at the far right side of the range. The only sound remaining was a faint clicking.

Brent's face was blood red, his teeth gnashed against one another and the blood vessels in his forearms looked like a road map. He gripped his pistol with white knuckled fury and continued to squeeze the trigger even though his weapon was empty.

Every muscle in his body was taut—rigid. Although his eyes were cold, Brent's demeanor was on fire. It wasn't intensity, it was near insanity. The expression shouted revenge. It was the look of a soldier about to snap.

Brent was indeed on a mission, one of self-destruction.

Seven gently reached over and slid the gun from his best friend's hands. "We're finished, buddy," he said.

Brent looked back with pupils dilated. A slight twitch was visible: the eyes of a killer. Facial muscles so tight, it seemed his skin would tear like a piece of paper. He opened his lips, but his teeth remained welded together. "I haven't even begun," he growled.

Seven watched as the man he most respected, unraveled in front of him. Brent turned to leave. Seven put his hand on his friend's shoulder, and stopped his progression. Brent snapped his head toward him. He was a man possessed.

"Easy, Colonel, you're among friends. This ain't no mission."

Brent's continence didn't change. He glared back. There was a void in his eyes where compassion once lived. He turned and walked out of the armory.

"Mandatory meeting at thirteen hundred hours," Seven yelled.

Brent stopped.

"Please," Seven chewed on his lower lip and spit again. "Don't make this even harder than it already is."

Brent gave a quick head nod and walked away.

Dejected by what just happened and about to leave, Seven looked down range. He flipped a switch, the target moved and stopped inches in front of him. His shots found its left shoulder. Brent's were kill shots. Twelve holes in the head of the target.

CHAPTER 3

Brent, dizzy on adrenaline, made his way to the locker room. He stripped down and eyed his reflection in the mirror. His eyes, sunken and surrounded with black circles almost took his breath away. He was a mere shadow of the man he had been just four weeks ago.

So much had occurred in the past month, it was hard to make sense of it all. He had spent his waking hours trying not to think about it, but the memories kept coming. Reflections of Chloe asking . . . no . . . begging him not to go in search of the Ark of the Covenant. Flashbacks of the operation in the Middle-East; one of the bloodiest objectives he had ever taken part in, and images of realizing that Red—second in command of the Brotherhood of Gaza—held Maddie and Chloe captive. He gripped the sink with both hands as the room began to spin. His vision clouded by the memory of Chloe's death, a death he was responsible for.

Thirteen hundred hours approached. The directorate sat in the conference room so still they could hear each other breathe. Maddie glanced up at the clock as the final seconds ticked away. Brent still hadn't arrived. As the second hand hit the twelve, everyone jumped at the sound of the door's air-lock. He stepped through in battle fatigues.

"Why the uniform, Colonel?" she asked.

"It just seemed fitting," he answered.

Maddie swallowed hard. He wasn't going to make this easy.

He eyed the table. It was round like all the tables inside SIA. Maddie believed everyone was an equal and therefore she insisted on round tables. No one should sit at the head of the table. After a while, everyone had staked out his or her own territory and always sat in the same chair.

Maddie observed Brent as he eyed the configuration of the chairs. She saw his expression change when he realized the one usually occupied by Chloe had been removed. As he dropped his head, Maddie could almost feel his heart break. No one made eye contact.

Before he could say anything, Maddie brought the meeting to order. As usual, Joan typed as the director spoke. Her fingers moved so fast and light on the keys the sound was barely audible.

"I've called a special meeting of the directorate because of the de—" she couldn't finish the word, "—because of the happenings of the past few weeks." She looked over at Bishop Jessop and gave a weak smile. "The first order of business is to welcome the new member of the board. I have asked the bishop to join the SIA directorate. Over the past year, he has shown his worth and resolve in matters dealing with national security and I believe he has earned that right. President Dupree and the National Security Council agree."

Maddie stood from her chair and walked to the front of the room. "We have always been open with one another, so if you have any objections to the bishop's appointment, speak now." The room was silent. "Good," Maddie said. "That matter is closed."

Her expression changed as she brought the next item up for a vote. "All our lives have been changed drastically due to the passing of our beloved Chloe. None more so than Brent's. I have asked the colonel to take some time off, but he didn't think it was a good idea." Her attention shifted toward him. "Colonel, I'll ask you once again, not as your superior, but as your friend, please accept a leave of absence from your duties so you can get your personal affairs in order." She hoped beyond hope that he would agree.

He looked up. Eyes dead. "No," was all he said.

Dejected, she inhaled and exhaled slowly through pursed lips. "Then you leave me no choice but to relieve you of your post." With anxious urgency, she continued. "All those in favor, raise your hands." Hers was the first to go up. Slowly, all but Joan raised theirs.

Brent noticed that even though the arms of those he considered family were raised, their heads were not.

Maddie stood tall and in a firm voice said, "The board has voted. Effectively immediately, Colonel, you are relieved of your duties at SIA and the Phantom Squad." Brent continued to look in her direction. He didn't appear to look at her, it was as if he was looking through her. His effect—nonexistent.

She turned and faced the room, "Any questions or comments?" No one spoke.

"I have one." Maddie swallowed hard as she heard Brent's voice. "Will I still have access to HQ?"

Maddie had hoped to address this in private, but that was no longer a possibility. "No, Colonel. You have one hour to remove your personal items from your office. Effective at fifteen hundred hours, codes will be changed and your palmer recognition will no longer be valid."

She turned her attention to Joan. "Please see that these changes are made in the security system."

Joan pinched her eyes closed, wrinkled her nose, and swallowed hard. "Yes, Madame Director."

Maddie turned her attention back to Brent. "Colonel Venturi, in ninety days, you will have the right to apply for reinstatement. If there are no further questions, this meeting is adjourned."

The director gathered her papers and quickly left the room. Brent took one quick glance around the table, gave a head nod and followed suit, leaving everyone else still seated in their chairs.

Seven spit in his cup. "That went well," sarcasm bled from his words.

"He's hurting," Bishop Jessop said. "Isn't there anything else we can do?"

"He's not responsive to anyone or anything," Seven replied. "He has declined to speak to the staff psychiatrist and won't talk about what happened. We were left with no choice."

"But . . ."

"But nothing, Padre," Seven scolded. "You run the homeless mission in Coral Cove. You know what it's like when someone comes in and won't accept any of the help you offer. I know for a fact that if they won't seek help, you personally ask them to leave until they've had a change of heart."

The bishop stood and flashed daggers at Seven. His arms flailed with every word. "Brent is no bum, drifter, alcoholic, or addict. He is our best friend." He pointed a finger in Seven's direction. "How many times has he pulled you from the fire? How many times has he saved your ass?"

Seven stood in the bishop's personal space. His breath could be felt on the bishop's face. "Plenty," he yelled back, "and that's why this is necessary. I'm trying to save his life."

Bishop Jessop pushed his way past Seven and headed toward the door. "You sure picked a coward's way to do it." He punched the scanner, but nothing happened. His head snapped back towards the room. "Will someone please get me the hell out of here!" he yelled.

Joan, closest to the door, laid her palm on the black, glass plate and opened the door. The bishop stormed out of the room leaving everyone stunned.

"The colonel left us with no choice," Joseph said.

Joseph Conklin was the agency's past director and the last Ambassador of the Endowment before Brent.

"His emotions may be void," Joseph said, "but underneath they are about to boil over. Any one of his decisions could cause irreparable harm to himself or anyone else in this room."

CHAPTER 4

Omar, dirty and tired from his trip to Pakistan, finally made it back to Khan Younis. The Palestinian stronghold along the Gaza Strip had been his home and base of operation for the past forty years. He made his way to al-Qal, the ruins of a once majestic building back in the time of the Ottoman Empire. He traveled the main floor and passed camera ready tourists snapping pictures of every conceivable thing. He made sure to blend in and more importantly to stay out of the eye of the lens.

The tourists turned left into a small stairwell that would take them to a gift shop. He lagged behind and turned right past a sign which read, "stay out: structure unstable." He smiled. He had placed the sign there himself. He wasted no time and traveled the centuries old hallways down into the bowels of the ruins.

In the deepest recesses of the catacombs, Omar had set up his headquarters. His accommodations were sparse. On one side of the room there was a cot and on the other side a desk and chair. He sat at his desk and thought back to the conclave that occurred just a few days ago. It had been necessary to bring the Brotherhood together. After the failure of securing the Ark Trilogy, the Brothers had been devastated. A new destiny had to be discussed. The organization had waited hundreds of years for the opportunity to get their hands on the arks. His second in command, Red, had been captured by

Colonel Venturi, this generation's Ambassador, also known as the Enlightened One, and a group known as the Phantom Squad. He personally held its leader responsible for defeating them.

Internal turmoil and grumbling of the brothers made it impossible for him not to show his face at the meeting. A thousand strong had shown up to find out what the Brotherhood of Gaza would do next, but most came to meet their mysterious leader. No one but Red had ever seen him before.

He drummed his long, boney fingers on the top of his desk and thought about his decision to bring in an outsider. He didn't like the idea, but he knew the man's knowledge of the enemy could prove invaluable. His long nails made a distinctive ticking sound as he continued to tap his desk.

"Excuse me, Holy One, but the visitor has arrived. What would you like me to do with him?"

Omar looked up at one of his minions. "Have the proper precautions been instituted?" he asked.

"Per your orders, sir."

"No one saw you enter al-Qal?"

"No, sir. I brought him through the concealed entrance."

"Then show him in."

The servant turned and ran out of the room. Moments later, a man—hands tied and blindfolded—was led into the room. Omar looked at his new ally. He was dressed in khaki pants and shirt. The clothing typical of a mercenary. Clothing Omar found offensive.

A buzz cut topped his scarred head and stubble covered the stranger's sharp jaw line. His muscular shoulders were visible under his loose clothing.

"You may dispense with the rope and blindfold," Omar ordered.

Once the man was freed from his confines, Omar ordered his underling to give them privacy.

"Was all that necessary?" the man asked.

Omar could hear a southern drawl. He nodded. "I'm sorry for any inconvenience it may have caused, but under the circumstances I saw no choice."

The man rubbed his wrists where the ropes had been and blinked repeatedly trying to get used to the dim light. Once adjusted, his eyes slowly moved about the room. "Nice digs ya got here." He oozed sarcasm.

It didn't escape Omar.

"One must do what one must in order to stay safe, I'm sure you understand that."

The man looked at his host. His eyes, daggers, pierced the old man. "Before we go any further, do you have what we agreed upon?"

Omar opened the top drawer of his desk and pulled out a thick envelope. "You Americans are direct. That has always been your problem."

His guest motioned with one hand for Omar to hand over the envelope.

As he counted the bills, Omar continued, "I suppose I should be grateful that you place financial gain above all else."

Satisfied with the cash, the American, known as Falcon, took a seat on the opposite side of the desk. "Whatever. Your message said that you would tell me what this is all about when I got here." He opened his arms wide. "Here I am. Care to explain?"

"My organization has been plagued by a group I wish to get rid of. If you are as good as they say you are, you may be able to help me."

"I am the best at what I do. Your *little* group of terrorists, The Brotherhood of Gaza, has developed quite a reputation, why do you need me?"

"I have learned that superior numbers don't always equate to victory." Omar stood and walked about the room. He clasped his fingers behind his back as he moved. He was still agile for a man in his eighties.

"Are we going to continue to play twenty questions or is there a point to this meeting?"

Omar stopped and faced Falcon. "Tell me, have you heard of a group known as the Black Militia?"

The visitor's hands balled into fists, his eyes squinted and his facial muscles twitched. "I may have heard of them."

Omar decided to press the subject. "And do you know what they call themselves?"

"They are known as the Phantom Squad."

The old man nodded. "And their leader, what is his name?"

The younger man stood up and mimicked Omar's actions. "Now that's a trick question."

"How so?"

"They are led by a Captain Venturi, Brent Venturi, but ..." He intertwined his fingers, squeezed and cracked his knuckles. Through gritted teeth, he seethed. "The brains of the squad is a little punk known as Seven."

Omar brushed his grey eyebrows from his vision. "It seems you're not as good as I was told."

Falcon stood nose to nose with the old man. "Care to clarify?"

"No." Omar took a step back, finding both disrespect and false bravado in the man's actions. "It is my understanding that you have connections within the U.S. Pentagon. I suggest you use them and then we will meet again at sunrise in forty-eight hours. If you come with the correct information, I will make you a very wealthy man. If not," he shrugged, "you keep your down payment and I will find another way to get the information I need."

Omar clapped his hands three times. Men entered the room and quickly retied the American's hands and blindfolded him before escorting him from the room.

The old man again took his seat and drummed his fingers on his desk.

CHAPTER 5

In his new office, the bishop placed a phone call. The voice on the other end was familiar. It brought him hope and a smile. "Hi," he said. "How have you been?"

Bishop Jessop could hear a quiver in her voice. "As well as can be expected. Is everything okay? Has something happened to Brent?"

The bishop paced the floor as he explained all that had transpired since Chloe's death. He finished with what occurred earlier at the meeting. He listened to shallow, stunted breathing on the other end. He opened his mouth to speak, but his words didn't come. He clutched the crucifix that hung from his neck for strength.

"He . . . he needs you." He waited for a response, but all he got was dead air. "Did you hear what I said?"

"Yes, but . . ." The words were soft and muffled. It sounded like she was choking down tears as she spoke. "Me? I tried to call him after everything happened. I felt somehow responsible since my husband was part of the Brotherhood."

There was an awkward pause and the bishop shifted his weight in trepidation.

"He didn't return any of my calls or text messages. I would think I would be the last person he would want to see."

Not knowing what to say, the bishop blurted, "He missed you at the funeral."

"He told you that?"

"Not exactly, but . . ."

"But what? What exactly did he say?"

"Well, he didn't actually say anything. After the funeral, he scanned the crowd, I got the impression he was looking for you."

"So this is all a hunch? A wild hunch."

"Let's call it intuition," the bishop said.

"Male intuition, that's comforting."

"Please. This may not make sense, but I know Brent. Come to Palm Cove. Your presence will help."

Again, silence engulfed the conversation.

"I'll think about it. I can't handle the rejection right now."

The bishop stopped pacing. "This isn't about you. It's about our friend who needs our help—your help."

She sighed heavily and said, "I'll think about it and call you back."

"Do more than think about it. Pray about it and listen to what God tells you."

The line went dead.

Halfway around the world, Alana hung up the phone. Her hand was trembling. She didn't know if she could bear to see Brent without falling apart. They had grown close during the quest to find the Ark of the Covenant. She had fallen in love. She placed a shawl over her head covering her long, dark hair, gathered her prayer book and headed to the local synagogue.

CHAPTER 6

Since Brent had anticipated the outcome of this morning's meeting, he had already cleared out his office. He had spent the past few nights copying all pertinent materials, including the software on his computer. With Joan's help, all of his security software was loaded on a new laptop and on an untraceable smart phone. He had moved everything to his Endowment office in the secret room behind the wall in the library.

The Palm Cove Public Library was originally owned by the Venturi family and when built, a false wall was designed adjacent to the head librarian's office. The secret room was also attached to the Endowment tunnel system which ran beneath the city.

He, too, had been busy changing codes. No one other than Joan and himself would be able to gain access to the room, either by way of the door behind the bookcase or the tunnel entrance. Two could play at this game.

He sat behind his desk at HQ, looking at his wedding picture when he heard someone knock on the door. "It's open."

The door slowly opened and a teary eyed Joan stood at the threshold. "May I come in?"

A grin creased his face. It felt foreign. "You know better than to even ask that question. You are always welcome."

Joan stepped, as if on broken glass, into the bare room. Brent met her halfway and she threw her arms around him and wept like a baby.

Brent squeezed, holding her tight. His thoughts drifted back to the details that had brought Joan into his life.

She had been like a daughter to him ever since the day he and Seven went to Washington D.C. and rescued her from what seemed to be an FBI lynch mob. Joan's mom, Monica, was the Pentagon liaison between the government and the Phantom Squad. She was one of the heroes that perished in the Pentagon bombing on September 11, 2001.

Two days later, Joan stabbed and killed the bastard that was her stepfather. He had been sexually abusing her since the age of nine. That night, too drunk to follow through with his desires, he beat her unconscious. She woke and found the strength to end the horror once and for all. She was sixteen.

The FBI had her locked up in a room and were drilling her as if she was a criminal, not treating her like a victim. Brent and Seven changed all that. Strings were pulled, charges were dropped and Joan was on a flight with Brent to her new home in Palm Cove within the hour. Seven was on a flight with the FBI agents to a backwater outpost, a post they still occupy.

Brent gave Joan the space she needed, but always kept a careful eye on her. He let her mourn in her own time and only spoke of what happened when she brought it up. A deep respect between them developed into a parental love.

Still crying, Joan began talking, choking back tears. "I couldn't raise my hand, you don't deserve to be treated like this. There was not one person in that room whose life you have not saved more than once. I . . ."

Brent held her at arm's length and wiped the green and pink bangs away from her beautiful face. "I would have done the same thing if the shoe were on the other foot. I would have lost respect for Maddie if she came to any other conclusion."

Questions flooded her mind. "Where will you go? What will you do now?"

"I will do what God wants me to do."

Joan was surprised to hear him use God's name. Since Chloe's death, Brent made it clear that he had lost his faith. "God?"

"Yeah, God."

Prying for information, Joan didn't let up. "And what does He want you to do?"

Brent shook his head. "I'm not sure. I only know what He has revealed to me. I know I have to go back to the beginning to make this right, to try to make sense of what has happened."

Joan wiped the snot from under her nose with her shirt sleeve. "The beginning? Where's that? What does that mean?"

He handed her a tissue and waited for her to blow her nose. She tried to hand it back to him.

Reaching for it, he had second thoughts. "Nice," he said. "Thanks, but no thanks." His eyes moved towards the waste basket.

She tossed it away while laughing in a congested, wheezy kind of way. "Seriously, Brent, what do you mean?"

He shrugged. "I'm really not sure. I'll step blindly."

There was no response of any consequence, so Joan changed the subject. "Everything you have asked for has been completed."

"Thank you."

"Will I see you again?"

Brent smiled as he lovingly placed his wedding picture in his backpack. "Every day."

The answer seemed to appease Joan, at least for the time being.

"Will you be at the house tonight?" he said.

"It's the baby's one month birthday," she smiled. "I wouldn't miss it for the world."

"In that case," Brent kissed her on the top of her head, "I'll see you at eighteen hundred hours at mom and dad's."

CHAPTER 7

Brent spent the rest of the day in the Endowment office going over ancient maps of Turkey, Armenia and the Khor Virap Monastery. He hadn't told Joan, but he did know where he was going, at least where he would begin his journey. He was going to leave before dawn of the following day for the monastery that sat at the base of Mount Ararat: the biblical resting place of Noah's Ark.

It was the beginning, the beginning of a covenant between God and Noah. A secret covenant known as The Endowment. It had been kept by one man of every generation. One who was of the highest moral and ethical fortitude. One who was known as The Ambassador. Brent was this generation's chosen.

He was going over what little information he had on the monastery when his squad phone rang. "Colon . . . Brent speaking," he corrected.

"It's Maddie," she said in a tentative voice. "I wanted to make sure you were okay. I checked your office shortly after the meeting, but you were gone. In fact, everything is gone."

"It didn't take a rocket scientist to figure out what was coming. I knew what conclusion you and the directorate would come to. I left you little choice."

"So, you're not mad?"

"No, I'm not mad," Brent laughed, "I would be if you came to any other decision. You did the right thing. I would have done the same, I just would have pulled the plug earlier."

"I have some papers I need you to sign. Tell me where you are and I'll bring them to you."

Smooth, he thought. "I'm out running around, but I'll be at the house later. Will you and Seven be there tonight? Lucille insists on throwing a one month party for the baby."

"We'll be there. Eighteen hundred hours on the nose."

"Good, I'll sign them then." Neither spoke for a couple of seconds until Brent said, "By the way, tell Seven to spit quieter when listening in on our conversation."

Brent could hear Seven's laughter.

"I'll work on that," Seven said. "And by the way, you're still a Colonel. Your rank hasn't changed."

Brent thought about his upcoming trip. *Not yet anyway.* "I'll see you tonight," he said. "Hey, do me a favor and tell everyone to be there on time. Then again, I'm sure they already know."

The speakerphone in the conference room went dead. Everyone that had been at the morning meeting was seated around the table. "I swear," Maddie said, "he has the entire world bugged. How could he know where we were? Or who was here?"

Maddie's expression was wrought with frustration. It had been a tough day. Hearing Maddie voice her feelings was somehow cleansing to everyone.

Seven stood up. There was a look of concern in his expression.

"What is it, Sev?" Scarlet asked. Scarlet was the newest member of the Phantom Squad and the president's daughter.

He sucked hard on his lower lip as if the answers might be hidden somewhere in the tobacco. "Something ain't right," he drawled. "Brent's been on edge ever since Chloe died. Today, we give him the worst news possible, and all of a sudden he sounds better?" He spit his juice and his worries into his cup. "He's up to something."

Everyone nodded, yet no one voiced an opinion. They were a collective black hole.

Maddie stood beside her husband. "The way this day has gone, I don't even want to imagine what Brent is thinking." She looked around the table. "But you heard him. Be there on time." She glanced around one more time. Her heart was heavy. The table seemed empty without Brent and Chloe. "You're all dismissed."

Seven saw Joan typing at demonic speed. "Did you get a trace on the line?"

"No, sir." She slammed her laptop closed. "Brent bounced his phone signal off of so many satellites, the point of origin still hasn't reached us."

Seven spit. "Thank god, he's still thinking like the colonel."

CHAPTER 8

Brent wiped the condensation off the bathroom mirror and looked at his reflection. He could see the scars through a month's worth of beard growth. Still wrapped in a towel from his shower, he pushed his long, dark hair away from his face. He gave thought to shaving, but didn't think for long. "The beard stays for now," he mumbled. He looked again at the scars. There was a time, especially after he left the squad following his encounter with the Butcher when he hated what they represented. Now, it was different. Each one reminded him of a different slice in his life.

He grabbed an elastic band and secured his hair in a ponytail. He never liked the idea of one, but his little girl changed all that. When he held her, she would grab hold of his hair in a death grip. It was either the ponytail or cut it off. Tail won.

At the top of his hairline, the faintest of scars was barely visible. A run in with a coral reef at the age of twelve while surfing. Touching it, he thought back to that fateful day.

He had worn a ball cap and feigned being ill when it was time for dinner. He knew his grandfather didn't allow hats at the table. He wasn't afraid his grandfather would be angry, he just didn't like disappointing him.

The surfboard was new. Only a week old. A birthday present. Now it was in two pieces. Not cool.

"What's wrong, buddy?" his grandfather asked.

"Nothing bad, just a little stomach ache," Brent answered.

"Come into the kitchen, I'll give you something to make it feel better."

Dejected and guilty, Brent opened the pantry door and squealed with elation. Leaning up against the wall was a brand new board. He reached out and ran his hand down the fiberglass.

Brent turned to his grandfather. "How did you know?"

"You should know by now, nothing goes on in this town I don't hear about."

Brent's parents had supposedly died when he was just two. His grandfather was the only parent he remembered and he didn't like letting him down.

His grandfather put his fingers under Brent's chin and raised his head. "You never have to feel shame with the people who love you. No matter what happens, you can always count on me being in your corner. Got that, buddy?"

Brent's eyes welled up as he threw his arms around his grandfather's waist. "I'm sorry, Gramps. It's just that I know how much you paid for that surfboard and I was afraid you would be mad."

"Did you break it on purpose?"

Brent shook his head with vigor. "No, I would never do that."

"It was an accident?" his grandfather asked.

Brent nodded.

"So why then would I be mad?"

Brent knew he had to come clean. He looked away from the man he admired most. He didn't want to see his expression when he told the truth.

"I was with Sam and Chris out at the Pointe."

Fisherman's Pointe was a rock and coral filled jetty where the waves had a tendency to dump instead of roll. Brent knew it was off limits.

Jake knew Sam and Chris were actually Samantha and Christine, two girls a grade or two older than his grandson. Now the picture was clear. "Leave the board and come with me," he said.

Brent followed his grandfather into his office.

"Have a seat." Gramps lifted his pipe out of the onyx ashtray and packed it with a vanilla smelling tobacco. "I'm going to tell you a secret that I have never told anyone before."

Brent sat a bit taller in the chair when he heard his grandfather's words.

His grandfather stalled long enough to flick his brass lighter open and light his pipe in one smooth motion. Exhaling, he put the pipe down. "When I was fifteen," he smiled, "I got my first vehicle. Your great grandfather gave me his old pickup truck. I was so excited to get that truck. I had just learned to drive and knew I wasn't allowed unless my daddy was with me." Inhaling again, he leaned back in his chair, lifted his head and slowly let out the smoke.

Brent watched the smoke leave his mouth in a single line. When it reached the ceiling, it spread out in an ever increasing pattern until it disappeared.

"Like that smoke," his grandfather said, "we know we're supposed to walk a straight path, but sometimes life puts things in our way that change what happens." He slapped the back of his pipe with the palm of his hand, emptying the ash in the onyx tray. "For me, it was a pretty little blond named Mary." His face lit up as he remembered her. "I didn't want to disappoint her, so I took her for a ride in the truck."

Brent leaned forward in his chair. Gramps never spoke of his past, so he didn't want to miss a word.

"We were almost back home when my dad drove right past me. I got nervous and hit the mailbox turning into the drive."

Anticipation was painted in Brent's expression. "What happened?" he asked.

"My dad calmly stood the mailbox back up, got in the truck with us, and told me to drive Mary home." Gramps shook his head, yet his eyes smiled at his grandson. "I was never so nervous in my life. When we got back home, my dad looked over at me and grinned. He said that women will make you do stupid things all your life. We just need to pick and choose when to be stupid."

"Did you get in trouble?"

"The guilt I felt for disobeying him was punishment enough." He leaned forward. "Do you get what I'm telling you, boy?"

A young Brent nodded. "Yes, sir, I do."

"Good, then this matter is closed."

Brent looked at the scar intently. His first lesson on the opposite sex. It certainly wouldn't be his last.

He packed his duffle bag with essentials and left his room to go be with his daughter.

Lucille, his mother, was feeding her and talking gibberish to the porcelain skinned beauty. She saw her son walk in and said, "Would you like to finish? I still have some final arrangements to make before our guests arrive."

Brent nodded and held out his hands. He looked at his daughter with unconditional love. She looked back up with big brown eyes and opened her mouth around the nipple in a drool-filled smile. She stopped sucking and reached up for his hair. When she couldn't grab it, a quizzical look shone in her eyes. Brent held her and the bottle with one hand and untied the ponytail.

"Is this what you're reaching for?"

She grabbed hold, her lips turned upward and her eyes closed as she began to again suck hungrily on the bottle.

CHAPTER 9

Everyone arrived promptly at seven p.m. They all ate and drank as if famished. It was something to do, so they wouldn't have to talk to Brent. The guests, the soldiers under the his command and the members of the SIA directorial board, tried to act as if nothing had changed, but nobody could get Chloe or this morning's proceedings out of their minds.

The townhome was the same one Brent had lived in with his grandfather when he was younger. After he and Chloe were married, they convinced Lucille to move in with them. They bought the home attached to theirs, knocked down the dividing wall, and made her a spectacular living quarters as well as a nursery for a future child. When Joseph, thought to be dead, was found alive, he too moved in to be with his wife.

Every detail in the home had Chloe's signature. Everyone could still smell her perfume and sense her presence. They started to understand how hard the past month must have been on Brent. What broke their hearts the most was how much the baby looked like her mother. She had Chloe's lips, skin and temperament, or maybe it just seemed so.

Brent was cordial, but as the night wore on, he became more subdued and more distant. Every conversation became stunted because it was so hard to talk about Chloe and even harder not to.

After the guests left, Brent tried to help his parents clean up, but Lucille would have no part of it. "Go be with your daughter."

He knew better than to argue with her, so he left them in the kitchen and went into the nursery. He picked her up from the bassinet and sat in the antique rocking chair that Chloe had meticulously restored. That was the moment he called her by her name for the first time. He looked at her, so comfortable in his arms, and knew she was to be Faith Chloe Adler.

Because of his involvement with the Phantom Squad, his name and identity had been wiped clean from every database known to man. Like all the other members, his born identity ceased to exist. As he rocked, his mind drifted back to his squad days.

After their final training mission, Seven gathered them in the hanger one last time. "When the powers in charge asked me to train this squad, I always envisioned it as a four man operation. Only three of you made it through." Seven packed his lower lip full of tobacco and spit. "I still see it as a four man op, so therefore you're stuck with me. I have asked Captain Venturi to lead the squad," he looked at Brent, "and he has accepted the position."

The men looked at each other in confusion.

Before they could ask any questions, he explained. "First, you have all earned a promotion and second, I know a leader when I see one. The captain was born for this. All of our orders will come directly through him from Washington. I am no longer your commanding officer and you are to no longer call me sir." He looked at Brent and smiled. "The moniker he gave me seems to have stuck, so from now on, I'm just Seven.

"I have papers for each of you to sign, making this little group official, but before you do, you need to hear me out. From here on out, we will be known as the Phantom Squad. Although Uncle Sam paid for your training and will continue to write your checks, they will never . . ." He raised his voice. "They will never acknowledge our existence. In the field, we are totally autonomous. If we get caught, no one will send help. We, the Phantom Squad, do not exist. Not as a unit and not as individuals." He picked up a pen, tapped the papers and then pointed it at each of them. "You will no longer exist to anyone. Your names, social security numbers, ranks and files will be erased. It will be as if God never put you on this earth."

Seven bent over and signed a sheet. "One of the reasons you were originally picked for training is because none of you have any immediate family. Whatever family and friends you do have will think you died . . . killed in action. It's like the witness protection program without new names and without government assistance. Think long and hard before putting your name to paper. Once inked, you will be wiped from the earth." Seven looked at the men, squeezed some flavor from the tobacco, and spit in his cup. "I'll leave the hangar, so you can talk about it."

Before he could move, Brent stepped forward and signed the paper. The other two, Sergeant Malcolm Jefferson and Sergeant Tommy Fitzpatrick followed suit. Seven smiled.

"I guess that makes it official then." He looked over at Brent. "Anything you'd like to say to your troops?"

Brent faced his squad. "I am honored to have been asked to lead you." He eyed each man. "Look around. This is your new family." He stepped forward and hugged each one and gave his promise to put their lives before his own. Each man did the same. "Okay then, you are to gather your belongings and get the hell off this godforsaken mountain. At your bunks, you'll find a satellite phone. It is set at a wavelength that no one can intercept, not even the President of the United States. Your documents will contain temporary identities and the location of your new homes. Go there and blend in with your community. You'll be called when we have our first mission. Everyone's dismissed."

When Brent married Chloe, he was disappointed that she could not legally take his name. Looking down at his daughter, he felt a different emotion. Her taking Chloe's last name seemed right. A fitting tribute to the mother she would never know. He smiled, genuinely, for the first time since her death.

As night turned to early morning, he decided to take Faith on a short walk. There was a lot he needed to say and this wasn't the place to say it.

CHAPTER 10

He walked to the beach and held Faith close to his chest. He sat on a bench on the boardwalk and cradled his daughter, one hand supported her head, the other held her tiny body. She opened her eyes, reached up and grabbed a handful of hair and gurgled. A lump formed in Brent's throat. He desperately wanted Faith to understand his actions, but he knew his words would be fruitless.

How do I tell a four week old that I have to leave because I am useless the way I am, because I can't be the father she deserves and needs until I get my head on straight?

He looked down at the miracle of life in his arms and sighed. He kissed her cheek and whispered, "I promise to return to you a stronger and better person."

Brent closed his eyes for a moment and when he opened them, Faith was sound asleep. He bundled her up and slowly made the walk back home.

When he arrived, Lucille was waiting for him.

"Where did you go?" she asked. "You had me worried sick."

"I just needed to take a walk and have a talk with Faith."

"You needed to talk to a one month old? That's a bit . . . did you call her Faith?" she smiled.

"Yeah," Brent beamed, "Faith Chloe Adler."

Lucille radiated with joy as she took her granddaughter from his arms. "That's a beautiful name. Chloe would have loved it."

"I think so," he said. "It just seems right."

Lucille leaned forward and kissed Brent on the cheek. She could taste the saltiness of his dried tears. "Get some rest. It's been a long day."

Brent nodded. "I will." As his mother began to walk towards Faith's room, Brent whispered, "I love you, Mom."

"I love you more." Without realizing it, she used the exact words Chloe always said when Brent told her he loved her.

Brent walked to his bedroom, but had no intention of going to sleep. He still had a lot to do before he left later that morning.

CHAPTER 11

Brent waited until he was sure everyone was sound asleep before he made his way to the basement. He removed the air conditioning grate and stepped inside the Endowment tunnel.

A little more than two years ago, he and Chloe found the tunnels buried under Palm Cove, thanks to the contents inside the Ark of the Endowment as well as a note that his grandfather had left him. The tunnels were only known to the Ambassadors and their most trusted allies. Each Ambassador had only a handful of people who knew his identity. They were known as the Inner Circle. Brent's had consisted of the members of the Phantom Squad as well as the SIA directorate and his family.

Memories flooded his mind as he flipped the electrical breaker and lit up the tunnel. He fondly remembered Chloe's words at first seeing the tunnels. She said it was a miracle that they existed at all.

The tunnels were ten to fifteen feet underground, completely handmade, and so close to shore that they were composed entirely of coral and shell. He could still hear her saying that it was archeologically impossible that they didn't flood and collapse. Their existence had to be divinely inspired. They dated back well over a hundred years.

Continuing to walk, Brent remembered bringing Charlotte Dupree, now known simply as Scarlet, into the tunnels. She was a bitter, scared, angry young woman who had been brought to Palm Cove against her will due to the escape of the Omega Butcher.

Jonas McFarland aka The Butcher had gone on a two-year killing spree centered on college sororities until finally apprehended. Scarlet had been his last victim and the only one to survive, thanks to the squad. Her ordeal left her psychologically scarred.

That memory alone was enough for Brent to bug out. He finally came to the spot in the tunnel which was a true miracle. When he and Jessop had followed the clues found in the Ark of the Enlightenment, they had found the hidden chamber that was an exact replica of the Holy of Holies: The tabernacle inside of Solomon's Temple.

He reached up and placed his hand on the etching of the alpha and omega. The wall began to vibrate so hard that each time he did this, he was sure the entire system would collapse. When the vibration stopped, the wall was gone and in its place was a purple curtain—the entrance to the tabernacle. Brent pulled it aside and walked onto holy ground. After he entered, the ground shook again. The curtain was gone and the wall had returned.

He looked around at God's glory. The only light in the tabernacle came from a luminescent glow which shined from the Sword of Truth. The sword he had been given by Archangel Michael, the one Brent used in his fight against Satan during a time known as The Enlightenment.

He dropped to his knees. "Father, I am lost," he prayed. "I need to find my way back to who I was. You have told me that I must seek the beginning in order to do so, so I ask you to please help me in my quest. While I am gone, please keep watch over Faith, my family, and those I love."

He blessed himself with the sign of the cross, stood up and approached the altar. On it laid the sword as well as the three arks, the Ark of the Endowment, the Ark of the Enlightenment and the Ark of the Covenant. Brent slid an envelope out of his backpack and stared at it knowing the magnitude of what he was about to do. He opened the Ark of Endowment and placed it beneath the letter Joseph had left for him. Joseph's letter explained the covenant forged between God and Noah and all of his descendents. The envelope that Brent placed in the Ark gave explicit instructions of what was to happen if he never returned to Palm Cove. An envelope he hoped would never be opened. He then closed the Ark and stood in front of Sword of Truth.

Brent lifted his arms and head towards the heavens and asked God to allow him to use the Sword of Truth in his quest. He lowered his arms and grasped it, knowing that he would not be able to lift it if God did not deem it so. It was weightless in his hands. The glow that came from the sword shot through him and filled him with the Lord's glory.

He sheathed the sword and tied it around his waist, thanking God for the gift. He turned to leave and saw that new words had been divinely etched over the curtain which once again appeared.

To find the beginning one must walk through the past and be willing to step into the future.

Brent didn't understand their meaning, but with all things, he knew God would help him to understand when it was time. Until then he would step blindly and follow His word.

He made his way through the tunnel until he came to the entrance which led to the rooms behind his office in the library. Flipping the breaker, the lights dimmed and the metal door slid open. He walked through the doorway to face his past and his future.

CHAPTER 12

As his sight adjusted to the bright light, he saw Joan staring back at him. She was once his ward and was now his confidant. She was a scared, emotionally distraught sixteen-year-old when he first met her in Washington D.C.

He thought of her mother. *She has grown into a beautiful, young woman, Monica. You would be so proud.*

She turned her attention back to the computer and continued typing. Brent opened his mouth to speak, but she held up a hand to quiet him. He walked closer, watching her type in an encrypted language to which only he had the key. Finished, she closed out the program, shut down the computer, stood and faced Brent with red puffy eyes.

"I've loaded everything you asked for and some other materials you may find useful."

"Thank you. I don't know what I would . . ."

Joan threw her arms around Brent and cried like a baby.

"Hey," he whispered. "Everything is going to be all right."

She wiped her tears on his sleeve and with sarcasm said, "All right, for whom? I'm only saying goodbye to the one person I trust."

He ruffled her hair. "That's not so, you have Maddie and everyone else here who loves you."

She punched him in the arm. "You know what I mean. With

you it's different. It always has been."

"Yeah, I know what you mean. I'm just trying to make this easier."

"The only way to do that," she said, pointing to the sword, "is to put that thing away and stay here where you belong."

Brent ignored her comments and placed the laptop in his backpack. "Are you sure the video feed will work and that I'll be able to communicate with you and Faith while I'm gone?"

A smile spread across her face. "Faith?"

He returned the smile and nodded. "Faith Chloe Adler. Like it?"

"It's perfect," she sobbed. "Chloe would love it."

Again he nodded. "I, ah . . ." Brent cleared his throat in an effort to stop his own tears from flowing. "I have papers here that have been notarized naming you as her guardian until I return." He handed them to Joan as he continued. "Are you sure you don't mind living in the townhome with Lucille and Joseph while I'm gone? It's not the penthouse you're used to."

"I wouldn't have it any other way. Besides, I'm sure Scarlet will like the place to herself for a while. She just better not get used to it."

He then handed her another note. "This is only to be opened if something catastrophic occurs."

Joan took the envelope and placed it in the top drawer of the desk.

An awkward silence enveloped the room as neither knew what to say next. Brent looked at his watch. "It's ten minutes after four. I better get going if I want to leave before anyone notices."

"Yeah, you better," she mumbled.

He turned to leave when she again wrapped her arms around him. "I swear," she said, "if anything happens to you, I will hunt you down and make your life a living hell."

Brent hugged her and laughed—nervous laughter—because he knew she could.

"Here," he said, handing her a letter. "I want you to read this to everyone after I'm gone."

Joan opened the note, read it, and sighed, "Kinda final isn't it?"

"It's the way I feel, the reason I need to leave."

Joan swallowed hard. Her words seemingly choking her as she

spoke. "I'll see that everyone hears it."

He kissed her forehead, turned, and stepped back into the tunnel. *One more stop before I leave.*

CHAPTER 13

Brent stepped on to the sand just as the sun began to rise over the water. The peace he once felt at the water's edge was nonexistent. His mind raced back to his marriage proposal on this very spot. He prayed that he would feel that joy again one day. As he stood looking out at the rolling waves, he heard a familiar voice.

"No goodbyes? No see you later? Is that how you treat your best friend, Professor?"

He looked up the beach and saw Seven standing in the sand twenty feet away. "It seemed easier this way."

"You were never the type to take the easy way out."

Brent shrugged, not knowing what to say. He noticed Seven carrying a guitar case. "Come to serenade me?"

Seven spit in the sand and tossed it to him. "Do you really want to hear me sing?"

"You sing about as good as you brew coffee, so I'll pass." He glanced at the case and then back at Seven.

"A long haired freak with no known identity and a sword attached to his waist is sort of conspicuous. I thought it might come in handy."

"Conspicuous? Big word for a southern hick."

"Yeah, well I picked it up hanging out with this Harvard tight-ass I knew." They both smiled and walked toward each other. "Are you sure you don't want some company on your trip?"

Brent shook his head. "You know I have to do this alone."

"Yeah, I know, but I had to ask. If you ever need me, you know how to reach me."

Brent nodded and walked up to his friend. They embraced, slapping each other on the back. "You take care of everyone while I'm gone, understood?"

"Is that a request or an order?" Seven said.

The left side of Brent's mouth rose in a half smile. "That's an order."

"Good. You're already sounding like the tight-ass I once knew."

"And you still sound like that gap-toothed hick I knew."

Seven spit the tobacco out of his mouth, pulled the tin out of his pocket and pinched off a fresh dip. "You better pack that geetar and git a move on."

Brent opened the case and saw a guitar.

"It has a false bottom. A place to put that." Seven pointed to the sword.

Brent placed the sword inside, slung the case's strap over his shoulder and looked up to see Seven walking back up the beach. "Love you, brother," he yelled.

Seven kept moving and raised his arm in a wave. "Git, before you see a gap-toothed hick get emotional."

As Brent began walking down the beach, he heard Seven yell, "Love you too, brother."

CHAPTER 14

Sitting at the train station, Brent couldn't help but notice the young man to his left. He appeared on edge. His demeanor was cool on the outside, yet he seemed ready to pounce at a moment's notice. His eyes and his posture were his tells. His eyes never stopped roaming the platform. His hands were in constant motion, relaxed and then balled up in fists. The pattern was repetitive. He sat Indian style, but looked as if he could spring from his coiled position like a cobra. The young man's hair was long, black and shiny. The Army tat on his bulging right bicep muscle flexed in a subconscious manner. He wasn't looking for trouble, but his posture stated that he was expecting it.

A few minutes later it arrived. Five men, his approximate age, mid-to-late twenties, appeared on the platform and fanned out around him. Their leader approached from the side. In his back pocket was a pair of Chinese nunchucks.

The young man on the bench surveyed the scene, never changing his position.

"You going somewhere, Tag?" the leader said. His anger seemed palpable.

The young man looked straight at him and spoke in a quiet confidence. "I have no beef with you or anyone from the tribe. I'm just looking to leave town."

"The problem is—the tribe has a beef with you." The aggressor whistled a bird sound and the other four closed in, blocking all portals of egress. "You know the tribal rules. We are an independent nation. Your stint in the U.S. Army violated our code. You were warned not to return."

"It's a free country. I just came home to see my family. Now, I'm leaving."

The leader of the gang stood directly in front of Tag. He shoved him on the shoulder in an attempt to agitate the young man. "It's bad enough you went and joined up, but then we discovered you and your family are not even tribal members. You lived on the reservation among our people, taking what is not yours."

"My mother is pure Seminole. We had every right to live there."

Brent noticed that the young man still spoke with a quiet confidence. This seemed to further infuriate the gang.

"She married a Cree. That makes you and your sister a half breed." He spit in Tag's face. "She will be dealt with later. You on the other hand, will be punished now."

Tag wiped the spit from his face and stared at his aggressor with a quiet anger. His eyes grew dark and menacing as he spoke. "Your problem with me has nothing to do with my parents or my sister. You leave them out of this."

A laugh of disgust burst from the leader. A laugh filled with hate. He brought two fingers to his mouth and whistled. A sixth man entered the platform pulling a girl, no more than fifteen, along with him. She was gagged and her hands were tied. When Tag saw his younger sister, his demeanor changed.

He sprung from the bench and pointed to her. "Let her go. Now!"

The leader smirked. "She won't be harmed. We just wanted her to witness what happens to those who break our rules."

"The elders made it perfectly clear that no tribal laws were broken. I had every right to join the military."

"The elders are wrong. Their ways are old. Our ways are now the way of the tribe."

Tag's eyes narrowed and his pupils dilated. His forearms and biceps surged with blood, becoming vascular in appearance. "Let her go and we finish this now."

Brent scanned the scene. The others pulled their hands out of their pockets revealing brass knuckles and knives. They closed in on Tag, surrounding him from every angle.

Damn. I just wanted to leave quietly. He slowly removed his backpack and stood. "Six against one. A coward's odds," he said.

The leader's head snapped in his direction. "Stay out of this old man. This is tribal business."

Brent rolled up his shirt sleeve revealing his identical Army tattoo. "I see it a bit different," he said. "Your anger seems to stem from this young man's patriotism. I have a problem with that."

The gang leader raised his hand and the others closed rank on Brent. "Our friend's allegiance was misguided. If he wanted to fight, he should have fought alongside of us, not alongside a nation that abandoned us."

Brent's smile disappeared. His eyes became blank. "You must be the group of punks I've read about. Outcasts from your own tribe. Even my friend, your chief, has tried to make you understand, but you refuse to listen."

The leader pointed a finger in Brent's face. "It seems you're the one who's misguided. The chief is a fool. This is our tribe now."

As they spoke, Brent saw Lieutenant Owens and three other Palm Cove police officers appear on the platform. He nodded in their direction and asked them to stand down.

Lieutenant Owens nodded and looked at the crowd of people who had gathered. "We'll make sure no bystanders get hurt." He smirked. "You need any help, you let me know."

The gang leader looked at the police and back at the other braves. "Don't worry about them," he said. "They have no jurisdiction over our nation."

Brent again addressed the gang's leader. "It seems you're the misguided ones. I will ask you one time to leave this train station before you and your friends get hurt."

"Someone's going to get hurt all right, but it won't be us," the leader fired back. "Why don't you just walk off this platform and let us settle this matter our way."

Brent shook his head. "Can't do. You see," he rubbed his hand over his tattoo, "I made a vow years ago to help a brother in need. You fight him, you fight me."

The nunchucks were now in the young man's hands. He put on a demonstration of his expertise with the ancient oriental weapon. With each forward motion of the sticks, he closed in on Brent until the colonel could hear the weapon pass by his ears with each movement.

Brent didn't move one iota, knowing even the slightest motion would mean being hit. "I'll ask you once again to put those away and crawl back under the rock you came from."

The leader's face turned crimson with anger. He took an offensive stance and attacked. With dexterity and speed, he flipped the nunchucks under his arms, across his body, and went for the strike. Brent's speed was even more impressive. As the weapon was about to hit its mark on his temple, his arms flew out in unison with the movement of the nunchucks and he caught the wooden dowel in his hand. The sting of impact was deep, but not even a wince of pain showed on his face.

He grasped and pulled the weapon from his attacker's hands.

Lieutenant Owens' men dropped their hands to their guns, but were given the command to stand down. "Watch and learn," Lieutenant Owen told his men.

Brent put on a blazing exhibition on how the nunchucks should be used. Just as he was about to strike, he pulled back and held both chained dowels in one hand. He threw them aside and waited for the attacker to react. A switchblade appeared in his hand.

"I'm going to enjoy gutting you, old man."

He attacked again. Brent crouched low and assumed an offensive position. With catlike dexterity, he spun and landed a roundhouse kick to the outside of the young man's knee. The sound of ligaments snapping could be heard by all those who watched. The attacker dropped, clutching his leg and screaming in pain. His eyes went to his followers. Through clenched teeth, he yelled, "Finish them."

They all attacked at once.

Brent glanced over at Tag, who was taking care of two of them. That left three. Brent spun, eyeing his prey. He picked out the weak link and drove his hand into the young man's throat. He felt the cartilage of his windpipe shatter as he went down, gasping for air. Seconds later, the gang was laid out on the cement slab clutching different body parts and moaning in pain.

"Are you all right?" he asked Tag.

Tag nodded, breathing heavily from the ordeal.

Brent's respirations hadn't increased at all.

Brent could hear the train approaching.

"You never cease to amaze me, Venturi," Lieutenant Owens said as he waved his men forward to make the arrests.

People started to cross in between Owens and Brent as they made their way toward the train.

Brent yelled above the crowd. "Please take the young lady back home," Brent said, "and I would appreciate it if you could put a watch on her family."

"I would love to," Owens yelled, trying to keep his eyes on Brent, "but you know tribal law. We are not allowed on their property."

"They no longer live on reservation property," Tag said. "My family's home is just off my peoples' land."

"In that case, consider it done," Owens said. He now stood next to the leader and pulled him up by the scruff of his neck, balancing him on his good leg. The young man opened his mouth to speak, but the lieutenant shut him up. "You'll get it looked at after we book you and your friends here on attempted murder with a deadly weapon."

When the police were busy rounding up the gang, Brent took the opportunity to disappear into the crowd.

CHAPTER 15

The two took adjacent seats on the train as it prepared to pull out of the station.

A half hour went by, yet no words were spoken. Brent feigned sleep until he heard Tag's voice.

"Thank you for the help, sir…"

Brent opened his eyes and peered over at the young man.

Before he could speak, Tag continued. "But I could have handled it myself."

"I don't doubt that you could." A smile crept onto his face. "I just had a little pent up aggression and the situation seemed like a good way to dispense with it." He waited for a response, but the soldier just stared back. "So, Tag, is that your full name?"

"Rowtag, it's . . ."

"Algonquin . . . Cree," Brent said. "I like it. It's a strong name. It means Christian, if I'm not mistaken."

Tag returned the smile. "You speak Cree?"

Brent shrugged. "In my line of work, I've picked up a few words here and there."

Tag's posture became more erect. Curiosity filled his expression. "May I ask what line of work that is, sir?"

"I'm a librarian, I read a lot."

Tag smirked. "Right, a librarian."

Brent pushed his hair away from his face. "Do I detect some sarcasm?"

Tag mimicked Brent's move. "Well, let's see." He held up a finger. "One, you seem to have a lot of pull with the police. You ask them to stand down and they do without as much as a single question." He held up a second finger and leaned forward. "Two, you fight with the moves of a seasoned Special Forces officer." Tag sat back in his seat. "That must be quite an interesting library you work in."

Brent sat back, mimicking Tag's movements. "Why would you think I was an officer?"

"Your confidence and movements gave it away. High ranking I would suspect."

Brent laughed. "Retired, full bird, and you?"

"I was a second Lieu when I opted out."

"Hmm," Brent again closed his eyes. He knew if Tag wanted to talk about it, he would without prodding. The young officer did the same. It seemed the time wasn't right for soul searching.

CHAPTER 16

That morning, the SIA directorate, sans the bishop, convened for its daily meeting. Before they adjourned, Joan told everyone that she had received a note from Brent that he asked her to read.

Standing in front of the room, she cleared her throat, "Ahem," and read,

> *Take care of each other and my baby until I get back. You know I'm no good to anyone the way I am, especially to her. She is to be christened, Faith Chloe Adler. She will carry her mother's name. Brent Venturi is dead.*

There was only silence.

Just about the time the train was leaving the station, a plane was touching down in Palm Cove. A plane piloted by Q. He worked for the Endowment network and was part of the Inner Circle.

"I hope you enjoyed your flight, miss."

The woman picked up her bag and looked out the window.

Q checked his watch. "Your ride should be pulling up right about now." As he spoke, a car drove onto the tarmac. "If it means anything, I hope you can help. Brent needs as many friends as possible around him right now."

Her full lips edged upward in an awkward smile. She pushed her long, thick, dark hair back from her face. "I appreciate the lift," she said in an Israeli accent. "It was a bit less dramatic than the last time you picked me up."

Q's expression broke into a full faced grin. "Yeah . . . and no gunfire this time."

She threw her bag over her shoulder. "You can't have everything."

Q laughed. "Maybe next time."

"Maybe," she said.

Outside the plane, Bishop Jessop waited, nervous with anticipation. When the door opened, he saw only Q. For a moment he thought she may have changed her mind. Alana appeared in the doorway, and he smiled. He knew this was the right thing to do, even if the colonel didn't warm up to it right away.

"Thanks for coming," he said.

She dropped her bags and hugged her old friend. "I just hope I'm not making a fool out of myself."

"You're not, but he's in a bad place. He might not give you the warmest of receptions. You'll have to give him time."

She opened the passenger door. "Time is all I have."

Arriving at HQ, the bishop looked over at Alana. "Everything from this point on doesn't exist. I'm sure I can count on your keeping a secret."

"I'm a woman, am I not?"

"That's my point."

Her eyebrows arched. "Sarcasm? I see Seven has rubbed off on you."

The bishop laughed. "His one admirable trait." He reached up and pushed the remote on the sun visor. The back wall of a concrete building began to open up.

"This should be interesting," she said.

"You have no idea."

The bishop had all the privileges and responsibilities that went along with his new position as a member of the SIA directorate, so he was able to gain access to HQ using palmer recognition. He knew it was silly, but he enjoyed someone watching him place his hand on the scanner and seeing the airtight door disengage. Once inside, he was greeted with respect and decorum.

"There seem to be a lot of check points," Alana said.

"This building is top secret. It was thought to be impenetrable. The Brotherhood changed all that. In the past eight months, changes have been made and the director brought the security to code red status."

Alana watched as the bishop's wrist was scanned at each point. "What's that all about?"

"One of the changes that I mentioned," the bishop said. "Since the infiltration and break in by the Brotherhood, we all had to agree to be micro-chipped. Each time I'm scanned, I'm followed by someone from security inside the inner sanctum."

"Inner sanctum?"

Bishop Jessop smiled. "The heart and brain of the Strategic Intelligence Alliance. It's where Maddie, the Madame Director, and her personal staff are located. It is also the headquarters of the Phantom Squad."

A thought suddenly occurred to Alana. "Do they know I'm coming?"

The bishop hesitated. "No. I didn't want anyone to accidentally mention it to Brent." He saw concern in her eyes and squeezed her hand. "Don't worry. They are all great. I couldn't ask for better friends. They're like my family."

"I hope I'm not the unwanted stepchild."

He could hear her apprehension. He stopped midstride and looked her in the eyes. "They're going to love you and they'll be happy you're here, you'll see."

As they entered the sanctum, they were frisked again.

The guard, heavily armed, flipped through papers on a clipboard. "Sorry Bishop, but I have to have prior knowledge of any visitors. I'll have to check with Joan before Alana is allowed to go any further." He looked up and asked for her last name.

The bishop opened his mouth and realized he didn't know. "I, it's . . ."

"Lavi," Alana said.

The guard nodded and told them to wait in the receiving area until he returned. Alana began biting her fingernails while they were detained.

"Sorry about that," Bishop Jessop said. "I just realized I never knew your last name. That was rude on my part."

"Brent knew. I guess he didn't tell anyone. Thinking back," she continued, "I guess there never seemed to be a reason for it to be brought up." She appeared to think for a moment. "Or, he didn't care enough to mention it." Her mood seemed to sully the more she thought about it. She shook her head. "This was a bad idea. I don't think I should be . . ."

The door's airlock hissed and interrupted her thought. The guard walked over and waved them through. "Follow me, please."

Bishop Jessop's heart rate increased with excitement and a little fear. He had never acted on his own when dealing with matters concerning the squad or the SIA. He hoped for a positive reception.

The guard stopped at the last set of doors. "I need to return to my post. You have been granted full access from this point onward."

The bishop's hand trembled as he placed it on the infrared scanner. His heartbeat increased as he wondered if he had made the right decision.

As soon as they entered the inner sanctum, he knew something was wrong. It was too quiet and Joan wasn't at her desk. Seconds later, she exited the conference room. Dark circles under her eyes. She plastered a reluctant smile on her face and walked to where they were standing. She glanced at the bishop and then stuck her hand out toward Alana. "It's a pleasure to finally meet you. I feel like I already know you. Those who have had the honor, speak very highly of you."

"Joan, what's going on?" Bishop Jessop asked. "Where is everyone?"

"Follow me and all will be explained."

Inside the conference room, a meeting was in full swing. Everyone stood as they walked in. Maddie was the first to approach them. "Hi, Alana, I'm Maddie. It's nice to meet you."

Seven came over and gave her a hug. "It's nice to see you again. Let me introduce you to everybody."

After the introductions, Maddie asked everyone to have a seat. Bishop Jessop and Alana looked around the table and then at each other. Each knew the other's thoughts. No Brent.

The bishop was aware that Brent had been relieved of his duties, but he was hoping that somehow he would be here. "Madame Director, I hope I didn't overstep my authority, but I thought Alana might be able to help with the situation concerning the colonel."

"You know your input is always appreciated, but Brent is not here," Maddie said.

"Where is he? Brent and Alana established a bond during our mission. I'm hoping he may open up to her in some way."

"You misunderstood. He's gone. We have no idea where he is."

"What? He just vanished?"

"There you go again, stating the obvious," Seven said, "but yeah, he just vanished."

Alana's shoulders slumped. Seven's words frustrated the bishop and seemed to tear a hole in Alana's heart. Bishop Jessop looked around the table. All heads were down. He saw Lucille wipe a tear as it slid down her cheek. "Can someone please tell me . . . us what's going on?"

"He left this morning, just before dawn," Seven said. "I had a feeling he might bug out and I found him at the beach. We spoke briefly and then he left."

"What? Where did he go?" The bishop glanced at his watch. "That was only a couple of hours ago. Maybe we can still catch him."

"We've looked everywhere," Maddie said. "He's cleared out. No signs of him anywhere."

Alana stood. "I knew this was a bad idea. I should get home. If I can call a taxi, I'll catch a ride to the airport."

"Hold on," Seven said. His mind was in overdrive. "With Maddie's permission, I would like you to stay. We could use you around here until he returns."

Alana looked confused. "For what?"

From the corner of his eye, Seven saw his wife nod her approval. "For one, the squad is a man down. I witnessed your military training when we were in Jerusalem. We could use your help if called into action."

She lowered her head. "I don't know, I . . ."

"And I could use all the help I can get taking care of Faith," Joan said.

"Faith?"

"Brent's daughter. I'm taking care of her until he returns. I hear you're a night person and frankly, I'm not. I could really use your help."

"Thank you, but I need to think about it. This isn't what I expected. I don't even have a place to stay."

"You'll stay with me," Joan said. "At Brent's townhome. It would mean a lot to me." She could tell Alana still felt dejected. "I think he would agree if he was here."

Those at the table followed up on Joan's statement. "I, for one, think it's a great idea," Lucille said. "I'm too old to raise a grandchild. As her grandmother, my job is to spoil her, not to raise her. You would be a big help."

"Seven can't stop talking about how great you were in the field," Jefferson said. "The squad is a five person operation and we are one short. We could really use your help. Your knowledge of the Middle East could be a huge help."

Fitz nodded. "I agree."

Seven smiled. "You'll get used to him. He doesn't say much, but he grows on you."

Their kind remarks made Alana feel a bit better. "Well, maybe for a little while. I don't have any reason to go back home. If you really want me to stay, I will." A slight smile emerged.

"Then it's settled," Joan said. "If it's okay with the Madame Director, I would love to take you to meet Faith and help you settle in."

"That's fine, but don't take all day. We still have an agency to run," Maddie replied.

"Thank you," Joan said.

"Yes, thank you, Madame—"

Maddie held up a hand to stop her. "Like it or not, you're now part of this dysfunctional family, so unless there is a need for formality, I prefer you just call me Maddie."

"I think I like it a lot." Alana blushed.

The girls started to walk out, but they were stopped by Seven. "It's o-nine hundred hours. I need Alana back here at twelve hundred hours to begin her squad training. No excuses, so git goin'."

"It would be faster if we went by . . . you know," Joan said.

Maddie nodded. "If Brent was okay telling Alana that he was the Ambassador, then I'm all right with her knowing everything else. You may use the tunnels. Help her get acquainted with their use and operation."

After they left, the rest of the team stayed put. "There are some things we didn't mention in her presence," Seven said addressing the bishop.

"Such as?"

"Brent took the Sword of Truth with him," Seven responded. "And enough gear to start a war."

The bishop's eyes grew wide. "God help us all."

Seven instinctively went for his tobacco tin, but thought better of it. "It's not us I'm worried about."

CHAPTER 17

The two continued to talk as the train continued to head north.

"Where were you deployed?" Brent asked.

"I did a stint in Iraq and three in Afghanistan," Tag replied.

Brent knew his meeting Tag was no coincidence. "Infantry?" he asked.

"Sniper."

Brent raised an eyebrow. "Unusual for an officer."

The young officer nodded. "I volunteered. I didn't think it was right to put one on my men in such a vulnerable position. I trained at sniper school. First in my class. The brass wanted me to teach, but I asked for deployment. At first, I was denied, but I was persistent."

Brent smiled. "Where are you headed, Lieutenant?"

"Hadn't given it much thought. I went back home to help my family. When my mission was accomplished, I knew it was time to leave."

Brent thought for a moment. "I planned on taking my trip solo, but you're welcome to come with me, if you'd like?"

"Where are you headed, sir?"

"Turkish-Armenian border. I have some business to take care of."

"Business, ha," Tag smiled, "I like the sound of that. It would be my honor to accompany you."

"Well, if that's settled, I suggest you get some sleep. We have a few stops to make before we get to our final destination."

Tag pulled his cap down over his eyes. "Yes, sir."

When the train stopped in St. Augustine, Brent nudged the lieutenant. "This is our stop. Grab your duffel bag."

They walked off the train and into the late afternoon sun. It was early September and the humidity was thick. Brent watched Tag to see how he reacted to the air quality. He didn't. The colonel liked what he saw.

"If I can ask, sir, why are we here?"

Brent stopped and looked at the lieutenant. "Let's get something straight. I'm not your commanding officer, so please call me Brent. You have the right to ask me whatever you want." Tag stared back at him. "And I reserve the right not to tell you."

The answer took the young soldier off guard. "Sounds like I'm still in the military."

Brent nodded. "Right now, I'm hungry, there's a great diner on Front Street. So, first we're going to grab some grub."

Tag's stomach growled. "Sounds good. Lead the way."

Tag looked around as they walked. "I've read a lot about this place, but I've never been. It's beautiful."

"It's the oldest settlement in the south. Some will argue that it is the oldest in the states," Brent said. "Great southern charm." They turned on Front Street. "And even better food. They serve breakfast all day." The sun began to set as they walked into the diner.

After a big southern breakfast, they both sat back. Their stomachs were full and Tag was full of questions. "I don't suppose we just stopped to eat. What other 'business' do you have here?"

"I . . . we have business here." Brent leaned forward in order to lower his voice. Tag mirrored his movements. "One of the best document forgers lives a couple of blocks away. We need new I.D.s and he'll be able to outfit us with passports and new military documents. That's our next stop."

Ten minutes later, they entered a back alley. Brent stopped at one of the few buildings that hadn't been restored. It looked abandoned.

"Nice digs," Tag said.

The left side of Brent's mouth rose in a half smile. "Sarcasm,

I think we'll get along just fine." Before he could knock, the door opened as far as the chain would allow.

"You didn't say anything about company," came a voice that sounded as rough as the building looked.

"You know me. Always picking up strays," Brent said.

"Has he been checked out?"

"I ran him through my contacts at the Pentagon. I wouldn't have brought him if there was a problem." Brent glanced around the alley. "How about we finish this conversation on the same side of the door."

The door closed and they heard the sound of the chain being slid off its mount. When the door opened, they followed an old man in a wheelchair. The occupant of the chair had no legs below his knees. The inside of the building was as rough as the outside. Dilapidated furniture and the stale smell of marijuana.

Hollow eyes encircled in dark rings looked up from the chair. "Sorry to hear about Chloe. I'm going to miss her."

Brent acknowledged the comment and quickly changed the subject. "You always spruce things up for company?"

"Screw you, Professor."

Brent emitted a belly laugh. The first in a long time.

Their host did the same. His was phlegm filled. "Damn, don't make me laugh. It kills the lungs." He reached for a joint and lit up. He took a deep hit and held it out for his guests.

"Thanks, but no thanks," Brent said.

"Ditto," Tag said.

Blowing the smoke out, the old man took another. "You don't know what you're missing. The government makes some of the best weed I've had since Nam."

"We'll take your word for it." Brent looked down at his watch. "We've got a tight schedule. How about we get down to business?"

The old man turned his chair around and rolled into the next room. "Follow me."

Tag couldn't help but ask, "What's your name?"

"You're kidding, right?" Not waiting for an answer, he added, "You can call me Wheels. That's what my friends call me. And you?"

"Rowtag."

Wheels looked at him, really looked at him for the first time. "Injun. That's a Cree name, ain't it?"

"Yes, sir."

"Sir? I ain't no soldier. Not anymore, anyway."

Tag looked to Brent for an explanation. "Wheels is one of your own. The best sniper the Army had. I'd put his skills up against anyone."

Wheels spit in a dirty glass on the table. "I had you pegged as an officer. You're a sniper?"

"Both," Tag answered.

"Well, I'll be damned," Wheels said. "It's about time the military did something right."

Tag nodded. No words were necessary.

Wheels flipped an envelope to Brent. "I have your documents ready, Colonel. His will take a little time. What do you need?"

Brent went through the contents: four passports, all under different aliases from different countries, and a new Army I.D. "Another set just like this one."

"Same price," Wheels said, "This ain't Walmart. I don't discount."

"Done."

He looked at Tag and then at the wall. "Stand in front of the white backdrop. I need your photo. I will also need your military I.D. so I can play with it a bit."

Tag pulled out his identification from his wallet and placed it on the table.

Once the picture was taken, Wheels said, "Give me a couple of hours. I'll put a rush on them for an extra ten percent."

"You mind if we leave our stuff here?" Brent said.

"It's safe here. Now, go do some tourist stuff or something. Everything will be ready at twenty-one hundred hours."

Back in the street, Tag said, "Interesting friends you have."

Brent thought of Seven. "You have no idea."

Two hours later, Brent handed Wheels an envelope full of cash and in return Tag was handed his new documents. He looked at his new military docs. "Billy Redman?"

Wheels laughed. "I liked the irony."

Brent just shook his head. "Let's go, *Billy*. We have a train to catch."

At the train station, Tag pulled his hair back in a ponytail and pulled it up under his hat. "Where to, Colonel?"

Brent grinned. "Washington, I need to say hello to an old friend. Then, we'll head back and board a flight to Turkey."

Tag just stared. He didn't know whether to press the subject, so he said nothing.

CHAPTER 18

The train began to rumble as it pulled out of the station. Tag pulled his wallet out of his fatigues. "I didn't come prepared for this type of expense. I . . ."

"Relax, Lieutenant. All your expenses are covered."

Fourteen hours and multiple stops later, the two walked through the train station in Arlington, Virginia. Not needing their belongings, they placed their bags in a locker and stepped out into the mid-morning bustle of the nation's capital.

"Now where, the White House?"

"Not today," Brent replied. He thought of his friendship with the president. *He would really flip if I took him to meet President Dupree.* "Where I need to go is a bit more important, at least at the moment."

The next thing Tag knew, he was exiting a cab and standing at the entrance of Arlington National Cemetery. They proceeded to walk about a half mile through the endless graves and monuments and finally stopped in front of the 9/11 monument.

Brent watched as Tag scanned the names of all those who had lost their lives that day. Tag's skin grew pale as he continued to stare.

"Are you all right, Tag?"

Tag blinked. Color and life flushed back to his flesh. "Yes, sir, I'm fine." He shook his head. "So much needless death."

Brent agreed.

"Why are we here?" Tag asked.

Brent didn't answer. "Stay here," he said, "I won't be long." He found Monica's name on the plaque and said a silent prayer.

Brent made his way to her gravesite, knelt and wiped the debris away from the stone. "I'm sorry I haven't been here to visit more often." A lump formed in his throat. He swallowed hard to suppress his emotion. "I just came to say I miss you. If it weren't for you, I never would have recovered from my injuries after my first run-in with the Omega Butcher. More importantly, I don't know if I would have regained my faith without you."

Despair came with his words. He wiped away a tear as he continued. "I could sure use you now, Monica. Losing Chloe tore my world apart. My faith is fleeting at best. I blamed God for letting her die and said some things I'm not sure even He can forgive." He placed both hands on the stone and looked up to heaven. "I know He is all forgiving, but I'm having a hard time forgiving myself." His tears poured down his cheeks. He took a deep breath to calm himself. Thoughts of Joan flooded his mind.

Brent focused on the marble stone. He closed his eyes and pictured Monica standing before him. "You would be so proud of your daughter," he smiled. "That wild child has grown up into an incredible woman." He choked back his emotion, but it was to no avail. His anguish poured forth and soaked the marble headstone. He wiped his face with his shirt sleeve. "I once promised you that I would take care of her if anything ever happened to you. I came to tell you that I stand by my promise. I needed to leave Palm Cove, to try to get myself together and to try to regain my faith. Although I won't be close to her, I will protect her and love her always."

Thinking back to the relationship he and Monica shared, Brent's despair became a bottomless chasm. "I wish we could talk about everything that is going on, but this will have to do. I don't know what the future holds, but I wanted you to be reassured that Joan will always be safe. I've lost too many people that I have loved and I pledge that I will not lose her." He took a deep breath and tried to bring himself out of his self-pity. "I promise to come more often and next time, I'll bring Joan." He bent forward and kissed the gravestone.

Brent stood and wiped the dirt from his knees. His eyes once again portrayed the soldier within—dark, empty openings to nothing. With a final glance at Monica's grave, he said, "Pray for me." With a renewed continence, he walked back to where he left Tag.

The young officer watched him approach. "Your wife?"

"Old friend. Died on 9/11 in the Pentagon." Brent could see that Tag had other questions. They would have to wait. "Come on, we've got some distance to cover. There's a rent-a-car lot a couple of miles up from the train depot. We'll pick a ride up there."

CHAPTER 19

At sunrise of the second day, Falcon stood once again in front of Omar.

"So," the old man said, "have you learned anything new since our last meeting or did you come to say goodbye?"

Falcon smirked. "My contact brought me up to speed. It seems the Phantom Squad is without a leader."

"Oh."

"Yeah. Your boys might not have killed Venturi, but indirectly, they killed his wife. She died during childbirth. She bled out due to scar tissue brought about by being tazed by one of your men."

Omar sat erect when he heard the news. Partly proud of what he was hearing, but mostly frightened because he knew what Colonel Venturi was capable of.

He was angry at himself when he noticed Falcon's expression. One that told him that Falcon could sense his apprehension.

Falcon smirked. "Seems the colonel went off the deep end and bugged out. No one, including the U.S. Government, knows where he went."

Omar rubbed his hands together in thought. "So, you are of no help to me then."

Falcon laughed in what seemed like arrogance. "I learned a few more things that might help your cause."

"Such as?"

"Such as, the president plans a little trip to the Middle East. A meet and greet with the troops."

"So?"

"So, no one knows of it. All hush-hush. He doesn't want a media circus."

Omar's mind went into overdrive. "No one knows?"

An evil smirk engulfed the American like a Cheshire cat. "Just you and me."

Omar waited for the American to continue.

"It seems to me, you may have a way of flushing out the squad, if you catch my drift," Falcon said.

Omar combed his boney fingers through his beard. "Do you know where President Dupree plans on stopping?"

"Not yet, but I will."

A belly laugh could be heard throughout the catacombs. "Sit," Omar said, "there are plans to be made."

CHAPTER 20

Joan watched Alana's demeanor soften the moment she laid eyes on Faith. She couldn't help but think of Brent as Alana held the child. She watched from across the room and saw an immediate connection between woman and child.

"It's time for her bottle," Joan said. "Would you mind holding her a bit longer while I heat it up?"

Alana didn't even look up. She just smiled and brought Faith's face next to hers and lightly kissed her cheek. Faith cooed at her touch.

Joan smiled as she walked into the kitchen. While she readied Faith's meal, she could hear Alana's laughter coming from the nursery. It was a hardy laugh, a soul cleansing laugh.

"Would you like to feed her?" Joan asked, returning with the formula.

Alana's eyes opened wide. Her full red lips broke into a joyous expression. "I would love to."

Joan handed her the bottle and watched the bond between them grow. She watched Faith reach up and grab Alana's hair. Something she had never done with anyone but Brent. Watching the two interact, Joan somehow knew Alana's feelings toward Brent.

"You love him, don't you?"

Alana's gaze slowly drifted to Joan. "I don't know what—I mean,

I . . ."

Not one to judge, Joan just shrugged. "It's all right." She leaned forward in her chair and her expression turned more serious. "I loved Chloe and I know Brent would never have done anything to break his vows. He loved her with all his heart, but," Joan hesitated and took a deep breath, "we all know he developed a special connection with you while the team was in the Mid-East."

Alana's eyes welled up with tears. "What do you mean, you all know? Did he say something?"

Joan shook her head. "It's what he didn't say. He—I don't know—I could just sense it. Everyone could." Joan stood up and walked over to the rocking chair. She removed a tissue from the changing table and handed it to Alana. She squatted down in front of her and continued to speak. "He was so adamant when Bishop Jessop suggested that you come to the funeral. It was as if your being there would somehow undermine his love for his wife."

"I don't understand."

Joan sighed. "It's hard to put into words. Brent was not one to show his emotions, but when your name was mentioned, it was if he wore his heart on his sleeve."

"I don't know that expression, 'wore his heart on his sleeve,' what does it mean?"

"It means his emotions were visible. We could all see how he felt about you."

Alana looked confused. "But his emotions were negative, were they not?"

Joan smiled. "I've known Brent since I was sixteen and the only other time I have ever seen him act that way was when he and Chloe were estranged."

Again, Alana's eyes filled with tears. "You have me so confused. Now, you are talking like Seven."

Joan laughed. "No wonder you're confused." She looked down and saw that Faith was sound asleep. "Here, let me take her and then we'll talk."

Alana removed the bottle from her mouth and kissed the milk from her lips. "Sleep well, little one."

After laying Faith down for a nap, the two sat at the kitchen table and sipped a cup of coffee. Neither saying anything. Alana put her cup down and swept her hair away from her face. "It's true."

"What?"

She looked away. She didn't know if she could handle seeing Joan's face as she spoke. "I fell in love with him the first time I met him. It was nothing he did or said, it was just, I don't know how to explain it. I just knew."

"Did he return the affection?"

Alana brought her cup to her mouth and drank. "He was caring and looked at me in a way no other man had ever done so before."

"There had to be something more," Joan prodded.

"I don't understand?"

"Brent has the ability to see people for who they really are, not as the world sees them." Joan thought of Maddie and how meeting Brent changed her. "Maybe someday, Maddie will tell you how Brent changed her life." Joan removed the empty cups from the table and sat back down. "All our lives have been changed because of him. But with you, it is different. The bishop knew it and that's why he insisted you come."

"How do you know Bishop Jessop insisted I come?"

A glint appeared in Joan's eyes. Her right eyebrow arched slightly higher. "I'm the only one who can contact Q outside of Brent. He works for the Endowment, not for SIA. The bishop asked me to make the arrangements. He explained the connection that had developed between you and Brent."

"I see. So you see me as a fool," Alana said.

Joan leaned over and clutched her hands. She spoke in a soft tone. "I see you as Brent's salvation, as the only one who can bring life back into him."

Alana looked down at their intertwined hands.

"I don't see you as a fool," Joan continued. "I see you as a woman who is in love and who longs for that love to be returned." She hesitated and planned her words carefully. "If you are patient and if you stick around, maybe you'll get what you long for."

Before Alana could speak, the front door of the townhome opened. Lucille stood in the entranceway. She was breathing hard as if she had been running. "There you are." She stopped to take a deep breath. "I was told that if you weren't back at headquarters in thirty minutes, your, and I quote, 'butts will be hung out to dry,' whatever that means."

They looked at each other and in unison said, "Seven."

The clock chimed twelve-thirty.

"We lost track of time," Joan said as she threw her messenger bag over her shoulder. "Faith was fed and is sleeping." She eyed Alana. "I hope you can run. We don't want to be any later than we already are."

Alana grabbed her bag. "You lead, I'll keep up."

CHAPTER 21

The girls were winded when they exited the tunnel at HQ. The grate to the air conditioning duct had already been removed. Standing on the other side were Seven and Maddie. Neither looked pleased.

Seven spit in his ever present cup. "Forty-five minutes late. Not the best way to get on my good side, soldier."

Alana looked at Joan and realized he was addressing her. "I'm sorry, it's my . . ."

"It's my fault, sir," Joan interjected. "It was my responsibility to watch the time. If anyone is to be reprimanded, it's me."

Seven sucked in on his bottom lip, "See that it doesn't happen again."

Scarlet was standing behind the two senior officers.

He gave Alana a head nod. "Scarlet will take you to the locker room and show you how to gear up." He turned his wrist and checked the time. "You have twenty minutes before you are to meet me in the armory, so I suggest you get moving."

Joan watched the two walk side by side down the hall. "It really was my fault," she said to Seven. "Don't be so hard on her. She has been through a lot."

Seven sucked his lower lip into his jaw and furrowed his brow. "You don't tell me how to run my squad and I won't tell you how to do your job. We clear on that?"

Joan swallowed hard. "Yes, sir."

"Good, now if you'll excuse me, I have a woman to break and a soldier to mold."

Joan looked over at Maddie. "That was a bit harsh, don't you think?"

"No I don't," Maddie replied. "Seven's not happy about having to give the orders. He thought he left those days behind him years ago. He's never been easy on a trainee and he sure as hell doesn't plan on starting now." She started walking down the hall. "Unless you have any other comments, follow me. We still have the world's top covert agency to run."

Joan knew when to shut up and follow orders. This was one of those times. "Yes, Madame Director."

As they continued to walk, Joan could see concern in Maddie's expression. "Has there been any news on Brent?" she asked.

"A little. I'll bring you up to speed when we get to my office."

Twenty minutes later, Scarlet and Alana entered the armory. Seven was waiting with Jefferson and Fitzpatrick. He glanced at the clock. It was all for show. He knew exactly what time it was. He glanced at Alana, "It's nice to know you can tell time."

Addressing Jefferson, he said, "Sergeant, you can cross telling time off your check list."

Jefferson took the pencil from behind his ear and scratched out the top line on his clipboard. "Can tell time. Check."

Seven handed Alana eye and ear protection and walked over to the gun range. "It's been a while since you were in the Israeli military. Let's scrape some dust off of your handgun skills."

CHAPTER 22

As they walked, Tag's curiosity got the best of him. "Where to, Colonel?"

"South. A Naval base, just this side of Jacksonville. There, we'll catch a short hop to Pensacola, then we fly into Germany, and our final leg will take us to Armenia."

Tag pulled up short, showing signs of surprise. "You weren't kidding when you said you were headed to the Armenian-Turkish border."

Brent looked at the lieutenant with a blank stare, one that brought apprehension to the young officer. "You'll find I don't kid. If you want to opt out, now's your time. Once we board the jet in Pensacola, there's no turning back." Brent tried to read the lieutenant's expression. "There's no dishonor in doing so. This is my fight, not yours."

Tag's heartbeat quickened. His nostrils flared. Air rushed in. His mouth opened slightly, letting the air out along with his nervous energy. His body tingled as if back in battle. He said nothing.

Tag stopped and looked Brent in the eyes. "It seems to me, you're used to going it alone, Colonel. Maybe it's time you had some company."

"Suit yourself," Brent said. He turned and walked west. "We need to get a move on if we plan on getting to the car lot before it closes." He glanced over at Tag. "You look like you're in good shape. Let's pick it up, double time. I'll lead."

As they ran, Tag's leg and arm movements mimicked Brent's. He saw Brent snap his head back in surprise. The expression made Tag smile.

They picked up a car, nothing conspicuous, and began the long drive south.

Like the car, the lieutenant's mind was in overdrive. "You mind if I ask what I signed up for?"

"I told you before, you can ask whatever you want." Brent checked the GPS and kept driving.

"You also said you retain the right not to answer. Is this one of those times?"

Brent turned his head toward the passenger seat, looked him straight in the eyes, and then turned his attention back to the road. "As a sniper, you've been taught patience. From what I observed back at the Palm Cove train station, I'd say it's pretty ingrained in your psyche. This is one of those times you need to put it into practice." He looked back at Tag. "All will be disclosed once we're in flight. In my line of work, nothing is left to chance and information is on an as needed basis."

Tag thought for a moment, "What exactly was . . . is your line of business, Colonel?"

"As a special ops officer, did you ever hear of a covert military operation that was more myth than reality?"

Tag laughed, but when he looked at the colonel, he saw the same vacant expression he saw back in St. Augustine. He swallowed hard. "Yeah, we all heard the stories. They were good entertainment when there was nothing to do, but no one believed them. They were too farfetched." As he spoke, his attention never left the colonel's face.

Brent's expression was pensive. He saw no humor in the stories.

"You mean to tell me they were real!"

A slight smile cracked the icy veneer. "As real as I am sitting here. I am, was the squad leader. We are only called in when all legal means to end a skirmish fail." He paused and looked over at Tag again. "We never failed a mission and never failed in bringing all our men out alive. I don't plan on changing either of those statistics."

"Does the squad have a signature?"

"Like I said, everything is on a need to know basis. Right now, you don't need to know that information."

"So, we're meeting the rest of your squad in Armenia?"

"Nope. This one is being run solo or a twosome if you still want in. It's only fair I give you that much information."

Tag's adrenaline level started to climb. He could feel his heartbeat speed up and his breathing increase. His eyebrows arched in excitement. "I wouldn't miss it for the world."

Not another word was spoken until they reached the airbase on the south side of Jacksonville.

They showed their military I.D.s at the security checkpoint approximately a half mile from the base.

"We'll have two more check points to go through before we're let onto the airfield," Brent said.

Tag nodded.

Once they arrived at their destination, Tag didn't see any jets, just cargo planes. "Where's our ride?"

"You're looking at her," Brent said, pointing to the C-130 cargo plane. "I hope you have some jumping experience. I bought the cheap seats. No in-flight movie and no landing. We deplane at 15,000 feet."

Tag laughed. "You really are crazy, you know that."

Brent chuckled. "You're not the first to call me that, but I've got a whole drawer full of psych evaluations to disprove it. The way I see it, I'm just thorough. Just covering all my bases and working through all possible contingency plans." He glanced in Tag's direction, "You can't follow what you can't see. We jump in the dark of night and board our next flight as soon as we land."

"Won't there be military record of us leaving?"

Brent nodded. "There would be, if they knew we're coming. The top secret part of this mission has begun. Follow my lead."

CHAPTER 23

It was a short jaunt from Jacksonville to Pensacola. They had just enough time to put on their jump suits and check their gear.

"I'm going forward to check with the pilot," Brent said. "Be ready when I get back."

Brent returned five minutes later. "We're two minutes from the jump zone. The pilot will count down from thirty seconds. When you see the back end of this bird open up, it will be time to fly. We can't deploy our chutes until we break the eight-hundred-foot ceiling, so prepare for a rough landing."

The last minutes were spent checking each other's equipment. As Tag tightened the colonel's harness, he couldn't help notice that Brent had the guitar case strapped to his back along with all his other gear. He was dying to ask about it, but he already knew he wouldn't get a logical answer. His thoughts were disrupted by the mechanical squeal of the gears as the rear end of the C-130 opened. He looked out and saw nothing but the dark of night.

Brent pointed to the coordinates on his altimeter and hand signaled for the lieutenant to set his to the same. Tag did as he was ordered and lowered his infrared goggles over his eyes. Everything took on an eerie green luminescence. His mind raced back to his last mission. Shaking his thoughts aside, he gave a thumbs up.

"Thirty seconds and counting," the pilot radioed. "Thanks for flying the friendly skies of the Armed Forces."

Brent and Tag gave each other a final nod as the pilot radioed, "I'll count you down from ten. When I give the go, there can be no lag time. You'll have a small window of opportunity if you're going to hit your landing site."

Tag shivered as the cold air of the high altitude permeated the inside of the fuselage. His heart rate idled like a tachometer on a hot rod.

The plane's radio cracked to life and the pilot gave the deployment order. "Three, two, one, go, go, go!"

Instinct kicked in. Brent ran for the back of the cargo plane and launched himself into the blackened sky. Tag was right on his heels. Tag hovered above him during the freefall as if they were attached. Seconds passed before Brent saw his altimeter drop below eight-hundred-feet. He and Tag pulled their ripcords in complete synchronization. Their chutes deployed at exactly the same time. The trip was quick, as all high altitude, low opening jumps tended to be. Terra firma struck quick.

They quickly gathered up the silk material of their chutes.

"We don't have much time," Brent said, "and the pilot meeting us is expecting one passenger. I'll radio ahead and let him know of the change of plans. The pilot knows to bug out five minutes after the expected meeting time. Let's move."

Brent led and picked up his speed to a six-minute mile pace. Twenty-four minutes later, they had skirted security and clipped their way through a barb wired fence. They stood at the edge of a battered, rut filled, old runway at the edge of the military base.

Tag looked around, but saw nothing but a Lear jet. "I don't see anything even close to military issue." Shadowing Brent's moves, he almost stepped in a pothole. "Please tell me this isn't the airstrip."

Brent pointed to the jet as they walked toward it. "As a sniper, you've been taught to see what can't be seen. You're target may be disguised, but you still know it's your target."

Tag understood. "You always talk in riddles?"

Brent laughed under his breath. "It seems to come naturally. It makes you think and keeps you on your toes." Tag heard Brent's phone vibrate. He watched as Brent retrieved it and read the message on the LCD screen. Before Brent could put the phone back in his pocket, Tag saw the inside lights of the jet flash on, off, and back on. They were dim and looked like emergency lights.

Tag watched as the door opened and stairs were lowered. One person, dressed entirely in black, deplaned. Even his face was entirely blacked out in a form fitting Lycra mask. Brent and the pilot hugged and communicated using hand gestures.

The pilot grabbed their bags and headed back up the stairs.

"We don't have much time," Brent said, as they climbed into the Lear. "The military saw the jet enter their air space on radar. The pilot has been able to scramble the signals and keep them from spotting his exact position, but it's only a matter of time before they unscramble the signal. We need to be quick."

Taking their seats and strapping in, Brent handed Tag a helmet, complete with communication gear. Tag was perplexed. "Won't they see us take off?"

"They can't find what they can't see," Brent answered.

Tag thought for a moment and then snapped his head toward the colonel. "You mean we're taking off without lights! That's suicide."

"Would be with anyone else but Q."

"Q?"

"Our host and the best pilot I have ever known." He saw Tag start to fidget. "Relax, Lieutenant. This isn't our first rodeo. We've done this before."

Tag shook his head and stared straight ahead. "I stand by my earlier observation. You are certifiably insane."

"I'll take that as a compliment."

The jet moved forward. The motion ended the conversation.

A voice came through their helmets. "Strap up, boys. Please replace all tray tables to their upright positions. This will be a fast, steep climb. Once I clear all structures, I'm going to roll this baby on her back and reverse directions. If spotted, they'll expect us to head out over open water. I'm headed due north over Alabama and Georgia. We won't see water until we clear South Carolina. As soon as I flip her back onto her belly, we'll hit mach one, one second later."

"What the hell have I—" Tag's words were cut short as he was glued to the back of his seat by the incredible thrust of the jet as it shot down the runway and launched upward. It seemed like an impossible angle and he waited for the fuselage to start to break up and crash land. Before he knew it, his world turned upside down and all his blood rushed to his head.

Q aimed the jet directly north. By the time it rolled back on its belly, Tag was dizzy and a bit nauseous. As he began to relax, the pilot punched the speed and the lieutenant heard the sonic boom as the small jet tore through mach one. They flew in total darkness until they were well over the Atlantic.

Tag white-knuckled his arm rest in a death grip.

"Loosen up, Lieutenant," Brent said. "We may need those hands later on. I'd feel much better knowing that you still have neurological control and dexterity in your trigger finger."

Tag hadn't even noticed that he was still clutching the armrests with all his strength. He slowly relaxed his grip and rubbed his hands together to aid his circulation.

The earpiece in his helmet crackled. "The no smoking sign has been turned off and you are free to move about the cabin."

Hearing Q's remarks, Brent unstrapped his harness. "Come on and I'll introduce you to the best damn pilot you'll ever have the pleasure of knowing."

Tag unbuckled and followed the colonel into the cockpit.

CHAPTER 24

Over the next hour, Q explained the Lear jet to Tag. Brent saw that the young officer was transfixed by what he heard.

"Do you mean to tell me that this jet is actually a B1-B bomber?" Tag's eyes glazed over in confusion. "How is that possible?"

Q looked over at Brent to see how much he could divulge. The colonel let him know he could divulge all about the jet.

"The skin of this bird is all Lear. It was designed by Colonel Venturi and the techies at the Geo-astronomical think tank. All the bells and whistles, including wet bar are pure luxury airliner, but the guts are pure bomber." Q reached above and pushed a red button. The 'dash' of the jet switched from luxury jet to military wonder. "I've been flying for thirty years and in all that time, I have never flown a better designed aircraft. There is no situation it's not equipped for. It is stronger, faster, and more maneuverable than the actual B1." Q's face lit up as he spoke. "The beauty is that even under the best radar the world has to offer, none of its true guts are detectable. X-ray and scanner can't even pick up what's hiding behind the outer shell."

Tag just stood, mouth agape. "Has she ever seen any action?"

"That's enough for now," Brent said. "What's our ETA for Munich?"

"Five more hours, sir."

Brent checked his watch. "Perfect."

Tag eyed Brent as he appeared to be in deep thought.

"Have you been in recent contact with the Knights in Germany?" Brent asked.

"Just before you came aboard. Everything is a go. We'll land at a private runway owned by one of the outer circle. They know members of the inner circle will be staying the night, but have no idea the Ambassador is on the flight. They're honored to have been called upon."

Brent hesitated for a moment. "How about back home? Any word?"

Q nodded. "Joan said the Madame Director and the team are making every effort to track you down, but they're not having any luck."

Brent smiled. "That's my girl."

"She also said that Alana is fitting in well with everyone."

"Alana? What the hell are you talking about?"

Q's eyes opened wide in surprise. "You didn't see her back in the Cove?"

"No! I had no idea she was coming. Care to fill me in."

"All I know is I received a message from Joan. I figured it came from you, but apparently I was wrong. I picked Alana up in Jerusalem and brought her to Palm Cove. The bishop met us at the airstrip."

"The bishop." Brent shook his head. "I should have known."

"I know it's not my place to say, so if you rather I say nothing, just cut me off."

"We've been through too much for me to tell you what you can or can't say. Speak your mind."

"Begging your pardon, Colonel, but we were all worried about your condition after Chloe's death. No one more than Bishop Jessop. He felt Alana's presence might somehow help. I tend to agree with him. I know you two shared a connection, a professional one, but still a special one. If you were to open up to anyone, it might have been her. It was worth a shot."

"Hmm," Brent mumbled. "You know what they say about opinions, Q."

The pilot laughed. "Yes, sir, I do, and now you have mine."

The colonel remained quiet for a few minutes. "Did you happen to hear what her plans were?"

"No, but I assume she'll be headed back to Israel. Dust doesn't gather around that one."

Again, Brent was quiet. "Well," he finally said, "everything happens for a reason. It's better this way."

"Beg your pardons, but I have no idea what the two of you are talking about," Tag said.

"I could use a drink," Brent said, "Tag, come with me and I'll fill in the blanks."

"I'd appreciate that. There seem to be quite a few." Tag followed Brent to the back of the aircraft.

"Pick your poison, Lieutenant. It will probably be your last for a while. Something tells me, they won't have liquor where we're headed."

"Jack on the rocks, sounds good."

"I don't normally drink," Brent said. "In fact, I haven't had a drop since I was inducted into the Phantom Squad," he took two glasses out from under the bar and poured two Jack Daniels, "but this seems like an appropriate time for one."

Tag downed half his glass. "The Phantom Squad? I guess that's the real name of what the terrorists call the Black Militia?"

Brent threw back his drink and nodded. "The number one rule between squad members is that there are no secrets." He gestured toward Tag. "It works both ways."

Tag nodded and raised his glass. "Fair enough."

"I'll go first," Brent said. "I'm sure you have a thousand questions. You deserve at least a few answers. What's your first question?"

"Tell me about the squad."

"We are a squad of five: some military, some not. We are called upon when all official means to an end aren't successful."

"So, everything I've heard is true?"

"I don't know what you've heard. You know how things get exaggerated."

Tag reiterated a couple of the stories he had heard about the squad's exploits and waited for a response.

"That's a first," Brent said. "The stories you've rehashed are actually milder than the truth. So, yeah, it's all true."

Tag almost choked on his drink when he heard the colonel's words. Gaining confidence, he asked his next question. "What's all this talk about Knights, Ambassadors and circles?"

"You stay on mission. I like that." Brent tipped his glass toward Tag. "Although, I'm sure you'll get to what's really on your mind soon enough." Brent took another sip, trying to figure out where to start. "I wear many hats. I wear the hat of an Army officer, though I'm not exactly in the military anymore. I also wear the hat of a covert government agent for the most clandestine agency in the world."

"CIA?"

Brent shook his head and pulled his hair back away from his face. "Not quite. This agency makes the CIA and the NSA pale in comparison. I am . . . was second in command of the SIA, the Strategic Intelligence Alliance."

Tag covered his mouth, trying not to spit out his drink. "We had heard of such an organization, but everyone thought it was made up."

Tag watched as Brent looked down and let his hair fall over his face. When he looked up, his expression was acute and sharp. "Everything I am about to tell you is far beyond top secret. Is that understood?"

Tag's posture stiffened, as if at attention. "Understood."

Over the next hour, Brent told his protégée a story that had the young officer asking for a refill on his drink. Tag opened his mouth to ask questions, but thought better of it and just stood at the bar and listened.

Tag looked like a child on Christmas morning.

"There are no questions out of bounds," Brent said, "what's on your mind?"

Tag swigged the rest of his drink. "I don't even know where to start. Let me see if I have this straight. You are the leader of the Phantom Squad, a squad of five soldiers, who aren't all soldiers, who don't exist, right?"

"Don't misinterpret soldiers for military personnel. Every

person involved in the squad is a soldier; the best you'll ever meet. The training they have undergone is more intense than anything the U.S. military could ever dream up. They not only underwent psychological and physical training but they were also trained to be assassins. Each is proficient in side arms as well as a compound bow, knives, oriental weapons, and hand-to-hand combat. They can strike without being heard or seen. As members of the Phantom Squad, our identities have been erased."

Tag put his hand up. "What do you mean exactly when you say erased?"

Brent smirked. "I mean that the man you are having this conversation with doesn't officially exist. No one outside of the squad, my immediate family and the directorate of the SIA knows I was ever born. I have no social security number, and you will not find any record of me: military, governmental or civilian. If I was ever fingerprinted, I would not show up in any database in the world." Brent's stare was so intense, it caused Tag to briefly look away. "That's why we had to visit Wheels. All my aliases can be tracked by the squad. Since I'm rouge for this mission, I needed a new identity, many, depending where I plan on going and what I need to accomplish."

"And what is that exactly?"

Brent checked his watch, "We can discuss that later. I need to go up and talk to Q for a moment."

CHAPTER 25

Brent returned after a few minutes. Taking his position at the bar, he asked Tag if he had any other questions.

"You still haven't told me about the knights." Tag spread his arms out wide. "Who are they and what do they have to do with anything of this?'

Brent dropped a couple cubes of ice in his drink and twirled them around with his finger, and looked at Tag with a dead-eyed stare. "They have pledged their allegiance to the Ambassador and are sworn to protect him and what he knows."

Tag had seen that look before. It was the same look he had seen on his friend after his life had been snuffed out by the enemy's bullet. He went to take another sip of his drink and realized it was empty. He swallowed hard. "Q had said that the Ambassador was on this flight. I take it you and he are one in the same?"

Brent nodded.

"What information do you have that would make these people put their lives on the line for you?"

"Before I say anything more, I need you to come clean. What was the real reason you left the service?"

Tag slid his glass forward. Brent opened a bottle of soda and poured him a drink. "It's not what you wanted, but it's all you get this close to Munich."

"What makes you think there's more to my leaving the service than just wanting to get on with my life?"

Brent gave a little shake of his head. "The military is your life. I can see it in every move you make and every word you speak." Brent pushed the issue. "Remember when I said there were no topics off limits."

Tag nodded.

"Well, that's a two way street. Why did you leave? If you don't want to talk about it, that's your choice. I'll just inform Q to drop you off anywhere you'd like and we'll part ways when we land. I can't, won't let you accompany me holding on to emotional baggage—potentially harmful baggage."

Tag fidgeted. His finger traced the condensation on the bar as it dripped from his glass. Did he really want to hitch his star to this crazy person? He looked around the interior of the jet and thought back to everything that had happened since they'd met. If he could trust anyone, he figured it was Brent.

"My last mission was in the mountains between Afghanistan and Pakistan. My spotter—a kid who I handpicked—had been with me for my last two tours." Tag held up his hand and crossed his fingers. "We were as thick as brothers. I would do anything for him and him for me.

"We had received Army intelligence that told us that there was a terrorist cell deep in the mountains on the Pakistani side. Off limits to the U.S. military."

"Al Qaida?"

"No, some new group. Well, not new, just new to us. Intel had been intercepting coded messages from all over the Mid-East and Europe. They were bounced off so many satellites that we weren't able to triangulate their position." Tag began to sweat and his hands started to tremble. "Man, they were so organized and so entrenched in every part of the world. They really had us dancing. Months were spent trying to track these guys, but no matter what we did and no matter what encryption busting methods we tried, we couldn't find jack.

"We had pretty much given up on them when an Afghani stumbled into Alpha camp. He was more dead than alive, delirious from fever and dysentery and high on poppy. I don't think he even knew it was a U.S. camp. He wasn't carrying any weapons and he was dressed in traditional Palestinian clothing; an ankle length robe, a throbe and a kaffiyeh, a black and white turban. The docs tried to help him, but he kept getting worse. When he slept, he talked.

"I don't sleep much and I was bored from being stuck in camp, so I asked to be put on night guard rotation. One night, out of the blue, he starts talking about his 'brothers' and how proud he was to be part of the Brotherhood."

Tag saw Brent's eyes widen.

"At first, I half listened," Tag continued, "but then he started rattling off coordinates in his sleep. Ones more accurate than we had." Tag's eyes dilated and the pitch of voice rose as he spoke. "I figured what the hell and started talking to him in Farsi. I was shocked when he began answering me. He told me that he got lost from his regiment during a sandstorm. He said they were headed to the Hindu Kush Mountains that border Pakistan and Afghanistan to meet with their leader."

"Did he give you a name of his leader?"

Tag shook his head. "No, but he said that the Brotherhood's last mission was a complete bust. Then, he starts rattling on about the Ark of the Covenant and how their second-in-command was killed somewhere in the West. I didn't give much credence to the whole ark bit. I figured the fever was getting the best of him, but with some prodding, I was able to get the coordinates of where everyone was to meet up in the mountains. It didn't take a rocket scientist to know he was talking about the Pakistan side of the ridge.

"Once I got all the information I could, I went to my commanding office. I wanted to leave that night and see if we could flush them out." Frustration washed over Tag. His facial muscles contracted as he clenched his jaw. "He didn't agree with me. His orders were to keep watch on the POW and see what other intel we might be able to gather." Tag dropped his head and shook it. "He died the next morning.

"It took days of hounding, but my captain finally agreed on a two-man mission to go and see if we could gather intel on the Brotherhood. The only stipulation was that we had to stay on the

Afghanistan side of the border."

Brent nodded.

Tag emptied his glass and continued. "The man who died said the meeting of the Brotherhood was scheduled for January ninth. My spotter, Bobby—Sergeant Delbach—and I left camp at o-one hundred hours, on the first of January. I decided we would make the trip on foot—less tracks to follow. From the coordinates the prisoner gave us, it was going to take us a good six days of constant moving and little sleep to make it to our destination. I wanted a couple of days to scout out the best position and get hunkered down.

"Everything went smoothly, maybe too smooth looking back at it, until we were perched high in the mountains. We found a deserted cave to set up and wait. It was the night of the seventh." Tag took a deep breath. "It was that night we heard voices close by. I wasn't too worried. I knew I could shoot faster and more accurately than a bunch of sand ni—"

Brent interrupted him mid word. "We don't need to disrespect their heritage."

Tag finished chewing the ice cube that was in his mouth. "Sorry, Colonel." He took a deep breath and continued. "Like I said, I thought I had the upper hand. I made my way out of the ant farm where we had set up camp. Through the night goggles, I could see them. There were so many of them. Hundreds. They kept emerging out of the holes in the rock like that game, 'Whac-a-Mole.' Knowing we were outnumbered, I retreated deep inside our 'hole' and sent an encrypted message back to Alpha Camp asking for air support.

"I stayed awake all night waiting for a response from my commander. I figured we would at least get air cover. It wouldn't take much to take out the whole lot. They were all gathered together on the ridgeline. When the response finally came back, it was short, three words." Tag looked up from his glass. Anger lined his otherwise smooth skin. "Two-man mission was all it said. That was it." His hands shook with emotion. "The bastard left us out there to die! I swore if I ever made it back to camp, I would make him pay."

"Why would an Army officer do that? It had to be personal," Brent said.

Tag nodded. "He was a desk jockey from D.C. He only took the assignment because he needed field time in order to make it up the ranks. Whenever the men had an issue or a question, they came to me, not him. He hated the fact that I had the men's respect." Tag gripped the glass tighter, hands still shaking.

Tag noticed Brent's attention shift from him to the glass. He loosened his grip.

"What happened on the ridge after you received the message?" Brent asked.

"We were perched right on the border. North Waziristan was just on the Pakistani side. We knew from surveillance that it was a strong hold for al Qaida, but we had no idea they were harboring other terrorists. The next morning, the enemy had disappeared. I figured they had crossed over. They had to be meeting in Waziristan. I made a decision to go further to see if we could pinpoint their stronghold.

"They left one sentry behind. He was dug in and camouflaged, but my spotter picked him up easily. I made the shot from a half mile and then we waited. I figured the terrorists would send reinforcements. No one showed, so we kept moving in the direction I thought they were headed. Four hours later, we found them. There had to be close to a thousand of them in a cave system just on the Pakistan side of the ridge. I noted the coordinates, took some snapshots, and we began our retreat. Six days later, we were in sight of camp. We figured we were home free and relaxed our posture. I made the call to Alpha to let them know we were on our way in." Tag stopped talking. He took a deep, labored breath, and closed his eyes.

"I still don't understand why you left the service."

Angry, Tag looked at Brent. "What command didn't tell us was that the man who died was gone. The night after we broke camp to begin the mission there was a raid and his body was taken from the morgue."

"Were there causalities?"

Tag nodded. "Eight of our men were lost and eleven of the enemy. That's why the Major was so adamant about not sending help. It had been a real cluster. The brass came down hard on him and was taking away his command. What I didn't know was that I was to replace him when I returned. Fifty yards from camp . . ." Tag leaned forward and spoke through clenched teeth, enunciating every word. "Just fifty yards from camp, I spotted an enemy soldier hiding behind a sand hill. Before I had the time to warn Bobby, the bastard shot and killed him. I emptied a full magazine into the son of a bitch before he could get off another shot." Tag's voice trailed off. "Too little, too late." He dropped his head. Chin resting on his chest. Tears pooled on the bar.

Brent reached out and squeezed his hand. "It wasn't your fault."

In a stilted voice, Tag clenched his teeth in anger. He balled up his fingers into a fist and punched the bar. "Yes, it was. I should have had Bobby covered. He was my responsibility. That bullet should have been mine, not his."

Emotions that had been pent up inside him since that day flowed down his face as if a dam had burst.

"I picked up his lifeless body and carried him into camp. Others came to help, but I wouldn't let him go. I carried Bobby into the Major's office and laid him on his desk. I don't know what I said to him or what he said to me, but I punched the S.O.B. and knocked him out cold.

"When the brass showed up the next morning, I fully expected to be taken into custody. No actions were taken. The colonel, Colonel Trenton, wanted to give me a commendation. I refused. He told me of his plans to have me replace the Major as base commander. I turned him down and resigned my commission. I wanted no part of an army that left its soldiers out to hang."

Tag's heart pounded with anger.

When he regained his composure, he listened as Brent told the lieutenant about Chloe and how she died. He told him about the Brotherhood of Gaza and of his plans to get even with all of them. Somehow, his unburdening did them both some good.

CHAPTER 26

Two hours later, Brent, Tag and Q were in the home of one of the Knights of the Endowment where they enjoyed a late dinner and got some shuteye.

Early in the a.m., they woke and again took flight.

Once Q had them at cruising altitude, Brent sat facing Tag. "I can't risk being seen entering Armenia so there won't be any landing committee." He pulled his hair back from his face and continued. "There won't be any landing at all."

Tag squinted and cocked his head to the side. Confusion seemed to engulf his expression.

"The SIA is looking for me." The lieutenant opened his mouth to speak, but Brent cut him off. "I'm not AWOL. They're looking for me because they're family and they care."

Tag nodded.

"I refuse to risk any more lives than I have to. Like your last mission, this is a two-man job."

"If the SIA is everything you say it is," Tag said, "won't their intel be able to track us?"

Brent smiled. "They would, if their tracker wasn't my inside person. She's scrambling all signals being sent out. Again, you can't find what you can't see."

Tag had to laugh at the colonel's ingenuity. "May I ask where our destination is?"

"We're headed to a monastery at the foot of Mount Ararat. The Khor Virap Monastery."

"Is it inhabited?"

Brent nodded. "It's a huge tourist attraction for Christians, so we should be able to blend in. As far as I know, it's not a working monastery. Just a place of pilgrimage with a church located on the grounds."

"What's there that's so important?"

The colonel shrugged his shoulders. "To be honest, I don't know. I just know it's where God is leading me."

"Beg your pardon, sir, but I don't quite understand. Why is God leading you halfway around the world?"

"It's where it all began."

Tag appeared exasperated. "Where all what began?"

Brent put his hand on his shoulder. "Sit down and let me tell you a story." He proceeded to tell Tag more details about The Endowment, about Noah's covenant with God, and about the lineage of his decedents known as The Ambassadors.

Tag leaned into the conversation. "At least the whole Ambassador thing is starting to make sense." He took a deep breath before continuing. "Okay, as farfetched as all that seems, I have no reason to doubt you, but what I still don't understand, is why you need to go there or what you hope to find."

"If you think it's farfetched now, I'm about to blow your mind," Brent said. "I had a vision . . ."

"You had a what?" Tag interjected.

"Just go with me on this, it's complicated."

Tag laughed. "Life has not been simple since we met, Colonel. I hate to see complicated."

Brent smiled. "You will."

Tag shook his head when he heard those two little words.

"Anyway," Brent continued, "in this vision, I was told that the answers to my questions would be found at *the beginning*. That's why I am going to the monastery and Mount Ararat. What I hope to find is two-fold. One, my faith and two, the ark."

"Noah's Ark? You must be joking. Right?"

"I've never been more serious," Brent responded.

"I'm no Biblical scholar, but I do know that a lot of people throughout history have tried to find Noah's Ark. What makes you think you can find it?"

Brent thought back to his vision when he was transported to a mountain range and spoke to God. It was as clear now as it had been on the day he was there in his dreams.

"I have already been there; I just need to retrace my steps."

"Damn it, Colonel. You're talking in riddles again." Tag stood and paced the compartment. "I hope I'm not out of line and I'm sorry if I am, but you're making my brain hurt. What do you mean you've already been there and what steps are you talking about? I'm just a lowly lieutenant, so please bring it down a notch and speak so I can understand." Tag sat back down and made eye contact. "I'm in for the long haul, but I need to understand what I'm in for." He shrugged his shoulders. "And what does any of this have to do with the Brotherhood of Gaza?"

It was Brent's turn to stand and pace the cabin as he tried to compose his thoughts in a manner that wouldn't put Tag over the edge. "First, you're not out of line. I appreciate your candor and I can understand your confusion. As far as speaking in riddles, get used to it. It just happens. Years ago, during a mission with the Squad, I had a vision. One that kept me alive during my captivity."

"What captivity? What mission?"

"It doesn't matter, what does matter is that it happened and in my vision, I was on Mount Ararat, and I'm pretty sure I was standing at the foot of Noah's Ark. I know in my heart, that's where I need to go back to in order for any of this to make sense."

"Okay, but I still don't see what this . . ."

"It's called stepping out on faith. You'll find I do it a lot. God has never let me down before and I have no reason to believe he will start now. I'm hoping to find clues to the ark's whereabouts at the monastery."

"But that place has been trampled on for hundreds of years. You said so yourself. How do you suppose to find something no one else has been able to find?"

Brent flashed back to his squad training.

"When you're looking for clues," Seven said, "don't be deceived by the fact that others have been there before you. If they don't know what to look for, it's possible they missed the obvious." Seven walked by his trainees. They looked disengaged. He spit his tobacco juice as he continued to walk.

"Professor," he yelled. His voice echoed off the concrete airplane hangar that had become their home.

"Sir?" Brent responded.

"Look outside and tell me what you find."

Brent took in his surroundings and answered. "I see trees, grass, dirt and mountains in the distance."

Seven smiled. "Anyone else find anything different?"

The other three recruits looked and shook their heads.

"Now, suppose, I rephrase the question," he said. "Professor, let's say you're not looking in general; let's say you're here because there was a terrorist attack yesterday and one of the men under your command was captured. Now, look around and tell me what you find."

Brent dropped into a squat position and closed his eyes. He tried to erase everything he had previously noticed. He wanted a blank slate when he looked again. He opened his eyes, stood and looked around. "I see the blades of grass to my right, broken and leaning in a northerly direction." His actions followed his thoughts as he walked outside the hangar where the grass led. "The low lying branches of the saplings are broken to my left, leading up into the foothills."

He closed his eyes momentarily to block out the sense of sight. "There is an odor of an extinguished fire. A camp site must be nearby and—"

"That's enough," Seven said. "Good job." He looked at the soldiers in front of him who now possessed a knowing expression. "You see, a thousand people could have been here, but if they didn't know what to look for, they would have seen the same thing the professor saw the first time. Of course, the more people who came through, the harder the clues will be to find, but they will still be there."

Brent opened his eyes and looked at the lieutenant. "I have two things that the thousands who have pilgrimaged didn't have. One, I have come for a different reason, and two, I have nowhere else to go. It's all I have and I hope it will be enough."

Tag shook his head and smirked. "I said before you were insane. I just wish you would stop proving it."

Brent was about to ask him a question when Tag interrupted. "You never did say what any of this has to do with the Brotherhood of Gaza."

Brent opened his shirt and showed Tag the tattoo over his heart.

Affectus mos adepto vos iuguolo

"What language is that and what does it say?"

"It's Latin. It says, 'Emotion will get you killed.' It's the Phantom Squad creed." Brent pointed to his own head and then to his chest. "If I can't figure out what's going on in my head then I can't get back to the soldier I was—the man I was—and I have no chance of defeating the Brotherhood. The only thing I will accomplish is getting both of us killed. That's why this place, this trip, this . . . quest is so important."

Brent watched as all the pieces of the puzzle seemed to connect in Tag's mind.

He waited a few minutes and then said. "There's one thing I've been meaning to ask you. When I asked you to follow my lead back in St. Augustine, you seemed to be able to mimic my every move and stay within my shadow. It was if we were just one person. Where did you learn how to do that?"

"It's a Cree battle trick that was used centuries ago," Tag said. "It made their numbers seem small to the enemy so they could hide their true strength. My grandfather taught it to me when I was a boy."

Brent's mind went into overdrive. "I want you to teach it to me. It could come in very handy when we go after the Brotherhood."

Tag stood a little taller. "It would be my honor, sir."

"Thank you," Brent said. "Oh, and by the way, I have a piece of information you might want to know. While we were flying to Munich, I had Q make some inquiries. The major you spoke of was given a dishonorable discharge for not sending in support and Sergeant Delbach was awarded the Purple Heart for bravery during his last mission."

Tag smiled ear to ear. "I don't know how you are able to do what you do, but I'm grateful."

"Two more things."

"There's more?"

Brent held up one finger. "The thugs we met at the train station are in custody and were thrown out of the tribe. Your family has been relocated back on tribal property with full tribal rights."

Tag stood, open mouthed and speechless. Without thinking, he threw his arms around Brent and thanked him.

"Don't get all sappy, I still have one more bit of information."

Tag straightened up and eyed Brent.

"I had Q contact SIA who contacted the Army. It's been arranged for you to be re-commissioned as an officer with all your privileges reinstated and if you'd like, to be assigned to SIA."

Tag laughed a full belly laugh. "Thank you, Colonel, and yes, I would like that. I would like that a great deal."

As they continued to speak, their conversation was interrupted by Q. "It's zero two hundred hours, Armenian time. You have a half hour before your flight ends. It's time you geared up and took your seats."

"Seats? How are we going to jump if we are in our seats?" Tag asked.

"That reminds me," Brent said. "Let me tell you about another little tweak I made to the B1-B."

Brent explained how since the bomber had the façade of a Lear, the only form of egress other than the door was for the bottom to drop out.

A half hour later, the bottom of the Lear opened up and they dropped, seats and all, into the night sky.

CHAPTER 27

Brent, having had experience with this type of landing was first out of his seat and harness. He helped Tag unbuckle his belt and gather his gear. They hid the seats and silks, grabbed their duffle bags and backpacks, and started the fifteen-mile trek to the Khor Virap monastery.

"What's with the guitar case?" Tag asked.

Brent looked back at Tag and grinned. "Need to know," was all he said.

Tag rolled his eyes.

Brent changed the subject. "I want to be there in time for the first tour, just after daylight."

Tag checked his watch. "Judging by the time and your pace, I don't think that should be an issue," Tag replied.

"It's always good to be early."

They stopped when they reached the outskirts of Artashat, the village closest to the monastery.

"We'll stop here and use the public restroom," Brent said. "We need to change out of our fatigues and into civilian clothing."

Once changed, they kept walking. Brent told Tag that their destination was just a half mile north of where they were, but he didn't get a response from the lieutenant. He thought Tag was getting tired and was lagging behind. An abrupt stoppage of movement proved him wrong. The young officer plowed into his backside.

"What the—"

Turning around, he saw Tag staring off into the distance.

Brent followed Tag's line of sight. As the sun rose over Mount Ararat, there appeared to be a light glowing on the upper northeast side of the mountain. Although the rest of the mount's peak was bathed in the early morning sun, one spot appeared to be illuminated in a brighter glow.

"If I didn't know better, I would swear that was a sign from heaven," Tag said.

Brent nodded. "I don't think you're mistaken, you can mark down this date and time for your first physical sign of God's Providence. He is pointing the way to the beginning."

As they stood admiring God's majesty, other Christian pilgrims came up from the village. The tour group stopped and took snapshots of the sunrise, yet none of them seemed to see what Brent and Tag were looking at.

"Why aren't they talking about the glow?" Tag whispered.

"Because they can't see it," Brent answered. "It is only meant for those God chooses."

Before Tag could speak, Brent told him to get in the back of the line and blend in. They walked in unison as the tour guide told the camera happy group about the area's history.

"When do we climb?" Tag asked. "We don't want to lose the light."

Brent smiled. "Like the star that led the Magi, the light will be present until it's time for us to ascend Mount Ararat. First, we have business at the monastery."

Reaching the outside of the monastery, Brent motioned Tag over to the side. "When the group enters the building, follow my lead. Shadow my movements."

Without a sound or movement, he saw the eyes of a sniper stare back at him. That was all the answer he needed.

The group entered the old stone monastery as the tour guide continued to speak.

"Grigor Lusavorich was imprisoned here for thirteen years by

Tridates the third, the king of Armenia," the guide said. "After his imprisonment, Grigor became the religious consul of the king and was later known as Saint Gregory. In the year 301 CE, Armenia became the first Christian country in the known world. A chapel was originally built in 642 in memory of Gregory. A larger church and monastery were built around it and even today regular church services are held."

The information, although interesting, was not news to Brent. He had researched Khor Virap extensively before departing Palm Cove.

When the group entered the chapel, a red rope blocked an alcove to the left. "What is beyond the rope?" asked someone in the tour.

"There are ruins under the monastery," the guide answered.

"Will we get to see where Saint Gregory was imprisoned?" said another.

"We will at the end of the tour, but we will make our way there by a different route."

Brent put his arm out as they approached the rope. "Lag back a bit."

Tag nodded.

When the group had all entered the chapel, Brent and Tag jumped over the rope and headed down into the ruins.

At the bottom of the broken stone steps, the ruins became more fragile. They stood in what looked like a cave from centuries past. The further they went, the darker it became. When he thought it was safe, Brent turned on his flashlight. The illumination shown on a dust filled room. It was small, but open. Rock and debris lay everywhere.

"Watch your step." Brent said. "Even the smallest mistake may take this place down."

"This is like entering the *Twilight Zone*," Tag said. "What do you hope to find down here?"

Brent shined the light back and forth around the open vestibule. In front of him were four passageways. He knew from his research that the monks had originally built them as a deterrent for their enemies. One led further into Khor Virap, the others were traps.

He went into a deep squat, closed his eyes and dropped his head forward.

Tag watched as Brent's shoulders and upper body went limp. For a moment, he wasn't sure if the colonel was still breathing. Brent began to sift loose gravel with his hands in a rhythmical motion. His breathing became so shallow that Tag couldn't see his chest rise and fall.

The deeper Brent went into his subconscious, the clearer his vision became. He saw the four passageways and was able to navigate each one. Three led to death. Only one led to . . . his vision became hazy as he sensed trouble.

Quickly, he brought himself out of the trance and stood up, drawing his weapon. Tag saw him reach under his shirt for his sidearm and did the same.

"What did you see?"

"Nothing good."

Before the words had fully escaped his mouth, they were surrounded by monks. Men wearing heavy brown robes and sandals. They were short in stature, carried staffs, and were unfazed by the fact that the two men they faced carried guns.

"We mean you no harm," Brent said. "I have only come looking for answers."

The monks didn't seem to understand his words and began to close in on them. Each twirling their staff with a deft ability. Tag repeated Brent's words in Armenian, but the monks continued to close rank. The colonel heard Tag release the safety on his semi-automatic and point it at the one who was closest. Still speaking in Armenian, he said that he didn't want to shoot anyone and asked them to put their staffs down.

The monks began to move in synchronized movements. Each spinning their bodies one way or another, all the while twirling their staffs in a faster motion.

"Stand down," Brent ordered the lieutenant. "Follow my lead." He slowly turned his pistol so he was now holding the barrel. He then squatted down and placed the weapon on the dirt floor. Tag followed orders.

From somewhere deep in the room, a question was asked. "Who

is it that wanders into our midst with weapons meant to kill?"

"The guns are meant for defense, not offense," Brent answered. "Your men move in silence. You have trained them well."

There was no response.

Brent took a step forward. He didn't look at Tag, but spoke to him. "Don't move, no matter what happens. That's an order, Lieutenant."

He continued to move forward in a cautious manner. He didn't stop as the staffs whizzed by his head so close he could hear the *whir* sound of their approach. Brent could feel the wind against his face with each pass. His head remained steady, but his eyes were in constant movement. "Who among you asked the question?"

"You have not earned the right to ask questions. I will do the asking."

Brent heard a tapping of a staff on the ground and immediately the monks stopped their movement and held their staffs in both hands so that the wooden dowels were perpendicular to their bodies. Each staff touching the one next to it, end to end, completing a circle. Two of the clergy parted so that their leader could come forward. He was a rotund, short man whose hood lay upon his head, blackening out all facial features. He reminded Brent of Friar Tuck from "The Adventures of Robin Hood."

"We don't take kindly to intruders," the monk said. "State your reasons for being here or turn and retrace your steps."

"I come in search for meaning," Brent replied. "I seek the beginning."

"The beginning of what?"

Brent knew his next words would change the complexion of the conversation. He would either cause discontent among the monks or bring peace to the situation. "I am the latest of Noah's lineage. I wish to discover the truth and find reason for what I do."

"If you are who you say you are, you are welcome among us. If not, you will find yourself at the bad end of the staff."

"How can I put you at ease?"

"Tell me the history of Noah's covenant with God."

Brent told the story of Noah and the herb of life. He told of the Enlightenment and of his fight with Satan.

Still not satisfied, the monk said, "Words are hollow, prove to me that you are who you say—prove you are The Chosen."

Brent thought for a moment and then asked if he could open the guitar case.

"You may, but don't do anything foolish. If you do, your friend will be dead before you can make your next move."

Brent looked over his right shoulder, back at Tag. "Stay relaxed, Lieutenant. No harm will come to you."

He slid his bags off his shoulder and gently placed the case on the ground. He opened it and took out the guitar that sat within. With deliberate movements, he removed the false bottom, reached in, and picked up the sheath that lay underneath. With his first touch, he could feel the power of the Sword of Truth. He held the sheath out in front of him and withdrew the sword from its place of rest. He stood in the middle of the circle of monks and held the sword by its handle. Slowly, he started to twist his wrist in slow, tight circles, allowing the sword to rotate in a vertical manner by his side. Brent then widened his stance and at the same time widened the circles made by the sword. Soon he was moving and spinning as if he was but a feather and controlled the sword with unseen dexterity.

Circling the room, he spun so fast that those watching could only see his hair flying and the glint of the steel of the sword. As he continued to move, Tag and the monks heard the sound of snapping wood, but no one dared move. When Brent finally stopped, he stood directly in front of the leader and held the sword out in front of his body in both hands. "Here is the Sword of Truth, given to me by Archangel Michael."

"What was the sound we heard when you put on that demonstration?" asked the monk.

Brent motioned for the brothers to separate their hands. When they did, their staffs were all cut in two equal halves, all shorn by the brilliance of his moves and the sharpness of the blade.

The hooded monk stepped forward and held out his hands. "May I?"

"You may, but I must warn you, you will not be able to hold it."

"Please."

Knowing what would happen, Brent placed it in his hands.

When he let go, the sheer weight of the sword dropped the monk to his knees and he screamed out in pain. The sword dropped and struck the ground with the sound of thunder.

The leader looked at the palms of his hands and watched them blister, burned from touching what was not his to hold. Instead of anger, the monk began to laugh even though his hands throbbed with pain.

Brent picked up the sword and with his free hand helped the man to his feet. "It's not a real burn, just a sign to let you know the truth."

The redness and inflammation quickly subsided along with the pain.

The brother looked at his hands and smiled. "We've been waiting for your arrival, Ambassador, but we thought you would come alone. Seeing you enter our home with another raised questions. Michael's sword tells me you are who you say you are." He waved Tag forward. "Why bring another on such a personal pilgrimage?"

"It's what God deemed. Who am I to argue with the Lord," Brent said.

The monk discarded his hood, revealing his face for the first time. His eyes were lined with age, but also bright with wisdom. They darted from Brent to Tag and back again. "If anyone could argue with the Lord Almighty, it would be you, my son. I'm glad to know even the Chosen has the humility to know his place."

Brent smiled at the brother. "To be honest, I tried it once and the outcome wasn't pretty."

The rotund monk smiled at his response. Placing a hand on Brent's shoulder, he asked, "Which way must we travel, Enlightened One?"

"The second opening on the right will not cause death and hopefully lead to answers."

The brother turned and walked towards the opening. He stopped before entering and said, "Are we to call you Ambassador, or do you have a name"

"You can call me Brent. And you, Brother?"

"You may call me Gregory. Every brother in charge of the true monastery has taken the name of our founder. Come and I will show you our home."

CHAPTER 28

Back in Palm Cove, things were in full swing. Alana's training was going as planned. She was in amazing physical shape. She had proven herself at the range with a variety of handguns as well as other handheld weapons, such as knives and swords. Sergeant Jefferson reported that she had great reflexes and was catching on fast to the martial arts used by the squad. What impressed Seven even more were her mental capabilities and her emotional fortitude.

Maddie had administered all the psychological tests that SIA trainees were put through. Alana passed with flying colors.

The final aspect of her training was conducted by Seven, and he pulled no punches. He was there to tear her down mentally, strip away her emotions and build her back up per his needs. A soldier who could act on instinct as well as intelligence, the best of the best who could meet the needs of the Phantom Squad.

The last stage of Alana's transformation had gone well, too well for Seven's taste, so he decided to throw a wrench into the training. He set up a scenario where she had to decide between saving the lives of her squad members or saving the life of Faith. He fully expected her to choose Faith.

The virtual scene was set in a bombed out building. It was a timed mission. He and the rest of the squad watched from the confines of Joan's lair where they could control the environment and the potential outcome. In the scenario, Alana had been given a cryptic message to follow. She was able to decipher the message without much trouble and entered the building with three minutes to spare.

"She's good," Jefferson said.

Seven looked around the room as the others watched with admiration at the calm demeanor of their recruit.

Seven thought back to when Alana got the slip on him back in Jerusalem. He fully planned on leveling the score with this final test.

He spat in a coffee mug. "We'll see," was all he said.

Alana moved in complete silence through the smoke-filled warehouse. A close up of her face was on one screen so Seven could look for signs of distress—signs that she would crack under pressure. He saw nothing.

Maddie stood in the background. Arms crossed. Foot tapping. She had argued with Seven the night before over this test. She had said that it wasn't fair, no member of the squad could make the decision he wanted.

His answer was rote. "God, country and squad before all else. That's the way it has been since the beginning and that's the answer I'm looking for."

"You're putting her in an impossible position and you know that," Maddie had answered. "You are setting her up for failure. What good will come of that? You will tear down her confidence and make her vulnerable in future missions . . . real missions."

Seven just stared back at his wife. "Not if she chooses correctly."

"You're an ass," Maddie replied. "You're only doing this because she showed you up in Israel."

When Seven opened his mouth to speak, she told him to shut up and turned off the lights in their bedroom. Those were the last words they had spoken to one another.

The tapping of her foot was getting on his nerves, but Seven was too bullheaded to say anything. He didn't even look in her direction.

Back in the warehouse, Alana faced off against four armed assassins. Two she disposed of with one headshot to each. Her last two bullets. The third man caught her off guard and jumped her from behind. She used her martial arts training and subdued the threat only to find herself face-to-face with a knife-wielding maniac. She could see from his eyes that he was high on something.

As he continuously lunged at her with the blade, he called her a whore and a loser, the same names her father and deceased husband had called her.

Still, she showed no emotion.

With a speed seen only by Brent and Seven, she reached down, slid a knife from her pant leg and in one fluid motion, let it fly. She missed her target high and to the left. Her assailant looked up and laughed at her ineptitude. As he began to lunge in her direction again, a loud snap could be heard in the warehouse. His head turned in the direction of the noise. He watched as a wooden truss, which had been attached by a rope, fell from the ceiling. In that split second, Alana used her other hand, pulled a second blade, let it fly and sliced through his jugular. He was dead before he and the board hit the ground.

Maddie couldn't help but smile at her ingenuity.

Back in the virtual mission, Alana made her way to the far room in the building and found Brent and Faith both tied up on opposite sides of the room. Each was wrapped in explosives which were attached by way of wire to a bomb placed against the back wall.

Seven, using a voice modulator said, "Well done, agent. Now comes the real challenge. The bomb is set to kill one or both of the people you see before you. To your left, you will find a pair of wire cutters. On the bomb, there is a clock. On my command, it will count down from ten. You only have enough time to save one. Choose."

Everyone in the room looked back at Seven with surprise. He felt their stares, but kept his attention on the monitor.

Alana surveyed the scene and mumbled, "You bastard." Picking up the wire cutters, the clock began ticking. Ten, nine, eight . . .. Dropping the wire cutters, she blew them both a kiss, ran towards the bomb and pulled two knives from her uniform. She dove for the bomb and in a final act of defiance, sliced both wires as they exited the explosive, landing on top of the device as it blew.

"I'll be damned," Seven spat.

Maddie looked at her husband and saw his mouth agape.

Seven regained his composure and whispered, "I never thought she would make that choice."

As the dust cleared, the lights inside the simulator turned on. Seven grabbed the mic. "Well done, Sister. Welcome to the Phantom Squad."

Like Lazarus rising from the dead, she rose from the floor. "I pray to God that none of us ever has that decision to make," she said. She then looked directly into the camera in the room and called Seven a name in Hebrew.

Seven looked over at Bishop Jessop and asked what she said. The bishop's face was crimson. "Nothing I'll ever repeat." The room erupted in laughter.

"A celebration is in order," Maddie said into the open mic. "Alana, you have proven yourself beyond measure to be all we could ask of you. Please get cleaned up and change into something nice. Dinner and all expenses are on my husband tonight."

Alana walked out of the simulation room. "He better bring some serious cash. I'm suddenly hungry for caviar and lobster."

Again, the room erupted in laughter. Even Seven couldn't help but smile.

CHAPTER 29

Dinner was held at The Loft with a menu chosen by Alana. She made good on her threat of caviar and lobster. Everyone, including Faith was present. She was the highlight of the night. The conversation soon turned to Brent.

"Has there been any word from him?" Maddie said, knowing the answer before she asked.

"None," Joan answered. "I haven't had any luck locking down a location and there is no way to get into the Endowment office to see if he left any information behind."

Maddie's eyebrow rose. "Hmm," she said.

"What about the guy Lieutenant Owens saw him with at the train station?" Seven said. "Have we had any luck identifying him?"

Joan nodded as she finished a bite of salad. "He's ex-military. His name is Lieutenant Rowtag Achak. He is a highly decorated veteran of both Iraq and Afghanistan. He was one of the best snipers in the Armed Forces."

Seven put down his fork and wiped his mouth with his napkin. "Sounds like a career man. Why did he leave the Army?"

Joan leaned forward. "That's where things get a little foggy. His last mission was on the Pakistan-Afghanistan border. A two-man recon mission. They had received word from a camp detainee that there was to be a gathering of terrorists somewhere on the ridge."

Seven stole a look at Maddie as he listened intently to Joan's intel. Maddie knew Joan had a Pentagon insider who had been a close friend of her mother's, but she never felt the need to question her about her sources.

"He and his spotter were somewhere dug deep into the anthills on the outskirts of Waziristan." Joan paused and looked around the table for dramatic effect. "They heard the terrorists talking about a group known as the Brotherhood."

Seven slapped the table hard causing silverware and plates to shake when he heard her mention the Brotherhood.

Joan leaned over the table and continued. "Lieutenant Achak overheard a conversation about a vast mission that failed and its connection to the Ark of the Covenant. The intel I received stated that all the members of the Brotherhood were meeting to devise a new strategy. It even mentioned that the mysterious leader of the Brotherhood would be present."

"What did the lieutenant have to say about the ark?"

Joan shook her head. "He didn't place any emphasis on it. He was more concerned that hundreds, possibly thousands of terrorists were to meet in one place." Joan was about to continue when her phone buzzed. She stopped talking long enough to read and answer the text.

Seven leaned across the table. "And . . ."

"And, if you stop interrupting me, I'll finish."

He nodded and leaned back in his chair.

Joan continued until her phone buzzed again.

"Who keeps calling?" Maddie said. "That's a secure line."

"The White House wants a video conference tonight. I told them we would make contact as soon as we returned. They acknowledged my message."

Seven motioned for Joan to continue.

"As I was saying," Joan said, "the major thought all the terrorists were dead, so he didn't send out a scout team to make sure. As Lieutenant Achak and his spotter approached camp, Sergeant Delbach, his spotter, was shot and killed. The lieutenant killed the attacker before he could get off his next shot.

"He carried his friend's body into camp and headed straight

for the major's quarters. He laid the body on the commanding officer's desk and then punched him square in the jaw. Knocked him out cold.

"He told the Army that if this was the way they treated their men, he wanted no part of the service and resigned his commission. He accompanied the sergeant's body back to the States and never looked back."

Seven chewed on his bottom lip. "I wonder how much of this Brent knows?"

"Knowing him, all of it," Maddie answered.

Seven spit tobacco juice in his cup. "Then we can assume that they are together. Wherever they are?"

The table was silent. It was broken by Benito, the owner of The Loft. "I thought this was a celebration," he said in a very Italian, animated style. "Why the long faces?" He looked around the table, stopping when he got to Seven. "And why are you spitting in my grandmother's china?"

Seven's face reddened. "Sorry."

Benny shrugged. "Nothing two or three washings in scolding hot water won't take care of. But just in case, this-a-cup is the one your coffee will come in from now on."

His remarks broke the tension.

"Benito, we need to get back to HQ. Would you mind boxing up the food?"

He looked at Maddie and smiled. "You know I can never say no to a beautiful lady. Go and I'll have it delivered."

CHAPTER 30

Everyone gathered in the conference room for the video conference with the White House. When the connection was made, they were all surprised to see the president at the other end.

"Is everything all right, Mr. President?" Maddie asked.

"Everything is fine." His eyes roamed the table and then brightened at the sight of his daughter. "How's my angel?"

Scarlet turned the color of her name. "I'm fine, Daddy. Are you sure everything is okay? It's not like you to call a conference for no reason."

"I didn't say it was for no reason, just that everything was fine. Call me later, so we can catch up. I miss you."

"I will," Scarlet said. "I miss you, too."

"Mr. President," Maddie interjected, "why the call?"

"I wanted to personally let SIA know that I've decided to take a trip overseas to visit our troops. Nothing official. No one will know I'm gone." The president twirled his pen between in fingers, something he did when excited. "This is no media junket, just an informal trip to boost morale. I'll be headed to Iraq and Afghanistan. I won't be leaving for forty days, but I wanted your help in securing the bases."

"I hope I'm not speaking out of place," Maddie said, "but do you think that's wise? There has been an increase in the fighting, especially in Afghanistan."

"I appreciate your concern, but yes, I do think it's wise. The increased fighting is why I feel the need to go. If the Commander and Chief of the Armed Forces thinks it's safe to be there, hopefully it will bolster the confidence of our brave men and women in uniform." He saw the deep concern of those seated around the table at HQ. "Don't waste your time trying to talk me out of it, my people already tried. I'm firm on this."

"I would like it on record that we agree with your staff on this," Maddie said.

"Duly noted," President Dupree acknowledged.

Maddie nodded. "With that being said, what can we do for you? Would you like members of the directorate to accompany you on your travels?"

"Not you specifically, but I promised my staff I would have your people secure each location and be on site when I get there."

"Send us a list of coordinates and I'll have my best agents deployed."

"I sent it just before the meeting began. Joan will have to decode—"

"Got it, sir," Joan said. She was typing like she was possessed. "Decoded and read, Mr. President."

The president smiled and shook his head. "You never cease to amaze me. It took my best people two hours to decode that message and they know the code."

Joan blushed. "Just doing my job, Mr. President."

"We'll make it top priority and let you know when our people are deployed," Maddie answered.

"I'd like to add one thing, if I could, sir."

"I never could stop you from speaking your mind, Seven, so speak up."

"If my people find anything that would put you in direct danger, I'm personally scrubbing this trip."

President Dupree pursed his lips in determination. "Like I said, I'm firm on this, so I suggest your people find a way to secure the locations."

The table was quiet as they tried to absorb the information they had received.

Some other small matters were discussed before the president got to the other point of this meeting. "What about Brent? Any word on his whereabouts or what he's up to?"

"Not yet, but we're working on locating him. We believe he is traveling with a young officer, a Lieutenant Achak; retired Army."

"Interesting," President Dupree said. "I guess it's good to know he's not solo. Send me what you have and I'll have the Pentagon do some digging. Maybe we can help track him down."

The president didn't know of Joan's Pentagon mole, and no one mentioned that they already knew what the government would find.

"That would be a big help," Maddie said. "Thank you."

The president's brow creased in concern. "You know how much I owe Colonel Venturi. Anything I can do, I will." The president's eyes moved from the camera to somewhere behind it. "I'm being called into a budget meeting. Stay in touch."

"Yes, sir."

As the feed was killed, Maddie saw that Joan looked concerned. "What is it you're not saying, Joan?"

"This list contains the camp Lieutenant Achak was stationed at. I don't like that."

Maddie tapped her pen on her pearly white porcelain crowns. "Me either." She turned her attention to the other end of the table. "Scarlet, when you speak to your father later, try to dissuade him from making this trip. If nothing else, get him to eliminate Alpha Camp from his list."

Scarlet swallowed hard. "When he gets his mind on something, it's almost impossible to change it, but I'll do all I can, Madame Director. I'll even throw a hissy fit if I think it will help."

CHAPTER 31

Brent and Tag followed Brother Gregory and the other monks through a maze of tunnels, traveling deeper underground. They came to a halt when they entered a small room which consisted of a kneeler for praying against the far wall. On the wall were three candles. All of which were lit.

"This was the cell that Grigor was kept in during his imprisonment," Gregory said.

Brent walked the perimeter. He felt the cool, damp, flat stones that made up the walls. "Not much room. No obvious means of escape. He must have been strong in resolve and spirit to have survived."

"One does not need much room to pray, Ambassador," Brother Gregory replied. He motioned around the room with his hands and asked his visitors, "Besides the obvious, what else can you tell me about this chamber?"

"May I move about the room?" Tag asked.

"By all means, young man."

Tag circled the room, feeling the walls with a soft hand, with a touch his grandfather taught him. His fingertips barely grazed the stone.

"And you, Ambassador? Do you wish to check out the room?"

"I'll wait until Tag has finished. I, too, want to see what he finds."

Tag finally came to rest where he started.

"Well?" the brother said.

"The walls are smooth as if they had been polished. There is no way anyone could have climbed them, so if there is a way out, it has to be a hidden exit."

He walked over to where there was a small notch in the wall, probably made to be a shelf of some kind. He placed his hand inside the opening and felt a small depression in the stone, one just big enough to place his finger. With youthful confidence, he stuck his finger in the hole and felt a lever.

He forced his finger deeper into the hole and pushed on the lever expecting a portion of the wall to give way. Instead, his finger became trapped, as if it were clamped into a pair of Chinese handcuffs. When he tried to pull it out, it was squeezed harder. Tag tried not to show pain, but relented and asked the monk for help.

Gregory laughed and walked to him. "Relax all the muscles in your arm. Start with your neck and shoulder and work your way down." He reached forward and placed his hand on the young man's bicep. "Feel the muscles relax as you visualize the same."

Tag closed his eyes and using his sniper training, began to relax the muscles in his arm. As his visualization reached his finger, he could feel the pain start to subside.

"Don't try to move your finger, just continue to feel the entire arm relax. Visualize a dead weight," Gregory said. He moved his own hand down near Tag's wrist. "It must be totally weightless in order for the wall to let go."

Tag kept his eyes shut.

Brent could see the lieutenant's breathing become slow and shallow. He knew the monk could feel his friend's pulse start to become thready and weak.

Five minutes later, Tag's arm fell by his side.

"I'm impressed," Gregory said. "The fastest any of the brothers have been able to negotiate their way out of there was two hours." He looked at Brent. "And you. Do you wish to hazard a guess?"

"I don't ever guess," Brent said.

He again walked the perimeter of the cell block, taking in all the nuances of his surroundings. Brent stopped, dead center in the room, and slowly dropped into a deep squat. He closed his eyes and remembered his training.

"Every trap, no matter how well designed has a way out," Seven said. "You just have to be able to sense it. Sometimes the most obvious will lead to safety, but sometimes . . ." He spit out the door onto a red ant hill. The ants gathered by the hundreds ready to defend what was theirs. "It leads to death. How well you decide your path will depend on how quiet and still you can be in times of trouble. Listen to what your environment is telling you. Sometimes they can be hard to find, but the clues will always be there."

Seven walked around the airplane hangar. All that could be heard were his boots on the cement floor. "Your senses will be your greatest ally in the field. But," he said in a loud voice. The word reverberated off the block walls. "Don't rely on sight. It's the last of your five senses you want to use."

His recruits heard everything he was saying, but he wasn't sure they were listening. He opened an equipment box and pulled out four hoods.

"Put one of these over your heads. We're gonna play a little game I like to call, 'the winner gets to eat dinner.' " The men's laughter was short lived when they realized he was serious.

They could hear Seven walk behind them and the sound of the light switch.

"The first one to meet me in the mess tent wins."

The last thing they heard was Seven shutting the door to the hangar. What they didn't know was that he had shut himself in the hangar with them.

"Now what are we supposed to do?" Sergeant Jefferson said.

"We could take the hoods off and find our way out of here," Private Jensen said.

No one answered Jensen. They figured he was joking. "We work as a team," Brent said. "That's our best chance to get out of here and then we all get to eat."

"Y'all do what you want," Jensen said. "I'm going solo. I'm gonna enjoy seeing your faces when I put that first piece of steak in my mouth."

He slid the hood up and over his left eye just enough to get a glimpse around the room. He surveyed the area, remembering what Seven had said about the answer sometimes being right in front of you.

While all this was happening, Seven was strategically placed in a spot where he was able to see and hear everything, but could not be seen. He watched as Jensen moved his blindfold to uncover one eye.

Jensen made his way to a window that had been left cracked open and slithered his way out like the snake he was. Safe on the other side, the corner of his mouth curled up like the first ember of a forest fire. An evil grin spread across his face.

Seven who had been hiding in an alcove right by a side entrance, followed him outside and watched with disgust.

Jensen turned to strut towards the mess tent when he felt a sting on the side of his neck. Before a guttural sound could emanate from his throat, his body crumbled to the ground. Seven bagged and tagged—tied up and gagged—the soldier.

Brent, Jefferson and Fitzpatrick worked as a team and found a way out. Seven congratulated them on their teamwork.

Brent's mind cleared as the memory faded. He blocked out all the sounds in the room and focused on the sound of his heartbeat until that too faded. He then repeated the process for his sense of smell, clearing his consciousness of all odors. Then there was nothing. No sound. No sight. No touch. No smell.

Everyone in the room stopped moving. They just stared at this strange man squatting in the middle of the stone floor.

In deep concentration, Brent heard a faint whoosh sound. He tuned it in, trying to figure out where it came from and what it was telling him. The longer he stayed still, the louder it became. Allowing his vital signs to stabilize, he opened his eyes, and stood up.

Brent made his way to the prayer bench. Kneeling, he said a prayer of thanks, stood, and faced the others. "There is little ventilation in this room. It comes from the passage we just entered.

The flames from the candles should flicker in that direction, towards the oxygen supply."

"Ah, so you think that is our way out?"

Brent turned his head toward Brother Gregory. "I said should. If you look at the wall where the candle basin is attached, you will find slight burn marks. That's because they flicker toward the wall."

The brother nodded. "And what does that tell you, Chosen One?"

Brent didn't answer, but again knelt on the pew. Instead of placing his hands on the top of the prayer rail, he slid his fingers under it and felt a slight depression. With a soft touch, he felt the stone begin to depress. He knew there had to be a spring built into it. With added pressure, he felt the wall give way revealing a much larger room on the other side.

Gregory let out a hardy laugh. "It is true what we have heard about you," he said.

"And that is?"

"That you are a man not like many others. One like David. A man after God's own heart."

"Like you, Brother, I am just a man trying to do what God asks of him."

The old monk patted him on the back. "Come and we will show you what we have been working on for your arrival and then we will eat." He led them through the opening into the rest of the monastery.

CHAPTER 32

Brent stepped through and walked into the Twenty-first century. He stood in a large heated room with hardwood floors and walls. It was if he walked back into the Endowment office inside the Palm Cove Library. "Interesting place you have here, Brother."

"It took us eight years to complete. All the work had to be done in the pitch of night, but the arduous task was worth your arrival."

Brent's expression turned inquisitive. "I don't understand. How did you know I would come?"

"The light on the mountain. I'm sure you saw it on your approach to the monastery."

Brent nodded.

"It first appeared a little over eight years ago. At first, we didn't understand its significance. Two of our younger brothers climbed Mount Ararat to try to find out what it was shining on, but they didn't get far."

"What happened?"

"The light became brighter the higher they climbed. Soon it was blinding."

"So bright, they had to turn back?"

"No, blinding," Brother Gregory emphasized. "They began to lose their sight." He called two of the monks forward. Brent could see a foggy glaze covering their eyes, much like cataracts. "They had no choice but to return."

Brent pushed his hair back from his face and placed his hand in front of the eyes of one of the brothers. The monk reached out and grabbed his wrist. *Not completely blind*, he thought. "I still don't understand how you related those happenings to me?"

Brother Gregory smiled. "While on the mountain, they heard the word of God. They were told to expect Noah's heir to return to Ararat. They were also given instructions on what to build in preparation of your coming. We finished just days ago."

"What were they told?"

"Come and I will show you." He led them through the great room into another.

"Holy . . ." Tag said. "I wouldn't believe this if I wasn't seeing it."

They stood in the middle of what could only be described as a war room complete with what appeared to be the latest in electronics and maps of the world.

Brent moved about the room, studying each map and its layout. Each was similar to the ones back in the Endowment Office, complete with pushpins showing the location of a Brotherhood of Gaza stronghold.

"Do you know the significance of each map?" Brent asked.

"No, only that they are important to you," Gregory answered.

"Was that all God told the brothers?"

"No, they were also told to prepare you for what you must do."

Brent stopped his movement and faced his host. "And how are you going to help prepare me?"

"We are to teach you our ways. Our knowledge, and our ways of self-defense."

"Your ways of self-defense?"

"The use of the staff and how to move in complete silence. It has taken us a lifetime to learn what we know. I questioned how you would learn everything in a short span of time," he smiled, "but after what I just witnessed, I am beginning to understand."

Brent turned and sat in a chair in front of a large computer monitor. "May I?" he asked.

Brother Gregory held his arms out wide and swept the room. "This is all yours. We have no use for any of it."

Brent touched the keyboard and the monitor came to life. He typed an encrypted message and was soon connected to Joan and his home. More importantly, he had a way to communicate with Faith.

CHAPTER 33

Scarlet knocked on Maddie's office door.

"Come in."

She found the director, Seven and Joan in deep conversation.

"I'm sorry to bother you. I didn't realize you were in a meeting."

Maddie didn't look up from what she was doing. "How can I help you, Scarlet?"

She shifted her feet, not knowing exactly what to say. The silence was enough for the three of them to turn their attention towards her.

Maddie stood and crossed the room. "Is everything all right?"

"I spoke to my father, but I wasn't able to convince him to change his plans." She shifted her stance from one leg to another. "He won't change his mind about going to Alpha Camp. He said it would be a sign of weakness if he didn't go. I'm frightened for him. I have no reason, just a gut feeling."

Maddie looked at Seven. "We figured as much," he said. "So we came up with plan B."

"No disrespect, sir, but I hope it's better than plan A."

"None taken, and don't call me sir. I'm still Seven and this is still the colonel's squad. I'm just holding fort until he comes home."

She nodded and asked of plan B.

"Instead of SIA agents, the squad will be with him when he enters Alpha territory. We'll make sure he is safe. You can count on it."

She crunched her face in frustration. "He is so stubborn," she said. "Ever since I was a child, he's been the same way."

Maddie reached out and held Scarlet's hand. "His stubbornness, as you put it, is one of the reasons your father will go down in history as one of this country's greatest presidents."

Scarlet rolled her eyes. "Yes, ma'am."

"Call me anything," Maddie said, "but not ma'am. It makes me feel old."

Joan tried to hold back a laugh, but a giggle made its way from her throat. Soon, Scarlet joined her. Maddie retook her seat and rolled her eyes back at the two of them. "You two will be the death of me yet." Her remarks made them laugh even harder.

"When you're done laughing, have a seat, soldier," Seven said. "I want to go over our plans with you, and I would also like to talk to you about Alana."

He spit in his cup. When he looked up, he was all business. "Since your acceptance as a member of the Phantom Squad, this has been a five man . . ."

Maddie cleared her throat.

It was Seven's turn to roll his eyes. "Person," he corrected. "A five person team. I see no reason to change that. Alana has proven herself to be more than capable and her knowledge of the Mid-East is a big plus. I want you to take her under your wing and fine-tune her skills with the compound bow." Scarlet went to reply, but he held up his hand. "I also want you to find her weaknesses and exploit them."

"I'm not sure what you mean?" Scarlet asked. "Didn't you already do that with the simulation exercise?"

"To a degree," Seven replied. "She is a tough nut. She has had a hard life that has made her cold in many ways. This is good and bad. She is good at keeping her emotions in check, but I don't want them to come out at the wrong time, she is a ticking time-bomb. There is something deeper that has her wound so tight. Find out what it is and bring it to the surface."

She nodded. "Why me?"

"Alana has a huge wall when it comes to men. I'm hoping

another woman will be able to break through it." His eyes glanced at his wife and then to Joan. They both gestured for him to continue. "You have both been the victims of violence. I need you to use your past experiences to bring her to a boiling point. Once she cracks, I can use that emotion to make her stronger."

Scarlet thought back to her torture while in the hands of the Omega Butcher. A shiver ran up her spine. "I'll do the best I can," she mumbled.

"You'll do better than that." Seven stepped forward so he was inside of Scarlet's personal space. "I'm counting on you. The entire squad is counting on you."

She swallowed hard. "May I be dismissed?"

He nodded. "We can go over the mission plans tomorrow."

When she had left, Maddie addressed Joan. "Go with her. Have a girls' night and find out how she really feels."

"Great, just what I wanted," Joan said. "A night of bitching and moaning."

Seven laughed. "Git."

CHAPTER 34

That night, Joan invited Scarlet over for pizza and wine, they asked Alana to join them, but she declined.

"So," Joan said between bites, "what do you think of what Seven said today?"

Scarlet twirled her goblet, watching the red wine slowly spin and twinkle from the overhead lighting. She shrugged. "It's an okay plan, I guess." She raised the glass to her mouth and took a sip. "But you know how hard it is for me to talk about abuse."

Joan took a sip of her wine. "I remember how difficult it was for me to talk to Brent about everything that happened with my stepdad." She put the glass down and twisted the ring on her right hand. "But I also remember the weight that was lifted off my shoulders when I did."

Scarlet lowered her head, thinking about how much she had hated life and how she had trusted no one before coming to Palm Cove. It had been cathartic to tell Joan about her time in captivity, held by the Butcher. She also knew she wouldn't have said a word if Joan didn't first tell her about the abuse she underwent at the hands of her stepfather. It made her think about how Alana must be feeling about her past.

A subconscious grunt emanated from her throat. "I think I'll go see if Alana is still awake."

Joan chewed on her lower lip. "I'll just clean up while you're in there. If you need me, you know where I am."

As if it were a death march, Scarlet walked to the other side of the townhome.

Alana opened the door, placed her finger to her lips, and whispered, "I just got Faith to sleep."

Scarlet looked in the crib and smiled. "Such innocence."

Alana nodded and kissed Faith's cheek.

"It's a beautiful night," Scarlet said. "A full moon. I thought you might want to take a walk down to the beach."

Alana shook her head. "I want to be here in case she wakes up."

Scarlet reached out and took her by the hand. "Come on, it will do you some good to get out. Joan will watch her."

Before she could rebut, Scarlet led her out of the room and down the stairs.

"It is a gorgeous night," Alana said as they walked.

They chatted about the squad and how Alana was adjusting to life in Palm Cove as they made their way to the water. Standing on the beach, they both looked up at the moon and stared.

"So amazing," Scarlet said. "I don't know how people can look at such wonder and deny God's existence."

"It is easy to think that way if you've never experienced the sorrow in the world."

Scarlet closed her eyes and silently asked God for the right words.

They wandered down to where the water could break over their feet and felt the warmth of the Atlantic wash over their toes before it receded back into the ocean.

"We don't know each other very well, and since we're going to be working close together, I thought I'd tell you something about myself," Scarlet said.

Alana pushed her thick, dark hair away from her face. "Let me see," she said, "you grew up in Connecticut. Your father was an attorney, before running for state senate. Your mother passed away when you were just eleven-years-old. You went to the best schools and your father eventually became the leader of the free world. Am I missing something?"

The air between them became tense. "You are direct."

"Some would say it's a good thing," she answered.

Scarlet tilted her head back and stared at the moon and then out at the open water. "When you were in Israel, did you follow the news from the U.S.?"

"All the time, why?"

"Did the news of the Omega Butcher ever reach your country?"

"Of course. Bad news always travels fast and far." She cocked her head to the side. "Why?"

Scarlet began to unbutton her blouse. She pointed to the top of her chest. "These are the scars, the visible ones that he left on me," she said. Her hand quivered as she touched them. She quickly pulled her hand away. "I haven't touched them since I was released from the hospital." Tears welled up in her eyes.

Scarlett could see the look of shock on Alana's face as she covered her mouth.

"I never knew," Alana said. "I mean, no one has ever spoken of it. I'm sorry for assuming, I . . ."

"Don't. Don't apologize. You said nothing wrong." Scarlet brought her hand back up to her scars. "When I woke up in the hospital and was able to think clearly, I asked what happened to the man who rescued me. I was told he died from the burns he incurred saving me."

"Did you ever find out who he was?"

The tears flowed freely. Again she looked at up the moon and then down as the ocean broke over her feet. "It was Brent."

Alana's big, brown eyes opened wide. "I don't understand?"

"It's a long story, why don't we sit."

Scarlet drew a cross in the sand and began to tell of her ordeal with the Butcher and what life was like after her rescue and before she was brought to Palm Cove. She left out no detail. She told of her humiliation of being forced to strip in front of him. She told of being called a worthless whore. She told of her fear when he threatened to peel off her flesh and knowing that she was going to die like all of his victims that came before her.

Alana's mouth was agape. She appeared mesmerized by Scarlet's words.

When Scarlet finished, she was trembling. When she finally calmed down, Alana turned away from her and lifted the bottom of her blouse. Her back was full of deep, purple scars.

"These are the marks left from my father and then my husband. They would call me a whore and whip me when they were drunk."

The tables had been turned. Scarlet timidly reached out and traced the deep lines on her flesh. Alana instinctively pulled away.

"Don't," Scarlet said. "I knew there was a connection between us, but I didn't know what it was."

She felt Alana tense up.

"No one has ever seen my scars before, never mind touched them," Alana said.

"Do you want to talk about it?" Scarlet said.

She shook her head, pulling her shirt back down. "I can't." Alana stood up and ran back up the beach.

Scarlet didn't get up and run after her, she knew exactly how her friend felt. She knew Alana needed to be alone. She sat holding her knees to her chest and dropped her head in despair and mouthed, "That went well. I hope you have a plan C, Seven."

Twenty minutes later, she stood and wiped the sand from her pants. As she turned to walk back, Alana was standing a few feet away. Through the moonlight, Scarlet could see her tear stained complexion.

"Why did you have to bring up the past," she cried.

Scarlet was breathless and she wished the ocean would suck her in with the tide. She took a deep breath and gathered strength. "Because," she finally said, "if you don't talk about it, it will eat you alive. You will never be able to love yourself again and more importantly, you will never be able to love anyone else."

Her words pierced Alana's heart. "It was all my fault," she screamed. "I deserved it."

Scarlet reached out and hugged her. "No it wasn't," she said softly. "I thought the same thing. I thought I must have done something so bad that I deserved the punishment I received." Holding Alana's face in her hands, she continued. "But I didn't and neither did you."

Alana cried harder. "I was so young." Her anger erupted. "They took my youth and they took my innocence. Why would God let that happen?"

Scarlet choked back her emotion. "I don't know the answer. I asked the same question. Brent told me that it was Satan who allowed it to happen and that it was God who stood by me and helped lead me out of my despair and hatred."

"Damn him," Alana said. "Why does he always have the right answers?"

"Because no one has been through more than he has. I think that's why he is God's Chosen."

Scarlet's words brought comfort to Alana and her tears began to subside. They walked back to where they had been sitting earlier. Scarlet listened as Alana talked of her youth, growing up outside of Jerusalem and of her mother's death and how it changed her father. Alana spoke of how she refused to marry the man her father promised her to at an early age, and when she did, her father thought she must have been a whore. She revealed everything that she had never expressed to anyone before, not even Brent.

They discussed Brent and how he had treated them when they first met him. They spoke of his kindness, his generosity, and most importantly, his spirit. By the time they had finished, both had a renewed hope.

"Why did he have to leave?" Alana said. "I was so scared to come here and have him reject me, but to have him gone is even worse."

Scarlet laid back and looked up at the sky. "He changed after Chloe died. He felt it was his fault."

"Why? How?"

"Before he left for the Mid-East in search of the Ark of the Covenant, they had an argument. Chloe didn't want him to go. She told him he was being selfish, and that he should stay home and be with his family. She told him nothing good could come of it and if God had wanted the Ark found, it would have been found many years before."

Alana lay back next to her. "When we first met, I told him the same thing; that nothing good could come from the search, but I was wrong."

Scarlet turned her head and looked at Alana. "How so?"

"I never would have met him nor would I have had the courage to leave my homeland, and I wouldn't have come to Palm Cove."

Scarlet just nodded.

"You said he changed. What was he like after . . . you know?" Alana asked.

"He grew more distant with each day. He became detached— cold." Scarlet tried to think of a way to say what she meant. "Have you ever seen how he gets when he is on a mission?"

Alana thought back, "Yes, it was as if he was no longer there. I mean he was there in the flesh, but his spirit, the things we just spoke of, were gone."

"Right, well that's the way he seemed after her death. It was as if he was just walking through life, not living it." Scarlet shook her head. "No one could talk to him. Not his mother, not Maddie or Joan, not even Seven. He seemed bent on only one thing . . . revenge."

"Do you think that's why he left? To seek revenge on the Brotherhood? That would be suicide!"

"No, well, I don't think so," Scarlet said. "Brent managed to leave Joan a note before he left. In it, he mentioned going back to the beginning, back to where it all began, back to a place and time where he could make sense of what happened and become the man he once was, the friend and leader he once was, and the father Faith needed. In the note, Brent said he needed to leave because he was no good to Faith in his current condition."

"I pray he finds what he is searching for. I pray Joan finds some way to reach him."

"If anyone can, it's her."

Joan was getting worried. It had been two hours since her friends left and her imagination was getting the best of her. She was about to wake Lucille and tell her she was going to look for them when she heard the front door open. When she looked at them, she smiled and a small laugh escaped her. Joan saw that Alana's posture was more relaxed and she sensed a slight vulnerability in her that only came from unburdening oneself.

After everyone went to bed, Joan's laptop alarm went off. She scrambled out of bed hoping to get it before anyone heard it. By the time she opened the lid and hit the off button, it was too late. Both Alana and Scarlet were standing in her doorway. Alana was holding a none-too-happy Faith.

"Is everything okay?" Scarlet said.

Joan didn't seem to hear her, she kept her head down and continued to stare at the computer monitor.

"Ahem," Scarlet said. "I know you can hear like a dog, so I know you heard me. What has you smiling like you just saw God?"

"Not God," Joan cooed, "but maybe a Greek or Indian one."

The girls looked at each other and went to stand next to Joan. They noticed she was watching a video feed of a young man with long, shiny, black hair and an olive complexion. "No wonder you're smiling," Scarlet said. "Where have you been keeping him?"

"Him, I . . ."

"Hello, earth to Joan. Come in, sister."

Joan closed the laptop and turned to them, red-faced. "What'd you say? I wasn't listening."

"No kidding." Pointing at the computer, Scarlet asked again. "Who's the hunk? I didn't know you were seeing anyone."

Scarlet's words snapped her out of her funk. "I'm not seeing anyone. I've never even seen him before. He just . . ." Joan's eyes opened wide. "Oh crap, that must be the lieutenant who's with Brent." She pushed her way past the others and hooked her laptop up to the television.

"With Brent? Now I'm confused. What are you talking about?" Alana said.

Joan knew she couldn't keep her secret any longer. "Sit here, facing the TV with Faith on your lap and see for yourself."

She backed the video to the beginning and hit the play button. The widescreen flashed to life and Brent seemed to magically materialize on the screen. Alana waved her hand in front of the screen to see if she could garner a response. "Can he see us?"

"No, it's pre-recorded," Joan answered.

"Hi, Sweet Pea. It's Daddy," he said in a hushed tone.

Scarlet and Alana watched in astonishment as he spoke to Faith for about five minutes. Joan could sense their shock. She stared at the screen and bit her nails down to the quick. She wasn't sure how she was going to talk her way out of this one.

When Brent blew Faith a kiss goodnight, she leaned towards the set expecting to see the man she saw earlier on her laptop, but instead was taken aback by Brent's words.

"Joan, I went and visited your mom."

"You what?" she exclaimed.

"Monica was my rock when I fell apart after my first encounter with the Butcher. Without her by my bedside, I don't think I ever would have recovered to the degree I did." He pushed his hair back. A gesture he used when he was nervous. "Since Chloe passed away, she's been on my mind constantly. I hoped that if I spoke to Monica, visited her, it would somehow help me make sense of it all." Joan stared intently as he took a deep breath and slowly exhaled. "I had a real heart-to-heart with her. I told her what's been going on and how much you reminded me of her. I let her know how proud I am of you and I . . ." Brent's voice began to crack. "I promised to bring you with me the next time I came to visit. I told her I loved you like a daughter."

He leaned into the camera, his hair falling in his face. "I heard that Alana was in town. I wish the bishop would mind his own business, but then again, why should he start now."

Joan glanced over at Alana. She saw her expression turn to one of disappointment.

"But to be honest," he continued, "I'm sorry I missed her. I don't know if you had a chance to get to know her in her brief stay, but I hope you did. She is an amazing woman and if it's God's will, I'll get to tell her myself one day."

Alana's expression changed. The disappointment was gone, and a smile of radiant hope seemed to canvass her face.

The girls watched as someone tapped Brent on the shoulder. They watched as he turned and spoke to the person who was off screen.

"There is someone here who would like you to get a message to his family. I'll let him talk. Take care of Faith and I'll talk to you tomorrow."

Tag sat down and Joan leaned in, almost falling off her chair.

"He's even more gorgeous on the widescreen."

He asked her to get word to his family that he was fine and that when he finished doing what he was doing, he'd be home. He thanked Joan by name for helping him and she quivered as he said her name. She typed the address and phone number he gave her and then before he could continue, they saw Brent's hand come forward and pull the plug from the wall.

The three women sat there staring at the black screen for what seemed like seconds, but it was actually much longer. They jumped at the sound of Lucille's voice.

"What in the world are the three of you doing up, staring at a blank screen and why do you have my granddaughter up so late?"

"We, um . . ."

Alana jumped in before Scarlet could say anything else. "The little one woke up crying, so we were watching *The Little Mermaid.* I guess we all fell asleep."

"Well, go to bed, it's late. Do you want me to take Faith?"

"No, thank you," Alana said. Faith had a death grip on her hair. "I'll put her to bed. Sorry we woke you."

"I don't sleep much anyway. Between my arthritis and not knowing anything about Brent, I'm surprised I sleep at all." She kissed Faith on her forehead. "Goodnight, my angels."

When Lucille was gone, Alana turned to Joan. "Tomorrow, we talk."

"Okay, but only if you promise not to tell a soul. Promise?"

They all promised, turned out the lights and soon fell into fitful sleep.

CHAPTER 35

The morning started early in Khor Virap. Brent and Tag were awakened at o-four-thirty.

Tag exited the shower, teeth chattering and hands shaking. "With all the modern upgrades the brothers installed over the past eight years, you would have thought hot water would have been at the top of the list."

"They use the runoff from Mount Ararat as their water source," Brent said. "We better get used to it. We'll be here for a while."

Tag stayed silent as he tried to button his shirt. His teeth still chattering. "Nu, nu, now I know why they wear robes."

Brent emerged from the shower with none of the same signs of hypothermia. He was dressed in the woolen robe of a monk. "Here," he said, throwing one to Tag. "They're actually quite warm."

Tag put it over his head and let it fall around him. "And easier to put on."

Brother Gregory entered their small room and saw Tag shivering. "I apologize that our ways do not have the conveniences that you are used to. There is hot running water in the village. May I suggest you go into town to bathe from now on?"

"That won't be necessary," Brent said. "If we are to learn your ways, then we will live as you do. We are appreciative of your hospitality."

Gregory smiled. "Then come, morning vespers are in five minutes. The morning meal will be served afterward."

They followed their host through a maze of tight tunnels until they reached a small chapel. All of the monks were gathered in the pews awaiting Brother Gregory's arrival. He led mass which was concluded with the Lord's Supper: Holy Communion. At the conclusion of mass, the brothers waited for their leader to exit the chapel first. They then followed by rank. The youngest ones were left to wash the chalice and put the Bible in its rightful place on the altar at the base of the cross.

Tag stood to leave, but Brent grabbed the hem of his robe and pulled him back down. "As a show of respect to the younger brothers, we should wait for them to leave first," he whispered. "If we are to gain their trust, we will always be the last to enter and the last to leave the chapel."

When all was completed, the young monks filed past them and nodded their thanks. Brent and Tag stood, fell in line and followed.

The dining hall consisted of one long wooden table with benches on either side. Brother Gregory, seated in the place of honor, waved for them to come and sit at the head of the table.

"With all due respect, Brother, it is our place to sit at the far end of the table," Brent said. "It would also please us if we could serve you and the brothers. When the meal is concluded, we will also clean off the plates and put them away. It is only right."

Brother Gregory looked at Brent with admiration, as did the rest of the brothers.

Because of the monks' vow of silence, Brent and Tag learned by example. The meal consisted of figs and a homemade porridge. Tag was pleased when he realized that hot tea was served with breakfast. Once everyone was served, Gregory stood and blessed himself with the sign of the cross. The others followed suit. A short prayer was said in Latin and then once again the brothers blessed themselves.

The meal was eaten in silence. Brent looked about the table and saw that everyone ate at a slow pace.

Brother Gregory watched as the Brent observed the others. "The brothers eat in reverence for what God has provided," he said. "Each meal, no matter how meager, is appreciated and eaten in a certain manner. All the hot food is eaten first, followed by the raw foods, and finally the dried foods. Bread is not permitted to be eaten with the other foods. Dairy," he continued, "is prohibited from our diets as is meat. We eat what you would consider to be a vegan diet. We eat to sustain ourselves and for no other reason. It is the way it has always been and it is the custom we continue."

Brent and Tag nodded their understanding and ate in the manner they were taught.

When all of the dishes had been washed and put away, they were led from the banquet hall into an open room to begin their training.

Brother Gregory gathered with the rest of the monks and explained their routine. "Every day begins with meditation and private prayer. The brothers pray for strength and that their thoughts and actions will be pleasing to the Lord."

"I see that that you sit in the lotus position when meditating and praying," Brent said. "Would it be disrespectful if I choose to squat instead?"

"Not at all," Gregory smiled. "We wish to learn from you as much as you wish to learn from us. May I ask why you choose to squat when you meditate and pray?"

"It's not for religious reasons," Brent explained, "it's just a position I have found which allows me to better concentrate on God and therefore block out the rest of the world."

"It is not our intention to have you do anything that would separate you from our Father. It is safe for me to say that no one is closer to the Lord than God's Chosen One."

"No one is closer than anyone else," Brent said. "It's just my way."

Addressing Tag, Gregory said, "Am I to assume that you too find this position to your liking?"

"Actually, Brother, I am more comfortable when sitting in the same position as you." He bowed his head in shame. "To be honest, I am not a man of prayer. The things I've seen and done have taken me out of relation with God."

"I will pray that your time spent among us will change your heart."

Tag opened his mouth to speak, but he decided otherwise.

The time of meditation and prayer lasted longer than Tag

expected. Every now and then he opened his eyes to see what the others were doing. He noticed how everyone seemed to be at peace and wondered at Brent's ability to stay in his position for so long. Every muscle in the Brent's body looked relaxed. Tag's eyes traced Brent's body. Nothing moved except his hands.

Tag changed his position and dropped into a deep squat, he imitated the actions he witnessed. Minutes passed before his quads began to cramp. Shaking his head, Tag opened his eyes and returned to his previous position. Minutes dragged on like hours until finally Gregory clapped his hands twice, a sign that it was time for them to end their private time with God. The noise brought Tag relief.

The brothers stirred at the sound of Gregory's gesture. They all began to stand up.

All but Brent.

Brent heard Gregory clap his hands, but he was under too deep to respond. He was back on Mount Ararat where he had spent time with Christ.

He was on his knees in the same crevasse near the top of the mount. His hair blew across his face as the bitter cold bit into his flesh. As the frigid air tore through him, he realized he could feel the cold. *This can't be good*, he thought.

"Why am I here, Lord?" The words seemed to burn as they passed his lips.

No answer.

He closed his eyes. His lids felt like an ice scrapper dragging across the windshield of a car. It was if he could feel ice shards tear into his eyes. They began to water and his tears froze as they touched his cheeks. The darkness seemed to soothe him in some way. His muscles spasmed from the harsh conditions. *I need to block out my senses. Relax*, he thought. *Let everything go.*

With each exhalation he tried to relax his muscles. He knew the shivers and spasms were his body's way of physiologically trying to stay warm. He needed to figure out a way to fight nature. To fight against self-preservation.

One sense at a time, he thought. *Hearing should be easiest.* Using everything he had been taught, he concentrated on suppressing all his senses, after hearing came sight. Prying open his eyes, he saw . . . nothing.

Now the hard part. Feeling. Bottom up, just like I was trained. He immersed himself to the task at hand. Soon, he was able to uncurl his toes as they began to relax. Working his way up, he did the same with his feet, legs, torso, fingers, hands, arms and finally his face.

His body fell forward as all feeling left him and he found himself face-down in the ice and snow. No sound, sight or feeling. A different type of darkness engulfed him. The darkness that came with death. With great concentration, he was able to control and slow his breathing and heart rate. It was then that he heard the voice of the Lord.

"Why have you come?"

"I needed to return to where it all began. The beginning."

"Why?"

"Knowledge. Understanding."

"Of?"

"My life," Brent said.

"That is only for God to know. Again I ask," said the Lord, "why have you come?"

Frustration and sorrow filled Brent's words. "Because I have nowhere else to turn. I can't do this by myself. I need your help."

"And you are willing to forget everything you know and start anew?"

"Yes."

"Is that the only reason you came?"

Brent lay prostrate at the feet of the Almighty. "No, I have come to ask for forgiveness."

"What is your confession?"

"I blamed you for Chloe's death, but I know that I'm the only one who was at fault."

"Look at me," the Lord said.

Brent lifted his head from the ice. He stared into a bright light and turned away from it.

"Look into the Light, my brother."

It took all the inner strength he had, but Brent looked into the

Light; into the face of his Lord. He tried to block out the feeling, but it burned. It burned deeper than anything he had ever felt before. He again tried to look away, but the hands of Jesus stopped him.

"You are not at fault," He said. "The world you live in is as much Satan's as it is mine. He, and he alone, is at fault for Chloe's death. Do you understand?"

Brent clenched and unclenched his fists. "I'm trying."

"Go back and learn from those you have sought. Use what they have been given. Only then will you be able to begin to understand. Only then will you be able to help those closest to you."

Brent began to hear the voices of Brother Gregory and Tag. The Light began to dim. "Wait, don't leave, I . . ."

"All will be revealed in time. You are forgiven."

Brent felt himself regain consciousness. He took a couple of deep breaths and opened his eyes. He saw . . . nothing. *My eyes must still be closed*, he thought. He once again tried to open them and realized that they were already open—wide open.

"Oh my God," Tag said. His voice barely audible, hoarse with fear.

Brent brought his hands to his eyes. He was able to touch his fingers to his eyeballs. The pressure caused tears to run down his cheeks. He heard the voices of Tag and Brother Gregory, but couldn't see them. He saw nothing.

In a hushed tone, the old monk said, "He has seen the eyes of God."

Tag was now more confused. "What are you talking about?"

"His eyes, they are white where there once was color, it is a sign from God."

Gregory grazed his fingers across Brent's eyelids, closing them in the process.

Brent dropped his head in anguish. "It's a sign."

Tag's voice rose in pitch and volume, reflecting his anger. "A what?" His voice grew louder. "Stop talking in riddles. What the hell are you saying?"

Brent spoke with a voice resolute of knowledge. "My eyes. My loss of vision is a sign from God, for both of us to put our faith in Him."

Brother Gregory placed his hand on Brent's arm and helped him to his feet. "This changes nothing. You have come here for answers and those answers begin with the learning of the staff as a method of defense."

Brent nodded his understanding.

"I have chosen two of our finest men to assist you in your training." Brent heard two brothers step forward. "For today and until I feel you are ready, you will listen to and follow your instructors as they go through the rudimentary use of the staff. Once I see that you have learned what is necessary, you will be instructed in how to form a staff from a tree. A tree that you will choose from the sacred mount."

Tag's anger escalated. "How is the colonel supposed to learn how to use the staff if he can't see what the monks are showing him? Answer me that one, O wise one."

His sarcasm was not lost on those around him. He went to push the brother.

"Don't," Brent said.

All eyes shifted to Brent. "Don't what?" Tag said.

"Shove him. Don't shove him."

Tag's voice quieted to a whisper. A smile broke through his confusion and frustration. "You can see?"

Brent's expression now showed the same confusion as his companion's. "No, I . . . I felt it."

"You what? You felt it?" Tag's voice was now barely audible. "What does that mean?"

Brent felt for a chair. Sitting, he placed his head in his hands. "I don't know what it means, I just did." He then began to tell the others of his vision. "When I was meditating, I found myself on Ararat. A place I had been before . . ."

"What the hell are you talking about?" Tag fumed. "Are talking about that vision you had?"

Brent nodded.

"But it was just a dream." Tag's voice rose in frustration. "How can you physically be impaired from a damn dream?"

Brent ignored Tag's outburst and directed his words towards Gregory. "When I was there, this time, I was told to have patience. To forget all I had been taught before and to learn from you and the brothers of Khor Virap." He lifted his head toward Tag. "That message was for both of us. We need to block out, to forget, our military training and learn what the brothers have to teach us. It is the only way."

Tag slapped the wall with the palm of his hand. "Stop with the freaking riddles! Only way to what?"

Brent began to match Tag's emotion with his own. "To help those who need us," he yelled. "To stay alive!"

CHAPTER 36

Joan woke to the aroma of freshly brewed coffee and Alana and Scarlet sitting at the kitchen table talking.

"How long have you two been up?" Joan asked, wiping the sleepers from her eyes.

"We're working on our second pot if that gives you any idea," Scarlet said.

"That long? It was a late night, what woke you up so early?"

Scarlet rolled her eyes. "Like you don't know. Sit down and join us. You have some splainin' to do, Lucy."

Joan swallowed hard. She poured herself a cup and took a seat. "What would you like to know?"

"You can start by telling us where Brent is?" Alana said.

Joan cupped her hands around her mug. "I don't know."

"But last night you received a message from him."

Joan looked up at Alana and then at Scarlet. "Before Brent left, he asked me for my help. He told me he would be leaving and that he would send a video each day for Faith to watch. He was afraid she would forget who he was." She shrugged her shoulders. "He wouldn't tell me where he was going."

"He didn't give you any clue?" Alana asked.

Joan shook her head. "That's all he would tell me."

"The squad knows none of this? Not even Seven?"

Joan looked over at Scarlet. "He made me promise not to tell anyone. Brent knew Seven would follow him."

"And now?" Scarlet asked.

Joan stared into the eyes of her friends. "And now, the two of you will keep this conversation and the videos secret." Scarlet opened her mouth, but Joan cut her off and pointed to each of them. "If you tell a soul, I will rain misery into your lives."

Alana threw her hair back and pointed her finger at Joan when Scarlet interrupted. "Trust me, Alana," she said, "she may be little, but she *is* capable of backing up her words."

Alana took the cue and kept her mouth shut.

The conversation continued for the next half hour. They moved on from the topic of Brent's secrets to what had occurred the previous night on the beach. Alana seemed at peace as she reiterated what had happened. Joan hated to admit it, but Seven was right. The emotional purging had done wonders. Their conversation was interrupted by the sound of Joan's cell phone.

"It's Maddie," she mouthed. Her expression became more solemn, the more she listened. The other two were glued to her half of the discussion which consisted of 'yeses' and 'I understands.'

"What was that all about?" Scarlet said.

"The president wants to move up his departure date. He plans on leaving for the Mid-East in four weeks. We need to get to headquarters on the double."

CHAPTER 37

Falcon stood in the catacombs of al-Qal. He was involved in a phone conversation with his Pentagon contact. A dark smile twisted his features as he listened. When his contact finished speaking, Falcon said, "I owe you a steak dinner when I return." He looked at Omar who was waiting anxiously for the call to end and said, "Or maybe my new friend will give you forty-four virgins as payment." A phlegm filled laugh filled the cavernous ruins as he listened to his reply.

Omar glared at the American's disrespect.

Falcon hung up the phone and eyed the old man. "I'm gunna enjoy spending your money."

Omar drummed his fingers on the table. "Don't spend what you have not earned. What were you told?"

"It seems President Dupree wants to move up his trip. He leaves in four weeks."

The drumming intensified. "That doesn't give us much time."

"That's the point." Falcon cleared his throat and spit on the ground. "It doesn't give his security team much time either. They can't secure all the locations in that period of time. The fool just dealt us the hand we've been waiting for."

"We still don't know where the president will visit," Omar said.

"That's where you're wrong, old man."

Omar's brow furrowed.

"We don't know all of his plans, but we know the most important part. He's making Alpha Camp his last stop. The same place where your boys infiltrated and killed those soldiers last year."

Omar smiled. "This is good news. How do you suggest we act?"

"My source tells me there are fifty-six men stationed at Alpha. We need double that amount to mount an appropriate attack."

Omar seemed reticent. "That's a lot of men."

"We need 'em," Falcon said. "Alpha has been on high alert since the attack. Once we take control of the camp, our men will have to impersonate the soldiers." He thought for a moment. "We will need members of the Brotherhood that look American. We can't have anyone who even slightly looks Mid-Eastern to take their place."

Omar nodded in agreement. "The Brotherhood is vast and our members are from all nationalities. I will assemble the men needed."

"I need them to meet me in the Afghani hills. Some place that resembles the terrain of Alpha Camp in order to train them on the attack and to teach them how to act like U.S. soldiers."

"Done. What else is needed?" Omar asked.

The American didn't even hesitate before speaking. "The rest of the Brotherhood needs to rendezvous at the same point in the mountains as your last conclave."

Omar shook his head. "You are asking for a lot. You expect me to place the entire Brotherhood at risk? To gather them all in one place? What for?"

Falcon stood nose-to-nose with Omar. "You think your *little* group is so strong. Next to al-Qaeda your numbers are weak."

Omar pulled at his own beard, his complexion grew crimson.

Falcon smirked at the old man's gesture. "You want to show the world how strong the Brotherhood of Gaza is? That's gonna take some shock value. If we show the world a thousand unified, armed rag-heads," he poked Omar in the chest, "then you will have the world at your mercy. The more fear you instill in the free world, the faster the American government will send the best to try to rescue Dupree. They will send the Phantom Squad." The American smirked. "Then we can both get some satisfaction."

"Our satisfaction?" Omar asked.

Falcon jerked his head from side to side eliciting a 'cracking' noise. "You can find out the location of your beloved arks and kill Venturi on worldwide television and I can put a bullet in the little punk who ruined my military carrier."

Omar paced as he absorbed his ally's words. He stopped in front of him. Close enough to smell his sweat. "I'll get word out to the Brotherhood."

Falcon nodded.

"And you will get us as much information as possible."

Falcon stood to leave. The sheik gripped his arm and pulled him back down. "If you ever poke me again or speak to me with disrespect, I will personally cut off your manhood and shove it down your throat." He released the man's arm. "We meet again in two days to finalize our plans."

Falcon began to walk away.

"This show of strength you demand of the Brotherhood; you had better be right, or it will mean your life," Omar said.

"If I'm wrong," Falcon said, "it will mean all of our lives." He turned and walked out of the ruins.

CHAPTER 38

A video conference with the president was underway as Seven paced back and forth in the front of the conference room. He reached for his tobacco tin, but it wasn't in his back pocket. He chewed on his lower lip like a smoker would chew Nicorette gum. "This changes everything," he said. "Explain to me again why you have to move up your trip."

"Do I need to remind you which one of us is the president?"

Seven was pacing like a caged lion. He hated being the one who had to try to talk sense into President Dupree. "I haven't forgotten, sir. It's just that I've always known you to be a rational man. And while we're reminding each other what our jobs are, do I have to remind you who is in charge of making sure you stay alive during this little photo excursion?"

The president slammed his open palm on the Eisenhower desk. "That's enough! I won't be disrespected by you or anyone else under my command."

Seven stopped and faced the video monitor. "I mean no disrespect, but I wasn't hired for my diplomacy skills."

"You should be thankful," President Dupree replied. "You'd be lucky to make minimum wage based on that skill set." The antique chair John Dupree sat in, creaked as he leaned away from his desk and stood. "To answer your question, while I was going over my itinerary, I realized I would be out of the country on a date of personal importance. I moved up the trip in order to be back on time."

Seven looked away and discretely glanced at Scarlet.

She mouthed, "Don't ask," in his direction.

He stepped to the side of the room where there was a video blind spot and motioned to Maddie to have Scarlet write down what she was talking about. While he waited for the information, he continued the conversation.

"John," he said, trying a more personal approach, "nothing can be more important than the safety of the Commander and Chief of the free world. This change in schedule only makes you more vulnerable." The next words poured from his lips before he could stop them. "No date is that important."

The president's face turned as red as the stripes in the flag behind his desk. "Don't tell me what is important in *my* life and what isn't." His voice rose in tone along with his frustration. "Where the hell is Venturi when I need him?"

"My thoughts exactly," Seven mumbled.

Maddie handed him Scarlet's note.

The date he is talking about is the anniversary of my mother's death. My father has never missed going to her grave on that date. Trying to talk him out of it will only make him angrier.

Seven fisted the paper, crumpling it in his grip. "Although I don't understand your reasoning, I will abide by your wishes," he said. "Maddie and I will speak to Tim Matthews," Seven said referring to the head of the head of the Secret Service's advanced detail, "and work out the arrangements. The one change I insist on is that the squad and I will personally accompany you to Alpha Camp."

The president sat back down behind his desk with a resigned look on his face. "If you think that's necessary, I will agree."

"One more thing, Mr. President," Seven said.

"And that is?"

"I need you to keep that bit of information secret. No one is to know that the Phantom Squad will be with you."

The president leaned forward in his chair. "Why?"

"Because," Seven said, "we don't exist. I don't care how good the Secret Service is or how highly trained the SIA agents are that will accompany you to your other destinations. If any of them catch wind that the squad is real, tongues will wag."

President Dupree smiled. "You're thinking more like Venturi already. Thank you, Seven. Thank all of you. Now, if everyone will excuse us, I would like a few moments in private with my daughter."

"John," Maddie said, "one more thing before we leave."

"Go ahead."

"Have your people had any luck tracing Brent's or Lieutenant Achak's whereabouts?"

The president sighed. "I'm afraid not. Joan had more luck than we did. My people lost his scent in St. Augustine. Somehow, she was able to trace him to Arlington National Cemetery. After that he went totally off the grid."

Maddie stared at Joan. She squinted and twisted her lips. "Do you have anything you would like to add?"

Joan didn't miss a beat. "No, Madame Director. I have the mainframe and the encryption software running twenty-four seven. Brent will make contact sooner or later and when he does, I'll trace him. He's not that good of a techie."

"If that's all, Maddie," said the president, "I'm crunched for time and need a few minutes with my daughter."

The directorate cleared the room and left Scarlet sitting at the conference table. Now it was just father and daughter.

"I've scheduled a memorial service for your mom. It would mean the world to me if you were there."

A lump formed in her throat. "Nothing could keep me away. I'll be there." There was a moment of awkward silence before she continued. "Dad, why is this trip so important to you? The security issues are a nightmare."

Her father once again began to pace the Oval Office. "I know it doesn't seem to make any sense, but deep in my soul, I have a need to be there. The men and women who serve our great nation are under severe duress. The chain of command over there has been breaking down for months. Soldiers have lost their trust in their leaders and there has been a great deal of turmoil within individual units."

"But . . ."

"I need them to know that the Commander and Chief is in their corner and that I understand their doubts and fears. I can't explain it any better than that."

Scarlet knew her father better than anyone else and she knew there was something he wasn't saying. She pressed the issue. "It's me you're talking to, Dad. What aren't you telling me?"

The president walked to the credenza and poured himself a glass of water. He lifted it to his mouth and began to chew on an ice cube. It was another 'tell' that he was holding back. "My Chief of Staff and the Secretary of Homeland Security have found a mole somewhere in the Pentagon, but they can't pin him down. Every effort made to flush him out has failed. It is their opinion and mine that this trip is the only way to find the leak and plug it for good."

"Send someone else, someone more . . . expendable."

"It has to be me. We know he has been selling intel to Hezbollah and other terrorist organizations. Homeland Security feels this is the only way to flush him out and I agree."

The president could see Scarlet biting the inside of her cheek—a sign of her pent up anger. "That's why I have enlisted the Strategic Intelligence Alliance and the Phantom Squad to front this operation," he said. "I knew Seven would insist on being with me when I touch ground in Afghanistan."

Scarlet glared at her father. She was about to blow when she saw something in her peripheral vision. She looked off to her right, to the corner of the room where the cameras didn't reach, to the corner of the room where Maddie and Seven were still standing. Maddie motioned for her to take a deep breath and calm down. Seven motioned for her to keep the conversation going. She thought long and hard before saying her next words.

"Things have been helter skelter here since Chloe died and even worse since Colonel Venturi disappeared. You couldn't have chosen a worse time for this little jaunt. As your daughter, I'm asking you, no begging you to reconsider."

"Believe me, I wish Brent were there too, but it was Seven who trained him and I have complete trust in him and Maddie and their organizations. Everything will be fine."

"I hope you're right," Scarlet said. "If not, I might be attending a memorial service for two."

"Don't talk like that," he scolded. "I have enough stress without you adding to it."

"She leaned on the table and stared at the screen. You're not the only one affected by your decision."

Her father inhaled deeply and slowly exhaled through pursed lips while sliding his hands through his hair. "I'm not only your father," he said, "I am your commanding officer and you will abide by my decisions." The president's tone of voice softened as he continued, "One more thing," he said "and I don't want any back talk, I am insisting that you stay in Palm Cove and not join your unit on the mission."

Scarlet's face turned crimson with anger. She eyed Seven who was frantically running the knife edge of his hand across his neck.

She blinked her understanding.

Scarlet eyeballed the screen. "I'll do as I am ordered," she said through pursed lips.

She watched as her father exhaled, breathing a sigh of relief. "Thank you, Sweetie. I'll sleep better knowing you're safe."

In her peripheral vision, she could see Seven telling her to wrap it up.

"Dad, Joan just walked in, telling me I'm needed in another meeting. I'll speak to you in a couple of days."

"See you at the memorial."

She pasted on a fake smile. "See you there."

The video went black.

"So that's why this trip is so important," Maddie said.

Scarlet's anger and frustration boiled over. "There is no way in hell," she screamed, "that I am staying here and not going on that mission."

Maddie looked to Seven to speak. "I have never disobeyed a direct order from the president." He spit in his coffee cup and then the left side of his mouth rose in a grin. "But I never received that direct order. I'll see to it that the message you just heard never gets to me. The squad needs you with us on our end, so you will be going with us."

Maddie shook her head. "I have a bad feeling about this," she said.

"Women's intuition?"

She glared at her husband. "Years of experience. You better call a squad meeting and bring them up to date on the new intel. I'll get Joan moving on trying to find the snake in the Pentagon. This mission just became Code Red."

CHAPTER 39

Battered and bruised, Brent sat alone on a wooden bench in the kitchen of the monastery. The frustrations of being blind had been building all day. Although he could sense where people were, his instincts were not sharp enough to block the advancement of his trainer's staff and his countermoves were too slow.

He began to bring a mug of hot tea to his mouth, but slammed the cup down on the table. The tea splattered on his hand and robe as his resentment spewed from his pores. His grip tightened, and his hand trembled with anger.

Like an explosive attached to a trip wire, all of Brent's anger and self-hatred exploded as the hot tea continued to drip down the side of the table. He first felt it in his gut. A minor tremor that built like an earthquake until it cracked his fragile veneer. A sound so guttural and vile that it erupted from his throat in a heat producing, bile-filled wail.

At the same instant Brent screamed, he reared back and launched the heavy ceramic mug across the hall. The sound of the plaster shattering was barely audible compared to the vocal blast that finally emanated from his wide-open mouth.

A cold sweat soaked his robe and drenched his thick hair. The fevered heat of anger became the ice cold of self-hatred.

He became acutely aware of another presence in the room.

He could hear another person breathing in the far corner of the dining hall.

"Don't just stand there, Brother," he seethed, "come over and have a seat."

Brother Gregory sat across the table from Brent. "How did you know it was me?"

"I know everyone by their breathing pattern and by their footsteps." Brent pulled at his beard. "Sometimes it's maddening." The veins on his neck and forehead pulsed with each spoken word.

Brent felt the bench shift as Gregory leaned forward. "The brothers tell me that you didn't appear for your training this afternoon. Would you like to talk about it?'

Brent looked up from the table. His sweat soaked hair hung from his head like the snakes of Medusa. "Do I want to talk about it?" he fumed. "Talk about what? Seeking the help of God and being answered with blindness. Talk about having the person you loved more than life being taken from you at what should have been life's most precious moment. Or maybe you'd like to talk about praying for answers and only receiving more questions." With each word his volume increased until it reached a crescendo. "Pick one, Brother, because right now, I don't give a damn what we talk about!"

Brent pushed off from the table causing the heavy wooden bench to slam against the wall. About to leave the room, he heard the monk speak.

"God tests those He has chosen in order to strengthen them for the next step in their journey."

Brent turned to in the direction of the voice. He still had the staff given him for his training. "If God wants to test me, than damn it, let's start now. I need to finish this, this . . . hell and move on." He pointed the staff at Gregory. "Call your best warriors to the training room."

"Chosen One, you are not ready for . . ."

"Now! And don't ever call me by that name AGAIN."

Brent gripped the staff, swung it with as much force as possible, and smashed it off the stone wall. Splinters flew like shattered glass. He dropped the piece he still held and walked out of the room.

Tag tried to calm and talk sense into Brent for the next twenty minutes, to no avail. Brent wanted to challenge the brothers to a fight and nothing and no one would change his mind.

"You're the one who brought me here, Colonel, but I'm the one who seems to be reaping the benefit," Tag said. "I know things have not gone as planned, but the one thing the military taught both of us is to always be ready to improvise. Situations change and in order to stay alive and accomplish your mission," Tag poked Brent on the sternum, "you must change with them."

Brent's anger and frustration had only increased since he left the dining hall. "Poke me again, and I'll make sure you lose the ability to pull the trigger on a sniper rifle."

Tag went to respond when he heard Brother Gregory clap his hands together, thus calling the monastery to full assembly.

"I have done as you have requested, Chosen—Brent," Brother Gregory said. "How would you like to proceed?"

Emotion was awash over Brent. He was a man who had lost all control. "First, I need to borrow a staff."

"He can use mine," Tag said.

Brent squeezed it in a death grip, so hard his knuckles and fingers blanched in color.

"What do you say, we get this over with," Brent said. "Put your three best in the ring and let's see what happens."

"I have some rules that must be agreed upon before this exercise begins," said the monk. "If you lose, you will abide by our methods and stay within these hallowed walls until I say you're ready to leave."

Brent nodded his agreement.

"And if you win?" Gregory asked.

"If I'm the last man standing, eyesight or not, I climb Mount Ararat tonight." He looked to where he knew Tag was standing. "Alone."

"So be it," the Brother answered.

The three best wielders of the staff stepped forward and tapped the end of their weapons on the stone floor.

"Don't patronize me," Brent said. "I know each of you by your smell and footsteps. It's a freaking curse." He pointed his staff at each. "Brother Ezekiel is on my right, Brother Matthew is in the center and my own personal trainer, Brother Peter is on my left." Brent spun his staff with one hand like a baton and waved them forward.

He could hear the sound of the individual staffs begin to spin. The 'whir' sound was like one hundred hornets in his ears. Under the noise, he could hear and feel their movement. Matthew stepped forward, his staff spun mere inches from Brent's face. The other two covered the flanks. Brent faked to his left and with his weapon, ducked low avoiding Peter's staff and plunged his rod like a knight's javelin into Matthew's pharynx, temporarily cutting off the monk's air supply. The brother dropped his weapon and clutched his throat in response.

Brent spun counterclockwise, the opposite of how he had been trained, and dropped Matthew with a swing of the staff behind the monk's knees. As he did, he could feel the breeze coming from his flanks. He knew they would go for his ribcage. They are the most exposed of all the bones and a strike there would make it hard for him to breathe. He tucked his arms in tight to his body and spun as fast as he could. At the same time, he brought his staff in tight to his body trying to protect his ribs.

The first blow came from his right. As he expected, it was aimed directly at his torso. The force of the blow was deflected by his rod, but it was hard enough to force the air from his lungs. He quickly countered, changing the position of his staff so that it was perpendicular to his body and slung low to once again take out the legs of an attacker. Brother Ezekiel easily jumped the oncoming weapon, and jabbed the end of his staff into Brent's right shoulder.

The shoulder was his Achilles heel. It had been dislocated so many times that when struck, the nerve supply to his arm temporarily malfunctioned, causing numbness in his hands and fingers. The strike caused him to drop his staff to the floor.

Brent placed his left arm over his face to deflect any blow that may be coming as he dropped low and twisted his body. He felt the staff with his right hand and went to grab it before the monk could react. The harder he squeezed, the less he felt. What he did feel was a jarring blow to the back of his neck. He slumped in an unconscious heap.

Brother Gregory spoke in whispered tones. "Please take our guest to his quarters and apply an ice pack to his neck."

Two monks stepped forward, but Tag stopped them.

"I'll take the colonel to his quarters and watch over him. I need to speak to him when he regains consciousness."

Bother Gregory nodded his understanding.

Two hours later, Brent moaned as he tried to open his eyes. He could 'feel' Tag's presence. "I guess that didn't go as planned."

Tag mumbled an obscenity. "I think that went exactly as planned. You knew you couldn't win, you just hoped the beating would help you erase some misplaced guilt you can't seem to get rid of."

Brent went to sit up, but the pounding headache dropped him back onto the rock-hard mattress.

He took the icepack from the back of his neck and placed it over his forehead.

"And what made you such an astute read of one's intentions?"

"I tried to do the same thing," Tag replied.

"Oh."

"I didn't return to the reservation to help my family," Tag said. "I knew the chief would keep them safe. I knew my presence would make the gang want to make an example of me."

Brent staggered, sat up and swung his legs off the side of the mattress. "You never planned on leaving the train station, did you?"

"No, I just wanted the confrontation to occur as far off the reservation as possible." Tag hesitated and swallowed hard before continuing. "Three times since Sergeant Delbach's death, I had placed the barrel of my service pistol in my mouth, but I was too much of a coward to pull the trigger." He looked at Brent for sympathy, but all he got was a blank stare. "So I went to plan B."

"You knew if you fought back against the braves, they would have no choice but to kill you," Brent said.

Tag's eyes smiled. "But you had to show up and ruin the party." Brent went to speak, but Tag cut him off. "And I'm thankful. I never expected them to bring my sister, and I never would have had peace knowing that she witnessed my death."

Brent dropped his head between his knees. Silence enveloped the small room.

When Brent looked up, he had a new determination. "It seems we have both been at a long pity party. Maybe it's time we both stop blaming ourselves for our losses and start trying to find a way to bring the guilty party to justice."

"The Brotherhood of Gaza," Tag said.

"The Brotherhood," Brent agreed.

There was a knock on the door.

"This is your home," Brent said, "there is no need to knock."

Brother Gregory stepped in. "The monitor on the computer is flashing an emergency signal. It says there is an incoming call from someone named Joan. The brothers can't override it. Please come."

Headache or not, Brent jolted from his bed and stumbled to the war room.

CHAPTER 40

Tag punched in the encryption code for Brent and brought Joan's image onto the screen.

Her attention first went to Tag, but settled on Brent. He was sitting in a very stiff manner and was wearing a sweatshirt with a hood covering most of his face.

"Joan, you have broken protocol. This better be worth it," Brent said.

"You know me better than that. We have been in contact with President Dupree and we felt it necessary to contact you about it."

Brent pushed his hair back. "Who the hell are *we*? I thought we had an agreement?"

"We did—do—things have just gotten a little complicated. You seem to have picked up an accomplice and I have inadvertently picked up a couple at my end."

Brent huffed. "Who?"

He sat waiting for an answer. His answer came in the sound of Scarlet's voice.

"It's good to see you, Colonel," Scarlet said.

"You, I can live with," Brent answered. "Joan did explain the ramifications of keeping this all very secret, didn't she?"

"Yes, sir."

Brent shrugged his shoulders, "Well," he said, "say something,

174

you didn't call this meeting so Scarlet could say hi."

Brent's abrupt manner had Joan a little freaked out. She hesitated before saying, "There is one more person who knows that we are in contact. I hope you aren't mad and what I really hope is that you are happy."

"Joan, just spill it." He was about to say something else when he heard a familiar voice.

"I never left Palm Cove. I have decided to stay and help Seven in your absence."

Brent was surprised, anxious and a little excited at the sound of the voice. He was at a loss for words.

"I hope you don't mind. Seven asked for my help with the squad until you return and—I fell in love with your daughter when I first laid eyes on her. I couldn't leave that precious angel."

"Please, don't be mad, Brent, it is all my fault," Joan said.

Brent remained stiff and guarded. "I'm fine with Alana being there. I'm not mad."

His mind shifted gears. "Joan, this is all interesting information, but nothing that couldn't have waited until our next video conference, what aren't you telling me?"

Joan cleared her throat. "President Dupree plans on going on an unannounced strip to Iraq and Afghanistan. He doesn't want a social circus so it is all hush-hush."

"What is Seven's take in this?"

"He doesn't like it, but he spoke to the president and got him to agree to have SIA agents accompany him to the different bases."

Brent tossed up his arms. "I still don't get the reason for breaking protocol. It seems everything is under control."

"The next two things I am about to tell you will change all that," Joan said. "He plans on making his last stop Alpha Camp deep inside terrorist territory and . . ." Joan hesitated, "there is a mole in the Pentagon. We are afraid he or she is feeding information to the Brotherhood."

Brent tentatively stood and moved about the room. His body still bruised and sore from his fight.

The girls noticed his tentative movements.

"Are you hurt?" Joan asked. "And what's with the hood? I can't even see your eyes."

Brent ignored her comments and continued to pace. "I need you to contact Sam at the Pentagon," he said, "and have him check all the outgoing transmissions, both encrypted or not. If it is encrypted, I'm counting on you to decipher it." As Brent looked straight in the camera, his demeanor changed from a wounded animal to a hardened soldier. He pointed a finger directly at the screen. "When you find the mole, do not break his cover, just get his name to me. Understood?"

"Yes, sir," Joan answered.

"One more thing before I hang up." He addressed his next comment to Alana and pointed in the direction her voice had come from, "For what it's worth, I appreciate your flying to Palm Cove to help. I'm sorry I missed you, but I am very happy for the connection that you and Faith have developed. Thank you." As he finished speaking, he lifted his head toward the monitor causing his hood to fall off the back of his head exposing his eyes.

He quickly disconnected the satellite hookup.

Brent reached over and squeezed Tag's shoulder. "It's time we start to train as monks."

Tag gripped Brent's forearm. "That's what I've been waiting to hear, Colonel."

CHAPTER 41

A single tear streamed down Alana's cheek.

"Why the tears?" Scarlet asked.

Joan logged out of her computer, but her attention was on Alana.

"Did you see his eyes?" Alana asked.

Joan looked at Scarlet who shrugged.

"He looked tired," Joan said, "but . . ."

"He's not tired," Alana said, "He's blind!"

Joan's instincts kicked into overdrive. She knew there was something wrong with the way Brent acted, but until now, she couldn't peg it. "Are you sure?"

Alana swallowed hard. "Positive, I've seen the look before."

The girls stared into space, each trying to comprehend what they just learned. Faith's cry from the other room brought them back to the present.

Alana stood. "I will go see to her."

"Wait," Joan said. "What are we going to do with this information?"

"Exactly what Brent asked us to do."

Joan and Scarlet looked confused.

"Which was?" Joan said.

"Nothing," Alana answered.

"She's right," Scarlet said. "If Brent wanted us to know, he would have told us. We need to do what he ordered us to do and nothing more."

Joan shook her head. "Damn him. Sometimes I just want to rip his hair out."

Her words made the girls smile.

"A shared feeling," Alana said. "Now, let's do what needs to be done."

Joan stood and took her laptop into the other room. "It looks like I have a lot of work to do," she said, "so if you will excuse me, I better get to it."

"How will you contact the Pentagon without Maddie and Seven knowing?" asked Scarlet.

"I don't need to keep it a secret that I'm using my Pentagon contact to help find the mole." Joan smiled. "The interesting part will be tapping into their software undetected, so I can find him myself. If Sam finds him, he will have to break it to his supervisors and then it will climb the chain of command. If I find him first, I can block anyone else from doing so, and get the information to Brent."

The next day, Seven began to discuss what procedures and security measures he wanted implemented for President Dupree's trip.

Normally dressed in jeans and a tee-shirt, Seven stood in front of the squad in full black uniform, including side-arms. "This mission starts now," he said. "We have twenty-two days before we depart for Afghanistan. In order to ensure the president's safety, we will be working on every possible scenario including . . ." His eyes circled the room and settled on Scarlet, "illness, injury by insurgent bombing, possible camp infiltration and death." He watched as Scarlet closed her eyes momentarily, before reopening them. "If any of you have a problem with dealing with any of those possibilities, speak now."

No one spoke. Scarlet set her jaw and blocked out any personal ramifications.

Seven packed his lip with tobacco and grinned.

"Good," he said. "I want everyone dressed in uniform and in the armory in twenty minutes. The first half of the day will be spent on refining our silent attack weapons. The second half of the day will be spent in the simulator."

Everyone nodded.

"Dismissed."

Maddie intently watched Joan as she tried to trace Brent's whereabouts.

Joan huffed. "You're not helping by stalking me."

"I'm not stalking, I'm learning," Maddie replied.

In reality, she was stalking. She knew Joan was holding something back, but couldn't figure out what it was. She thought if she shadowed her moves, Joan might slip up.

Maddie had been intermittently rubbing Joan's neck while in actuality she had been taking her carotid pulse looking for an increased heart rate, a sign of deception. What she found was . . . nothing.

"Well," Maddie said, "I have a lot of logistics to get to as well as a call to make to the head of the Secret Service. If you find anything, let me know."

"I will," Joan replied.

As soon as Maddie was out of her office, Joan clicked a button and brought up the Pentagon's internal security software. With all of the employees and contract workers, it was going to take some time to narrow down the list of suspects. She sat back and stared at the long, ever-growing list of names that was being generated on the screen. She tapped her pen on her desk, wondering how best to narrow it down.

Her eyes dilated as she quickly typed another address onto the computer. Numbers filled the screen so fast that she couldn't keep up. When they stopped, she used the Pentagon's encryption software to decipher the code. When it finished, she stared at the names and the corresponding code names of all of the U.S. government's foreign agents.

"Something's not right," Joan mumbled.

She pulled up another screen, this one had a list of all outgoing messages from the Pentagon to the agents. Her eyes scanned the screen looking for any anomaly.

Two hours later, she found what she had been looking for, one code-name without a corresponding agent. A name she was familiar with, a name that sent chills down her spine.

She needed to talk to Brent.

CHAPTER 42

Brent and Tag had spent their day in hard training. Beaten and exhausted, they made their way back to their small room after evening prayer.

Tag flopped himself onto the paper-thin mattress. "Even this rock under me feels good," he moaned.

Brent sat straight up on his bed staring at the Tag's bed. "Our day has just begun," he said.

Tag raised an eyebrow, "What are you talking about?"

"I need you to teach me the Cree shadowing trick."

"Now?"

Brent nodded.

Tag slowly sat up. "I don't mean to sound disrespectful, but it's the middle of the night."

Brent brought his hand to his watch. He had removed the glass from it earlier so he could feel the hands and tell time. "It's seventeen hundred hours, five p.m. for you civilians. Not exactly the middle of the night."

"Damn, is that all it is. My body tells me it's at least midnight, zero hour for you tight ass officers."

Brent smiled. Tag's words brought thoughts of Seven. He reached forward and slapped Tag's knee. "Sorry about your luck."

"Why now? Why not wait until morning?"

"Our daily activities are up to Gregory's discretion. We have to do this at night."

Tag huffed.

"Stop whining and gear up. We are about the same size so you can borrow some of my stuff. We will gear up in squad uniforms and head outside as soon as the sun sets. That gives us forty-five minutes to shower and get ready."

Tag stood and shook his head. "I stand by my previous assumption, you are insane."

Brent stood and smiled. "I will meet you at the entrance to the monastery."

"Why? Where are you going?"

"To let Brother Gregory know of our plans."

Forty-five minutes later, the two stood at the entrance to the monastery. They heard footsteps behind them.

Brent listened to the footfalls. "It's Brother Gregory."

The brother entered the small room where they had first entered days before. He placed a staff in each of their hands. "Whatever you need to do, do it with the staff. When you leave here, it will be your first and last line of defense. You must learn to do everything with it."

They nodded and took what Gregory had to offer.

Tag turned to climb the steps into the modern-day church. Brent stopped him and handed him a piece of black cloth.

"What is that?" Tag asked.

"Your hood. It's the same one you saw Q wearing when he picked us up. Even though it's doubtful at this time of night, I want to be sure that we are not spotted by a bystander. The hoods will hide our identity."

Tag inspected the hood. "There are no eye holes."

Brent smiled. "Exactly."

"Wow," Tag said when he put on the hood, "It's amazing how well I can see through the material."

Outside, Tag took four pieces of rope from his back pocket. "To learn to shadow, we must be tied together."

Brent nodded.

"I'm going to tie our ankles together and then our wrists. The first thing we must learn is how to move as one."

"When I was a kid," Tag said as he tied their ankles, "I used to watch the young braves as they learned the art of shadowing. It reminded me of a type of dance." Standing he took the other pieces of rope and tied his and Brent's wrists together. He again spoke while he tied. "I asked my grandfather if I could learn. My grandfather, the chief, was proud that his grandson wanted to be a Cree brave and learn the traditional battle secret of his people."

"Why was it used?" Brent asked.

"To hide their numbers. It allowed the braves to appear to be few, and then they would splinter off at just the right moment and overpower their enemies."

Brent smiled at the explanation.

Once Tag had finished tying himself to Brent, he huffed. "We have three things working against us. Shadowing is learned with the aid of sight, this terrain is not flat, and you are not Cree."

"Amuse me," Brent said.

For the next four hours, Tag taught Brent how to match his movements. They spent most of the first two hours on the ground or trying to stand up in unison. The staffs made it harder for them to move, but easier for them to get off the ground. The final two hours were a bit better. Brent began to feel Tag's movements before he made them. He was able to shadow his arms and feet as they walked and jogged along the hillside.

"You've come a long way since we began," Tag said. "I think this would be a good time to stop, we can pick back up tomorrow."

Brent agreed.

Tag untied the ropes and began walking back to the Monastery. Brent shadowed his movements.

Tag shook his head. "Amazing."

CHAPTER 43

Brent's emergency signal from Joan beeped at o-three hundred hours. He and Tag sat in front of the monitor and listened intently.

"I did what you said and hacked into the Pentagon's security system."

"I don't remember asking you to 'hack' into their system."

"Six of one, a half dozen of another," Joan said. "That's not what's important, what's important is what I found."

"Which is?"

"I found out that the mole is sending encrypted messages to someone who is near Gaza."

Brent leaned into the monitor, "Gaza?"

Joan nodded, "Gaza, and that's not all. The mole is sending them to someone calling himself Phoenix."

"What!" Brent's emotions were so stirred that he threw off his hood. "That was Seven's code name. Who the hell would know his code name? Not even the Pentagon knew him by that name."

It was Joan's turn to lean in to her computer. "I don't know. That's for you to figure out. And what the hell is going on with your eyes?"

Brent was quick to put his hood back on. "Don't worry about my damn eyes. Find the mole." He disconnected the transmission.

CHAPTER 44

Three weeks later, Omar and the man known as Falcon sat in a makeshift command post deep inside the anthills bordering Pakistan and Afghanistan.

"So, do you think we are ready?" Omar asked.

"I do. I'm surprised at the number of Americans you have inside the Brotherhood."

"The truth is important to all people," Omar responded.

"Whatever," the American answered. "We leave tonight for Alpha Camp."

"One more time, I want you to go over your plan," Omar said.

"*Pff*, for what?" Falcon said. Indignation oozed from his words. "Is it too much to get into that brain of yours?"

Omar had enough of the American's flippant attitude. He picked up a knife off his desk and lunged toward him. The American went to sidestep, but Omar's guards grabbed and held him in place.

Omar stopped with the tip of the blade pushing against the man's cheek. "I've had enough of your rudeness. You can either treat me with the respect I deserve, or I can kill you and complete this mission without you."

Falcon gave a slight head nod in response. It was enough for Omar to lower his blade.

The corners of Falcon's lips curved upward and his eyes gleamed as he spoke. "You need me as much as I need you. We don't have to like each other, we just need to live with each other for a little while longer."

Omar again asked the American to go over the attack plan.

"Your men will be my prisoners," Falcon said. "I plan on marching them straight into Alpha Camp."

Omar paced. "It is risky?"

"That's why it will work. Alpha has been in a state of flux since their attack. Leadership has changed hands three times and the soldiers are demoralized. A straightforward approach is the only way we will get in unnoticed."

"You better be right."

"I'm always right."

"Hmm. So what have you heard from your informant at the Pentagon?"

"Dupree leaves in three days for the Mid-East. He will be at Alpha in five days. We need to be set up and ready for his arrival in four. We move out in an hour."

Omar stood nose-to-nose with the American. "If you are wrong, I will personally kill you."

"If I'm wrong, you won't have to. I will already be dead."

Omar began pacing.

"If we're finished, I'm going to go prep the men. We have no time to waste."

Omar waved him away. Falcon started to leave and turned back toward Omar.

"The entire Brotherhood was supposed to be here. So far, all I've seen are the men who are going to Alpha. Where are the rest?"

"They will be here."

"They better."

Omar balled up his hands into fists. He was practically foaming at the mouth with hatred.

Falcon laughed when he looked at the old man.

Omar cringed. The infidel's laughter was like nails on a chalkboard.

Omar kept his eyes on his new ally until he was no longer in view. "Mark my words, you American pig," he fumed, "you *will* be dead when this mission is over."

Later that day, one hundred and six men, some in U.S. uniforms carrying U.S. weapons, others in traditional Afghanistan throbes marched out of the mountains and began the trek toward Alpha.

CHAPTER 45

The directorate and Phantom Squad met for one last meeting with President Dupree in the conference room.

"I would be remiss if I didn't ask one more time," Maddie said. "Mr. President, your trip is a logistical nightmare, will you please call it off."

"No."

Maddie sighed. "Very well."

"It is my understanding that all the pieces are in place," President Dupree said.

"They are," Seven responded.

"Then why the meeting? Did you find the mole?"

"Not yet, sir," Joan answered. "I have narrowed it down to ten possibilities, but I don't have a confirmation yet."

"Keep working on it. I would love to know who it is before I leave."

"That's one reason I've asked for the meeting," Seven replied. "I would like you to postpone until Joan has a definite on the identity of the spy."

"No can do, you know my schedule is tight. I need to be back in D.C. one week after the junket. I want the leeway," President Dupree said. "You said one reason, you have others?"

Seven glanced over at Scarlet. "Just one. I received a message last night from your office that you asked for Scarlet to remain behind."

"It wasn't a request," the president said. "As your Commander and Chief, I am ordering my daughter to say in Palm Cove."

Seven bit his bottom lip. He looked at Scarlet who was looking back at him with pleading eyes. He then addressed President Dupree. "The squad is a five-man operation. Just because Brent is not here, that hasn't changed. Scarlet goes with us."

President Dupree pointed to the monitor. "Damn it!" he yelled, "I told you, my daughter stays here."

Seven spit in his cup. "Yes, you did. And I told you that I would keep you safe. For me to keep my promise, Scarlet needs to be there."

The president stood, placed his hands on his desk and leaned into the camera. "If anything happens to her, I will hold you personally responsible."

"I don't mean any disrespect, but if anything happens to Scarlet, it happens to all of us."

The president's face turned crimson as he stared into the camera. Seven stared back.

Maddie finally broke the stalemate. "If there is nothing else, sir, we will see you in a few days."

The president broke his stare. "My plane will touch down in Palm Cove in three days at exactly five a.m. Be ready to leave. I want no further communication until I see you in person."

The screen went black.

"That went well," Joan said.

Seven looked at her and spit. "Better than I thought. I thought he would put up a bigger stink about Scarlet being part of the mission."

"He wants to protect me, but he trusts your judgment," Scarlet said.

Seven nodded. "I wish it wasn't my judgment. Where the hell is Brent?"

Everyone turned to Joan. She stared back like a cat that had swallowed a bird.

Maddie decided to press the issue. "How is it that you can break the Pentagon's security software, the best in the world, but you can't find a technologically inept man?"

Joan didn't even flinch. "The technologically inept man hasn't tried to use the internet, his phone or any form of communication. He is totally off the grid."

"What about the young officer who is with him?" Seven asked.

"The same. He is totally black. I spoke to his family yesterday. They are worried about him. They said that even when he was deployed, he always managed to contact them at least every couple of weeks. It's been forty-one days since he left Palm Cove and they haven't heard anything."

Maddie glanced at Seven and then back at Joan. "Keep trying. I want them found before the squad leaves for Afghanistan."

"Yes, Director. If there is nothing else, I have a lot of balls to juggle before President Dupree arrives."

"Dismissed," Maddie said.

Joan left and the airlock engaged.

"She's lying," Maddie said.

"I've seen her frustration build over the past few days," Alana said. "She is up half the night trying to find Brent. Why do you think she is lying?"

Maddie leaned over the table, and pointed a perfectly manicured nail at Alana. "Because I know her like a mother knows her daughter. She might be able to fool the rest of you, but not me." She pointed to Scarlet. "Press her. Find out what she knows."

"But . . ."

"But nothing. I want Brent found. I need Brent found." Maddie placed her palm on the scanner and the door hissed open. She turned back to the squad. "We all need him found."

Seven shook his head. "This day just keeps on getting better and better." He eyed each person in the room. "I want to run through a final scenario today."

"What would that be?" Jefferson asked.

"Helter Skelter."

"What's Helter Skelter?" Scarlet asked. "I've never heard of it."

Seven eyed the squad. "That's the scenario if everything goes to shit." He tapped his tobacco tin out of habit. "We meet in the armory in thirty minutes. Dismissed."

CHAPTER 46

Brent heard Brother Ezekiel approach from his left. He remained still as he tried to determine the monk's next move. Before he could adjust, Ezekiel swept his feet out from under him. Brent hit the stone floor hard.

"Perhaps all your late nights are impeding your progress," Gregory said.

Brent's frustration grew as he picked himself up off the floor. "Perhaps, you should go check on Tag and see how he is doing."

"I already have. Your young friend has mastered the staff and is sparring with Michael."

When Brent heard Gregory's words, he white knuckled his staff in frustration.

The monk placed a hand on Brent's shoulder. "Come, I have something to show you."

Brent shrugged off his hand, "I need to train."

Gregory replaced his hand and squeezed. "You need to follow my lead. Right now, I need to show you something, and then you can train." Gregory let go of Brent's shoulder. "Come," he said as he walked out of the room.

Brent sat on the wooden bench in the dining hall with a hot mug in his hands. His nostrils flared as he inhaled deeply. "Coffee, you've been holding out on me, Brother."

Gregory took a sip from his cup. "Brother Jonah picked it up in the village. I thought a little reminder of home would be nice."

Brent took a slow lingering sip. "You have no idea." Placing the mug on the table, he pulled his hair back and waited for Gregory to speak.

He didn't.

Brent began to rise from his bench. "If this is just a coffee clutch moment, I have training to get back to."

"Please sit, Ambassador," Gregory said.

"My name is Brent."

Gregory lowered his voice. "I think that is the problem."

"Come again."

Gregory reached over and clasped both of Brent's wrists. "You *are* the Ambassador, you *are* the Chosen One, you *are* the Enlightened One. Whether you choose to be called by those names or not, it doesn't change who you are." Brent opened his mouth, but Gregory squeezed his wrists harder. "I noticed you had a tattoo on your chest. '*Affectus mos adepto vos occidit*.' Latin for 'Emotion will get you killed.'" Brent swallowed hard. "I imagine those words must mean a lot to you?"

"They're not just words, they are what keep me alive," Brent answered. "They are part of me."

"Ahh," Gregory said. "It sounds like those words are part of your identity."

Brent nodded.

Gregory let go of Brent's wrists and rose from his bench. "Maybe you should have had Ambassador, Chosen One and Enlightened One tattooed below it."

Brent took another sip of coffee as he heard Gregory leave the room. He sat quiet for a moment as the brother's words reverberated in his mind. He brought his hand up to where the tattoo was and traced the words. In that moment, he knew what he had to do. Today and tonight.

Back in the training room, Tag and all the monks gathered in a wide circle. In the middle of the circle, Brent and Brother Ezekiel were about to face off in a duel.

Brent clutched his staff and squatted in the middle of the room.

He could hear the whir of Ezekiel's staff as the young monk circled the room. Although he was blind, Brent could see the movements inside his head. The image of Ezekiel was cloudy, as if he was looking through turbid waters. But it was clear enough. He knew where the monk was and he was able to predict his movements.

Brent closed his eyes and took a deep, cleansing breath. He rose from his squat and began to twirl the staff like a baton. He waved Ezekiel to approach with his free hand. The monk attacked, bringing his staff low as he tried to strike Brent behind the knees.

Brent countered and blocked his staff with his own.

Tag could see the look in Brent's expression. It was the same look he saw when they fought the tribal gang on the train platform. Brent's expression or lack of one made Tag smile.

For the next ten minutes, Brent blocked every attack of Ezekiel's. He could feel the strikes becoming weaker and knew it was his time to attack. He again stood in the middle of the room and waved for the young monk to approach. When he did, Brent turned, took three steps toward the wall, jumped, sprang off of the wall and flipped over Ezekiel's head. In the same fluid movement, he landed and swung his staff, clipping the monk's and knocking it out of his hand. When Ezekiel bent to pick it up, Brent swung again with both hands. His staff was aimed directly at the young monk's face. At the last second, he checked his swing and stopped the momentum of the staff inches from his face.

A collective sigh could be heard from everyone in the room.

Brother Gregory began to clap and the rest of the monks, including Ezekiel followed suit.

"Come, Brothers. We shall celebrate."

The monks began to funnel out of the room, but Brent and Tag waited to be called.

"The celebration is for the two of you, I hope you are coming," Gregory said.

"We are just being respectful, Brother," Brent said. "We are waiting for you to call us."

"I did," Gregory said. "You have proven yourselves worthy to be called Brothers. Come."

After dinner, Gregory asked Brent and Tag to follow him outside. Once they were in the cold night air, he handed them each an axe.

"What are these for?" Tag asked.

"You have proven yourselves worthy of your own staff. Come and follow me."

They walked up onto the foothills of Mount Ararat. Brent spent the time shadowing Tag and then Gregory. Even with his blindness, he never missed a step.

"Here," Gregory smiled and pointed at the two trees in front of them. "It is our tradition that all brothers choose their own tree, but I have had my eye on these two. They grow strong and true. If you would permit me, I would like to give you these trees to carve your staffs from."

"Are you serious," Tag said. "These trees must be thirty feet tall and four feet in diameter." He then brought his small hand axe up in front of his face. "You expect us to cut them down with these?"

Gregory's smile widened. "It is our custom."

Tag turned and clinked his axe blade with Brent's. "It's going to be a long night, Kimosabi."

Brent felt the tree with a soft hand, blindly looked up into a starry sky and belly laughed.

For the best part of the next five hours, Gregory instructed them how to fell the trees, how to peel back the bark and finally how to trim each layer of wood from the tree until all that was left was the core—the heart—of the tree.

Once the staffs were cut, the three men made their way back down into the monastery and there they saw the monks standing in a circle tapping the ends of their staffs off the hard stone floor. A form of celebration. Gregory led the brothers in a short prayer service before they all went to bed.

CHAPTER 47

Brent waited until everyone was sound asleep before slipping out of his room. He made his way towards the staircase which led to the Khor Virap chapel. He hesitated, waited, and listened. A smile came to his face as he heard the familiar footsteps of Brother Gregory.

Brent turned toward the monk. "Good evening, Brother."

"And to you, Brother. It seems you have me at a disadvantage."

"Oh?"

"You knew I was coming, but I don't know where you are going."

"Do you ever sleep? You seem to be everywhere."

Brother Gregory looked at Brent's heavy backpack. "That's funny, I was about to ask you the same question."

Brent's expression turned serious. "It's time I went in search of the beginning."

"Alone?"

Brent nodded. "It's what God is telling me."

"How will you climb without sight?"

"Since I have been out at night with Tag, I have discovered that I can see the light from the star."

Gregory handed Brent a leather bag. "Here, you will need this."

Brent felt the outside of the pouch. "What is it?"

"Dried fruit for your time on the mountain."

"How did you know I would be leaving?"

"The star you speak of. It has been getting brighter over the past few nights. Tonight, it is shining like the sun."

Brent tucked the pouch inside his backpack. "Thank you, Brother. I have a favor to ask of you."

"Ask, Chosen One."

He handed the monk a note. "Please see that Tag gets this note and make sure he doesn't leave until I get back." Gregory grasped the note, but Brent didn't let go. With his free hand, Brent grabbed Gregory's wrist. "Don't let him leave here, no matter what he hears, no matter what happens."

Gregory tugged again. This time Brent released the note.

"You are expecting bad things to happen?"

"Yes, not here, but . . . yes."

The old monk turned to leave. "We will do what you ask, and we will await your return. Go with the love and protection of God."

"Always," Brent said as he ascended the stairs.

The air was crisp as Brent walked the foothills which led to the base of Mount Ararat. He could see an eerie glow being given off by the star, and his other senses were in tune with his surroundings. The staff came in useful as the climb became steeper. He could still feel the rock and gravel under his boots. He knew from his visions that the ark would be found high on the summit where the mountain was covered in ice and snow. Based on his research, Brent knew he had at least a day's climb before he would feel anything other than rock.

He continued his climb for the next ten hours before he had to stop and rest.

That should put enough distance between me and Tag, he thought. He lay down in a protected crevasse, away from the wind, closed his eyes and fell fast asleep.

Back at the monastery, Tag became furious when Brother Gregory gave him the note and told him Brent left to climb the mount. He ran for the exit, but was stopped by the brothers. He swung his fist at the stone wall when his efforts to leave were countered by the monks. Luckily, Gregory blocked the strike with his staff.

CHAPTER 48

Joan and the girls sat in front of the television in her bedroom getting ready for the best part of their day. She had received a signal from Brent asking for a live video conference at eleven p.m. Joan returned the message asking him to push it back until one a.m. She wanted to be sure Lucille would be sleeping.

The four of them—they now referred to themselves as 'three ladies and a princess'—waited in front of the screen for Brent to connect from his end.

"I'm a little worried about Brent," Joan said.

"Why? What do you know that we don't?" Alana asked.

"Brent didn't encode his message earlier. That's not like him."

"Hmm."

Joan's thought was interrupted by the beeping signal on her laptop.

All attention shifted to the screen. Even Faith had grown accustomed to the sound. Instinctively, she reached up and took hold of Alana's hair. The connection went live and they were taken back when they saw Tag staring back at them.

Joan's spidey sensors were firing on all cylinders. "Lieutenant Achak, where is Brent?"

Tag's demeanor lightened momentarily when he saw Joan. "Please call me Tag."

Joan blushed and she fumbled with her words.

Alana rolled her eyes. "Lieutenant, I will ask the question again, where is Colonel Venturi?"

Both Tag and Joan snapped out of their fog.

"That's why I called this meeting. That and I don't know how to prerecord a message."

"Where is Brent?" she asked again.

"He is . . . he is on a mission, but he left me a note and asked me to get this to you as soon as possible."

"On a mission, huh," Joan said. "So, you don't know where he is, do you. He left you just like he left us."

"No and yes," Tag answered. "I do know where he is, sort of and, yes, he left without warning."

"Where is he?" Alana asked.

The side of Tag's mouth slid up in a crooked smile. "He didn't include that in his note, so I can only assume he doesn't want anyone to know."

Joan smiled. She liked his sarcasm. "What does he want us to know?"

"He left detailed instructions for the weapons development team. I will send them to you if you give me an email."

"No," Joan said. "We can't chance a trace. Read them to me."

"They are rather technical."

Joan rolled her eyes. "Read them."

Tag did as he was told expecting Joan to ask him to repeat them. She did not.

"He said to get the weapons as quickly as possible to Q and that he would deliver them."

"Fine," Joan said. "What else is on the note?"

"Just a name. He said to run it through the Pentagon security software and see if it pops up. If it does, you are to tell Seven, you found the mole."

"Give it," Joan said.

As soon as she finished typing, she said, "What's going on with Brent's eyes?"

Tag smiled. "You are exactly like Brent described you."

"Oh, how's that?"

"Direct, sly, intelligent, and . . . beautiful."

Joan's eyes opened wide and before she could respond, the transmission went black.

Scarlet and Alana looked at each other and winked. Scarlet then looked down at Joan's laptop monitor. "What are those directions for?"

Alana peered over her shoulder. "They are for some sort of a . . . hell, even I don't know what they are for."

Scarlet pointed to the screen. "The name, have you seen it before?"

Joan bit her lip. "No, but I think I know who it is."

"Who?" both girls asked.

"Phoenix."

CHAPTER 49

Brent woke to a biting wind. His fingers were cold and numb. Shivering, he ate some of the dried fruit and drank some water before continuing his climb. He had no idea where he was headed, but when he was on the right path, the light grew brighter. When he strayed, the light faded.

The vegetation grew thinner the higher he climbed. Every couple of hours, he found he needed to add another layer of clothing to keep from freezing.

Brent knew from his research on Mount Ararat that the glacier and ice fields began at approximately thirteen thousand feet. His visions took place in a frozen environment, so he assumed he needed to reach that altitude. If his calculations were correct, he had another full day of climbing ahead of him.

Brent continued to climb until he was so tired and cold that his dexterity began to falter. Shuffling his feet, he tripped over rocks or his own footing as he tried to press onward. When he came to an overhang where he could hide from the wind, he once again stopped to sleep. Sleep would not come without a cost. Nightmares infiltrated the darkness. Old nightmares. Nightmares he thought he left behind years ago.

In his nightmare, he was crawling through a duct-like system when he heard the cry of a woman, the cry of Charlotte Dupree. He stopped to radio the rest of the Phantom Squad. They had split up to cover as much ground as possible in order to discover where the Omega Butcher had taken the president's daughter. Her pleading became louder as he drew close to the opening that led to the Butcher's lair.

He watched Jonas McFarland *aka The Omega Butcher* and waited for the rest of the Phantom Squad to arrive. It was there that Brent heard Jonas speak for the first time. His voice went from effeminate and sing-songy to one that was deep and guttural. A voice that you felt more than heard and it brought fear to your soul. As his voice changed so did his eyes. They went from a piercing, diamond blue to the red, hate-filled eyes of a demon.

Brent closed his eyes and shook his head, trying to clear it of the image. He gripped his handgun and prayed for the arrival of his team. Charlotte's cries tore through him. He watched as the Butcher took a knife and slid the blade over her face and down her neck.

"I'm going to cut your clothes off, whore," he growled, "and then," he stopped speaking as he placed the knife between her breasts and cut the front of her shirt open, taking her bra with it, "I'm going to drip hot oil on your milky white skin." White, frothy sputum dripped from his mouth as he slid the blade over her nipple. The Butcher placed his lips up to Charlotte's ear. "The flame will cleanse you of your sins. If you don't scream like a little slut, I will let you live."

Fear caused a puddle to form between Charlotte's legs.

Brent took in a deep breath and tried to slow his heart rate. He knew his emotions would work against him. He could hear Seven tell him, "Emotion will get you killed."

As the first drop of oil seared Charlotte's flesh, her scream pierced his psyche and all his training became meaningless. He burst from the air duct and fired two bullets into the butcher; one in his thigh and one on his shoulder. He walked toward Charlotte and reached for her shirt to cover her up. That's when he saw two things in her eyes, the escalation of her fear and the reflection of the Butcher. He turned as the killer reached for the pot of boiling oil.

The Butcher screamed from the pain of his own burning flesh as his hands grasped the pot. In one last, dire attempt for pleasure he went to throw the oil on Charlotte. Instinctively, Brent threw himself in front of her and took the brunt of the boiling oil, passing out from the pain.

Still trapped in his nightmarish hell, he was gasping for air and surrounded by smoke. He smelled it but felt disconnected from it. His gasping soon became coughing. Out of oxygen, he opened his mouth wide and attempted to inhale. All he got for his effort was a chest full of smoke. He reached for his tee-shirt to pull it up over his mouth and nose, but he wasn't wearing one. It was then that he felt the first flicker of the flames.

Damn! Where the hell am I? he thought.

"Exactly."

Brent's head snapped all around trying to find where the voice was coming from.

Did I say that out loud?

"It doesn't matter. I hear your thoughts as well as your words."

Brent turned his head left and right, trying to see through the smoke. He looked down at himself and realized that his flesh was burnt and hanging from his body like wax dripping from a candle.

Laughter rose all around him with the flames. He knew the sound and it brought him to his knees. It was the laughter of the Dark One: Satan.

"Why am I here?"

"This is where you would have ended up if I had defeated you in battle."

Brent looked into the flame. "But you didn't."

The smoke became a shadow, a shadow of evil. Grey in color and acrid in smell, the odor of burnt flesh, it stopped in front of Brent and spoke. Its breath was putrid and made Brent gag. "Your God is not the only one who can perform miracles. I'm here to offer you one of my own."

Brent rose from his knees and opened his mouth to speak in defiance when a vision of Chloe emerged before him. Chloe and Faith smiling and giggling. The sound of a mother's love.

Satan pointed. "Your soul for that of the woman you love."

Tears streamed down Brent's face. He reached out to touch them, but his hand passed through them.

"If I defeated you," Satan whispered, "you never would have gone on the search for the Ark of the Covenant. Your wife would be alive and she would be with your daughter."

Brent fell on his knees in despair. The salt from his tears stung his seared flesh. "It's all my fault!" he cried.

The shadow grew and surrounded Brent. When Satan spoke, his breath now smelt like Chloe's perfume. "You can make it right. Just say the word and the woman you love will be with your daughter."

Brent looked into Satan's eyes. He saw hate and evil, but he didn't care. He then heard the sound of metal as Satan moved around him. Brent looked down and saw chains attached to the Dark One. He remembered that in defeating him during The Enlightenment, he sent Satan back to hell.

"And you?" Brent asked.

"And I will be free."

Brent knew he could not adhere to Satan's deal. As he was about to say no, he heard Faith's laughter. He looked up and saw the two people he would die for embrace as only a mother and daughter could.

He looked up towards heaven and snarled. *No loving God would ever take a mother from her child.* He looked into the eyes of hell and began to speak, but the smoke was so thick he choked on his words.

He woke from his horror and clutched his throat. He was still on the mountain. He tried to breathe, but couldn't. In desperation, he reached for his knife and was about to cut a hole just below his Adam's apple when suddenly his airway opened. He fell back and sucked in the cold air. It burned his throat and lungs as he continued to take deep breaths.

It was only a dream, he thought. Then he smelled Chloe's perfume. *Or, was it?*

Hate and scorn filled his heart as he mustered up the strength to continue his climb. He knew the answers would only come from one place. *The beginning.*

CHAPTER 50

President Dupree arrived on schedule in Palm Cove. He had expected to depart as soon as the Phantom Squad had boarded, but Maddie wanted one more meeting. One more chance to convince him to call off the trip.

It was fruitless, but while everyone was occupied, Joan was able to get a special package into Q's hands.

The squad and the president were soon in the air.

"We will land at Bagram Air Base, north of Kabal," Seven said. "From there we will have a two hour drive to Delta Camp, your first stop. Three days from now, we enter Alpha territory at zero-nine hundred hours and if everything goes as planned, we are airborne again twelve hours later."

President Dupree looked at the map spread out on the table in front of them. "Have you notified the Department of Homeland Security?"

Seven sucked in his bottom lip. "Negative. We notify nobody."

"But. . ."

"But, nothin'," Seven said. "You may be the leader of the free world, but from this point on until we land back in D.C., I'm in charge."

The president's hands began to ball up in fists.

Scarlet placed her hand on top of her father's. "We had Joan put word out through the Pentagon that you would be landing on the aircraft carrier, the *USS Enterprise* in the gulf, and then chopper in to Delta from there."

"She thinks she can flush out the mole with the fake intel," Seven said. "She has a trace on every line leaving the Pentagon and she should now be able to follow their transmission, no matter how many satellites the bastard bounces his signal off of."

President Dupree stood up. "Let's hope to God you're right." He nodded to the five people who sat at the table, the only five people he knew he could trust, the five people who had sworn to keep him safe. "I've had a long day and this is the last chance I'll get to sleep in a bed for a while, so if you will excuse me, I'm going to take a nap."

Everyone stood as he turned to walk away.

As the president exited the room, he mumbled, "Where the hell is Venturi?"

CHAPTER 51

Just before dawn of the next day, Falcon gathered his men for the last time before the onset of their mission.

He hand-rolled an Afghani cigarette, lit it and eyeballed them. "If one person as much as blinks the wrong way, I will blow your brains out." He heard someone mumble something about *jihad*. He grabbed the soldier by the hair, yanked him to his feet and blew smoke in his face. "If I kill you, there won't be a bunch of under aged virgins waiting for you, you pervert. You will be stuck in eternity fondling your grandmother. Do you understand?" He didn't give him time to respond. He just tossed him down onto the sand.

"I've sent word to Alpha that we are approaching with prisoners. When we crest the next sand dune, they will pick us up and send out a patrol. Everything goes exactly as planned. If we work together, we will control Alpha thirty minutes after entering, if we screw up, I will be the only one to leave alive.

"Move out."

As expected, Alpha Camp's security forces began tracking the Americans and their prisoners as soon as they passed the next dune and dispatched several troops. The dust cloud coming from the three Humvee's could be seen almost as soon as they left Alpha.

The soldiers from Alpha were leery of oncoming troops and stopped their Humvee's a distance from the men and took a defensive stance. Only after receiving confirmation from command, that the men they saw were from a U.S. outpost did they radio the camp that they were coming back with prisoners.

Falcon's orders to his men had been explicit. Once 'the prisoners' were locked up, his men were to blend in to Alpha Camp. He wanted them paired up with the real troops of Alpha. On his go, they were to shoot the soldiers stationed at the camp. All headshots and all fatal. The only one who would be allowed to live was the camp commander. His death would have to wait.

Everything went as planned.

Falcon looked at the carnage at his feet. He didn't see Americans or patriots, he only saw dollar signs. "I want the dead buried behind the camp and I don't want any sign of digging," he ordered.

As he supervised his men, he saw two of the Brotherhood kicking and spitting on a dead soldier. He walked up to them, pulled his gun and shot them dead before they had a chance to react.

He turned to the stunned expression of the rest of the Brotherhood. "You call that honor?" he yelled, waving his pistol. "Is that what your leader teaches you?" He walked between the men, looking each in the eye. "If I see any more of that shit," he spit, "I will cut off your *manhood*," he said mocking Omar, "and feed it to you before I kill you, is that understood?"

A rumble of dissent began to grow in the members of the Brotherhood. Falcon shouldered his automatic weapon and sprayed bullets at their feet.

"If you don't like my ways," Falcon yelled, "take it up with your leader. Until then, you do as I say or you will end up like those two."

The men glared at him with venomous hatred, but no one made a sound.

"Good, now bury the Americans as if they were your own family."

The commander, beaten and cuffed, looked up through a shattered eye socket and spoke through a busted lip. "That's a lot of compassion for someone who just murdered his own people."

The American swung and backhanded the colonel. "I don't give a shit about you, your men, or the United States," he seethed. "That little demonstration was all about keeping order. I needed to let these morons know who was boss before they started acting like fools just like your men did when we entered the camp." He grabbed the colonel's head and forced him to look at the men who had been under his command. "If you had any control over your soldiers, maybe some of them would still be alive, or maybe some of mine would be dead."

He dropped the colonel at his feet and turned to leave. "Take this piece of crap to his quarters and stand guard over him until I get there. Colonel Matthews and I are going to have a little discussion as soon as I get some grub."

The colonel was battle tested and put up more of a resistance than Falcon thought he would.

Falcon stood over the beaten, bloody, dead body of the U.S. officer. He looked down at the man and admired him in a way. "The bastard really did believe in God and country," he muttered. He reached over and grabbed the end of the American flag that stood beside the colonel's desk and used it to wipe the blood off of his hands.

He took one more look at the man lying at his feet. "In the end, they all talk," he said to himself. He spit on the floor next to Colonel Matthew's body. "Why do they make it so hard on themselves?"

Falcon gathered his troops in the mess tent. "My sources tell me that President Dupree will arriving the day after tomorrow. He will be accompanied by five soldiers."

He could hear snickering from some of the men.

The American leaned back and punched the one closest to him with such force that blood, teeth, and spittle landed on the four men next to him. The man dropped, unconscious before his head struck the ground.

The corner of the American's upper lip curled in anger as he clenched his bloodied fist. "These are not ordinary soldiers," he yelled. "These are the Black Militia! If I wasn't here, the whole lot of you wouldn't stand a chance."

A man in the back stood and asked, "What makes having you here any different? You are only one man."

Falcon smirked. "You have balls, I like that. What makes me different is that I have personal knowledge on how they think and how they act. I also know that their leader will not be with them. They will also be preoccupied with President Dupree's safety. These factors will make them vulnerable."

He paced in front of his men. "What we don't know or have any way of knowing is who may or may not come by the camp in the next thirty-six hours, so we have to look, act and breathe the part of American soldiers. Those of you who were brought in here as prisoners will remain in the brig."

He heard grumbling from the Brotherhood.

"Shut up!" he yelled. "It won't be locked and you will be armed." He turned his back to his men. "Everyone knows what they have to do. Go do it. We meet here again tomorrow morning for final prep."

CHAPTER 52

High on the mountain, the wind cut through Brent's flesh. He was on the verge of frostbite. His hands and face discolored, his beard laden with ice. He had climbed past thirteen thousand feet and Mount Ararat was a sheet of ice. The gradient of the climb and the ice had increased causing his footing to be less stable. For every twenty feet he climbed, he slid down five.

He felt for, reached, and grabbed a strong finger hold in the ice, took a deep breath and heaved himself upward. He lunged with both feet and felt his hold break loose. He fell backward, slamming his body off the frozen tundra as he tumbled. He came to rest on a slab of exposed rock. Rock he had climbed forty minutes ago. He lay still, afraid to move. Too tired to move. Distraught, and drained, tears began to fill his eyes. He brought a shivering hand, a hand covered in a torn, weather beaten glove to his face and scraped away the frozen tears.

As he lay on the frozen rock, a tornado of contempt tore through him. Contempt at himself, at the world, and at God. He clenched his jaw and his teeth began to chatter. He tried to relax his muscles, but to no avail. It felt as if his teeth would crack and his mind would break, but he didn't care. His resentment consumed him. Fists balled up, he slammed them off the jagged surface. He felt the electric shock of pain shoot from his fingers straight up his arms and find a home in his head. "Damn You," he screamed. The sound echoed off the mountain. "What do You want from me?" Brent stood on the rocky cliff and reached toward heaven with both arms. "I've given You everything, and You have taken from me the one thing that mattered."

Physically spent from his last outburst, Brent dropped to his knees. He lay, hoping God would take him at that very moment.

"You must continue your quest. The answers will be found at The Beginning."

Brent heard the words and slowly stood. "I'll continue the climb," he mumbled, "because I have nothing else to live for." His muscles spasmed and cramped as he lifted himself from the permafrost.

As evening fell on the third day, the light he could see through his blindness became so bright he squeezed his eyes shut trying to douse it. When he dragged himself over the next icy face, he felt the ground in disbelief. It didn't feel icy or cold, it felt like grass and was warm.

Touching the ground, the light became so bright it hurt, but with the pain came pleasure. Insurmountable pleasure.

"You have journeyed a long way."

Brent dropped to his knees when he heard the voice of God. "I have done as I was told," he scowled.

"You lay before God, and yet you are filled with anger."

"Don't I have a right to be angry?"

Brent could feel the presence of God step closer. As He neared, nature seemed to grow in reverence. Brent could hear birds chirp and the temperature continued to climb. "Stand, my son."

Brent stood, grass still clutched in his hands.

"You have the right to be angry, but not at Me."

Brent was speechless. Words seemed hollow at this point. He dragged his body to a standing position and found his voice. "I did everything You asked of me, and You let Chloe die!" he bellowed. "Who should I be angry at?"

"I too cried at Chloe's death. I held her hand as she passed from her earthly life and welcomed her with open arms when she entered her eternal one."

No longer able to hold his body erect, Brent fell at the feet of God. "Why did you allow her to die?" he wept.

"The wheels of time were put in motion when this garden was created. Man's choices have dictated what will and what will not occur. I comfort those who seek Me, but all other answers will not be revealed to anyone of this world."

Brent's tears continued to fall as God's words bore into his soul. "I thought I was climbing the mount to find the beginning of Noah's lineage, the Ark. Why do you refer to this place as the garden?"

"Where ever I step, the Garden of Eden will be found."

"Then, my climb must continue?"

"No, you have reached The Beginning."

Brent dragged himself off the ground, leaned on his elbows and looked toward the face of God. Confusion washed over him. "The beginning of what?"

"The beginning of everything. The cornerstone of creation. You have climbed to search for answers. All answers come from Me. I am the beginning and the end, the Alpha and the Omega."

"I don't understand," Brent said. "Why did I have to climb to find You? Why was this quest necessary?"

"Stand and walk with Me."

As Brent walked with God, he felt a peace never achieved.

"Why do you think you had to come here?"

Brent thought hard and long before answering. He just shook his head. "I'm not sure," he mumbled. "I'm not sure of anything."

God stopped and sighed. "All your life, you were kept in the dark. When you were young, you were kept in the dark about your family. As a man—as the Chosen, you were kept in the dark about your destiny. You needed to come to this place to see the Light."

"You speak in riddles," Brent said.

"Riddles to those who are in the dark, but my words are clear to those in the Light."

"So," Brent said, "is my destiny fulfilled?"

"Your destiny is what you make it. Do you think it is fulfilled?"

Again, Brent thought long before offering an answer. "No," he said, "my destiny lies in my daughter."

God nodded. "You must continue your quest as My Chosen so

that your daughter can live out hers."

Brent bowed his head.

"Must I continue blind?" he asked.

"That is up to you. Tell me, Chosen One, what do you clutch in your hands?"

Brent remembered that he still held the grass in his hands. He brought it to his nose and inhaled the scent. "Grass, a plant of some kind."

"And what plant would be found here that cannot be found anywhere else?"

Brent rubbed his fingers together feeling the moisture of the plant. As he brought it to his lips and as he was about to taste it, revelation struck him. He quickly lowered it from his lips. "The Herb of Life!"

"Well done."

"But I don't understand. How can this plant help me? I can't eat it. Your covenant with Noah and his descendants tells me so."

God stayed silent and continued to walk.

"Is there any other reason you came to the beginning?"

"I came because I seek understanding."

"Have you found it?"

Brent shook his head. "I don't know."

God reached out and held Brent by his shoulders. "You have spent most of your life hiding your true emotions. You have done so for good reason, but you must now release all that you have kept pent up in your heart. All of your hatred, all of your remorse, all of your guilt must be left here. You must leave all of your baggage at My feet if you are to be the father you wish to be. You must leave it all behind if you are to save the ones who need you."

Brent knelt at the feet of God and prayed for forgiveness. He prayed for God to take all of his guilt, all of his sins and all of his anger. He prayed for a new beginning.

"Your prayer for forgiveness has been answered."

Brent prostrated himself at the feet of God and wept. His tears were not tears of anger or of frustration, but tears of forgiveness and of peace.

CHAPTER 53

Brother Gregory ran through the monastery calling for Tag. Tag's pulse quickened when he heard the monk screaming. When Gregory found him, he grabbed Tag's robe and pulled him along.

"Wait," Tag yelled. "What's wrong? Where are you dragging me?" In his heart, he was praying that nothing bad had happened to Brent.

"Come," Gregory smiled. "You must come and see."

The two ran through the monastery, up the stairs, and out into the dark of night.

Gregory pointed to Mount Ararat. "Look."

Tag look out at the mount, but could see nothing. "See what? It's pitch black out here."

Gregory smiled. "Exactly!"

Tag thought the monk was crazy, but then it hit him. "The light—it's gone."

Gregory laughed as he clutched his knees in exhaustion. "He's done it," he said. "Brent has found the ark. He has found the beginning."

The two stared into the black of night and laughed with unspeakable joy.

Brent continued to kneel and as he did, he heard laughter. He then heard the voices of Tag and Gregory. *How can that be*, he thought. *How can I hear them up here?*

As he stood, he realized he was no longer on the mount but was now in the valley by the monastery. He brought his hands to his face and felt the herb caress his skin. His skin tingled when the herb touched it. His weather torn skin became new again. He opened his eyes and ground the plant into his eyeballs. Streaks of lightening shot through him as all the colors of the rainbow flickered past. Brent opened his palms and let the plant drop from his hands. He looked to the ground and watched as the Herb of Life disappeared.

His laughter mixed with the sound of his friends.

Tag and Gregory stared into each other's eyes when they heard Brent's voice.

"It can't be," Tag said.

Gregory leaned his head toward the heavens and laughed even harder. "All things are possible with God."

A shadow emerged from the darkness and around it glowed a heavenly light.

"Look!" yelled Tag.

Gregory looked wide-eyed at the shadow. "He has walked with God," he gasped.

Brent drew near and Gregory dropped to his knees.

"Get off your knees, Brother," Brent smiled. "I am just a man."

Tag ran towards Brent and threw his arms around him. "It is so good to see you."

"And it is good to *see* you," Brent emphasized.

It was then Tag knew Brent had regained his sight.

CHAPTER 54

The helicopter carrying President Dupree and the squad neared Alpha Camp. The past two days had gone better than Seven expected. The troops were as excited to see and hear the president as he was excited to see them.

"Alpha was notified two hours ago of the president's arrival," Seven said. "We take no chances. I want weapons drawn and ready when we touch down."

President Dupree peered down at the landing zone and saw three men, a color guard in dress uniform, holding the American flag. "No weapons will be drawn," he said. "This visit must be one that shows complete trust in this unit. Your weapons will reflect otherwise."

"They are soldiers," Seven said. "They will understand."

The president glared at Seven. "I said no! That's an order."

Seven glared back, packed his lip with tobacco and sucked in his lower lip. "You heard the man, weapons down."

The squad members flipped the safety on their weapons and let them hang by their shoulder straps.

As the helicopter landed, Seven started to get a bad feeling. Everything at and around Alpha was calm, a little too calm. He reached down and released the safety on his HK MP5 submachine gun. Jefferson and Fitzpatrick were out of the chopper before the landing gear had touched down. Scarlet and Alana flanked the president as he stepped down off the chopper. Seven followed close behind.

The soldier in the middle of the honor guard stepped forward and saluted. "Mr. President, the men of Alpha Camp are honored and welcome you to their home."

Seven stepped forward. "Where is your commanding officer, Colonel Matthews, Captain?"

"He sends his apologies for not greeting the president in person, but with the short notice of arrival, he felt his duty was to stay in the camp and make sure everything was ready."

Seven spit at the feet of the captain. He was about to continue when President Dupree stopped him. "Stand down, Seven," he said with a forced smile. "Everything is fine."

The president entered Alpha Camp to a standing ovation. The troops lined the entrance of the mess tent and clapped as he walked by. Colonel Matthews stood at the far end of the line, in full salute.

Seven was getting more uncomfortable as they approached the colonel. When the colonel brought his hand down from his face, Seven stared at a ghost. A distant memory flooded his mind. He drew up his MP5 and yelled, "Trap!"

He squeezed the trigger and shot anyone he could as he watched the soldiers draw their weapons and fire. In the instant Seven yelled, two things happened simultaneously. Falcon had grabbed the man standing next to him and used his as a human shield as he dove for cover, and the squad went into action.

Fitz kicked over a stable and Alana and Scarlet dropped to a prone position. Each had begun shooting even before they had taken aim. At the same time, Jefferson grabbed President Dupree by the collar and dragged him behind the barricade.

The squad mowed down everyone they could see. Members of the Brotherhood who had stayed hidden began firing at the squad from the rear flank. Bullets hit the dirt behind President Dupree causing three of the squad members to drop their weapons and jump on top of the president.

"Drop your weapons and I'll let the president live," Falcon yelled.

Seven clipped off another burst of ammo as he felt a knife-like pain bore through his shoulder. The bullet hit the nerve going to his hand and his gun dropped from his grip.

He looked to his rear and saw that his men and the president were completely surrounded. Any further action would result in the loss of lives.

"Cease fire!" he yelled.

Seven watched as Falcon moved from his cover and stood in front of him. His face was encompassed in a revenge-filled sneer.

Seven glared at him. From his peripheral vision, he saw the butt end of an automatic weapon slice toward his head. It was the last thing he remembered.

The next thing he felt was a kick to his ribs.

"Wake up, asshole, we're home."

Seven squirmed, but couldn't move. He'd been bagged and gagged. He and the rest of the prisoners were jerked into a sitting position. Through cloudy vision, Seven focused on the person in front of him. Private Jensen, the washout from the Phantom Squad.

"I'm gonna have my boys remove your gags so we can have a little talk," Jensen said. He walked the line of prisoners dragging his knife across their backs as he went. "If I get any lip from anybody, I start cutting." He stopped behind Seven while the gags were removed. "Is that understood?"

"Screw you, Private Jensen."

Jensen hit Seven on the back of his head with the handle of his knife. "One more remark like that, you piece of shit, and I'll cut your tongue out." He pushed Seven causing him to fall face first in the dirt. "The name's Falcon," he said as he kicked Seven hard, breaking a couple of ribs. He walked around Seven, grabbed him by the scruff of his neck, like a dog, and yanked his head up. A depraved grin on his face. "Although some of my friends at the pentagon know me as Phoenix." The expression on Seven's face caused him to laugh. "You like the irony, scumbag?"

"Enough!"

Falcon snapped his head up and stared into the barrel of a

semiautomatic handgun. A gun held by Omar.

"I like torturing my enemies as much as you do," Omar said. "but we have accomplished nothing if we cannot get their leader here. The Brotherhood of Gaza cannot extract its revenge if the leader of the Phantom Squad does not show. I want the entire world to witness the demise of the Black Militia and the President of the United States." He stepped in front of the president. "By killing both of you, the Brotherhood will stake its claim as the most powerful terrorist organization this world has ever known. We will bring about a jihad that others have only dreamt of."

President Dupree stared back at Omar, but said nothing.

Omar delighted in the silence. He turned and addressed Falcon. "And you," he said, "Falcon or Jensen or whatever you want to be called cannot collect the rest of your money if you cannot bring Venturi to me."

Falcon stepped into Omar so that the barrel of the gun pushed up against his gut. "I'll get him here," he snarled. He leaned into Omar and whispered, "The next time you draw a gun on me, you better pull the trigger or I'll blow your freaking head off."

Omar squeezed the trigger a bit harder. He wanted nothing more than to kill the pig who stood in front of him, but killing the leader of the Phantom Squad meant even more. He knew he still needed Falcon because of his Pentagon connection. He lowered the gun and walked out of the room.

Falcon turned and addressed his men. "I want two men for each of theirs at all times." He looked around the small cave. "You are to keep them up and walking around this shithole, twenty-four-seven. If they fall, pick them up. If they need to pee, they can wet themselves. They are not to be given food or water unless I give it to them. Is that understood?" He didn't wait for a response. "If any one of you fails to follow my orders, I will kill all of you." He looked around at his surroundings. "I've got a thousand more sand-niggers I can replace you with."

CHAPTER 55

When Q returned to pick up President Dupree and the squad, he found Alpha Camp vacated. He immediately called Maddie to alert the SIA.

Maddie ran down the hall of headquarters and threw open the door to Joan's office. One look and Joan knew something bad had happened.

Maddie's mascara was smeared and her eyes were red and swollen. Her words choked her as she spoke. "They've been captured."

Joan shot from her chair. "Dear God," she said. "By who? Where are they?"

"I don't know. Q just radioed. He said when he went back to Alpha everyone was gone. Everyone."

Joan slumped in her seat. "I'll reach the Pentagon and see if they have received notice."

"No," Maddie answered. "Call Brent and get his ass back here, now."

"But, I. . ."

Maddie got in her face. "I know you, Joan," she yelled, "and I know you can contact him. The president of the United States has been captured by the enemy along with our friends and family. I don't give a damn what he told you before he left or what deal the two of you made. Contact him and get him back here."

She watched as Joan sent a distress signal to Brent.

Joan's fingers trembled as she removed them from the keyboard. "That's all I can do," she mumbled. "Now, we have to wait until he answers."

"Or until we here from the terrorists," Maddie said.

They spent the night at headquarters along with Lucille, Joseph, Bishop Jessop and Faith. It seemed no one wanted to be alone and everyone wanted to be present when they heard from Brent or from the captors.

At two a.m., Joan's laptop buzzed.

CHAPTER 56

In the second day of captivity, Falcon watched as Seven, his squad and the president stumbled their way around the cave system. Omar walked up and stood beside him.

"I think they are ready," Omar said.

Falcon inhaled the smoke from his cigarette one last time before flicking it on the ground. "Bring the prisoners into the media room," he ordered. "It's time for their television premier."

Twenty minutes later, the squad was positioned on their knees in a row with President Dupree kneeling in front of them. Omar and Falcon flanked the group. Each wore a scarf around their faces and each held one of the HK MP5s they took off of the prisoners. When the light on the camera blinked red, Falcon began speaking.

"Next to me is the president of the United States and the group known to the world as the Black Militia. The authorities have forty-eight hours to find and bring the leader of the Militia to me or I start killing them. I will kill one person every two hours starting at o-two hundred hours on the second day and if he hasn't shown by the time I get to the last, I will put a bullet in President Dupree's head on live television."

Omar stepped forward. "We, the Brotherhood of Gaza, mean no harm to the president of the United States or his men. We just want to bring to justice the man who has killed innocent people for the past fifteen years. The Brotherhood has stood by while governments have tried to capture this man, but somehow he has managed to stay free. Even now, when the soldiers he leads were called into duty to guard the president, he has not had the courage to come with them." Omar stepped closer to the president and jerked his head back by the hair. "Forty-eight hours or this infidel dies."

CHAPTER 57

Joan and Maddie watched in terror as the broadcast ended.

"Did that go out over national television?" Maddie asked.

Joan typed in a few key strokes and shook her head. "No, it was patched to us through the Pentagon." Maddie went to speak, but Joan held up her hand and as the other danced along the keyboard. "The SOB just gave himself away."

"What?" Maddie said.

"The traitor inside the Pentagon. He must have been flustered when he saw the tape. He forgot to encode the message. We've got him."

"Have SIA agents stationed in D.C. arrest him and bring him here, now," Maddie responded. "I want to interrogate him, personally."

Everyone in the room jumped when Joan's laptop chirped.

"It's Brent. He said to go live in a video conference. I'll bring him up on the monitor."

A few key strokes later and an image came up on the screen. An image of Brent and Tag.

"Colonel, we have a clear transmission, how is it on your end?"

"We're good, Joan."

"Brent where the hell are you, you are needed back here, pronto," Maddie said.

"Where I am is immaterial at this point," Brent said. "I received a message from Q moments ago. Can you shed any light on the whereabouts of the squad and President Dupree?"

"We received a video from the Brotherhood of Gaza. I'm sending to you now," Joan said.

"Who is that next to you?" Maddie asked. "I assume it's Lieutenant Achak."

Brent nodded as he and Tag watched the tape.

Brent stared at the monitor as the tape ended. His squad was trained to endure pain and torture at the hands of the enemy. His worries were for the president. "Joan, rewind the tape to where it is scanning across the prisoners."

"Yes, sir."

"There," Brent pointed. "Did you see Seven's head twitching?"

Maddie's words got caught in her throat. "I . . . I thought it might be a reaction from some sort of torture."

Brent's appearance was intense, but he didn't show signs of despair. "No," he said pointing at Seven, "he's sending a message. He's using a code used by the squad. A form of Morse code. He said that they are in a cave system, but doesn't have a location."

"That's the weird thing. The terrorists said you have forty-eight hours to turn yourself in, but they didn't say where they were," Maddie said.

Tag leaned into the monitor. "Rerun the tape again, please."

As he watched the camera scan the room, his eyes opened wide. "Son of a bitch, I know where they are." Everyone's attention shifted to Tag. "They are in the Hindu Kush Mountains."

"How can you be sure?" Maddie asked.

"Because, I've been there."

"Are you certain?"

"Positive."

Brent and Tag made eye contact. Each reading the other's expression.

"How are you certain, Lieutenant?"

"That's irrelevant," Brent answered.

Maddie crossed her arms and tapped her foot in frustration. "Did you forget who your commander is, Colonel?"

Brent looked into the monitor with dead eyes. "The last I checked, I had no commander. I was fired the last time we spoke."

"Damn it, Brent, what the hell is going on?"

Brent used sign language to send a message to Joan. She immediately signed back.

Maddie eyed Joan. She was about to lose her composure.

"Joan says we're on a frequency that can't be traced," Brent said, "so I'll fill you in." He looked over at Tag. "Actually, I'll let Lieutenant Achak tell you."

"The place you're looking at," Tag said, "is the same place I was holed up in during my last mission."

"When Alpha Camp was raided?" Maddie interjected.

"That's the one," Tag nodded.

"Lieutenant, there are thousands of caves in those mountains, how can you be so certain that you were in that cave?"

"If you direct your attention back to the video, you will see scratching on the west wall at two minutes and thirty three seconds."

Joan rewound the tape to that exact point before Maddie could respond.

Pointing, Tag said, "Those scratches were the number of men Sergeant Delbach and I saw and if you wind the tape to forty-three seconds I'll show you something even better."

Joan smiled and rewound the tape again. She was more infatuated with Tag now than ever before.

Maddie was more confused. "They're just scanning across the prisoners."

"Not just," Tag said. "Joan, can you zoom in on the wall behind the president and squad?"

"I can do anything you want," she mumbled as she tapped the keyboard.

"There," Tag said. "On the wall, all the way up in the left corner."

Joan adjusted the point of view.

"That's a line drawing of the cave system. We had thirty-six hours to search it." He placed his finger on an X on the screen. "That is where we saw them exit the system on the Pakistan side of the ridge. The O," he moved his finger, "is the main entrance on the Afghani side."

Maddie and Joan smiled at the young officer's ingenuity.

"Joan," Brent said, "can you make a print of both of those and send them to me?"

Joan tapped a key. "Done."

Maddie saw the expression on Brent's face. A look she had seen many times before, the face of the leader of the Phantom Squad. "What are you thinking, Colonel?" she asked.

"Joan, do we have any knights in Pakistan near the Hindu Kush?"

"I'll have to tap into the Endowment network. That may take a moment."

"Do it after we end broadcast. Did you give the message from Tag to weapons development?"

"Yes, as soon as I received it."

"What message?" Maddie asked. She then rolled her eyes, "Never mind, continue."

"Q dropped off a package two days ago," Tag said, "the day after you went up the mountain."

"What mountain?" Maddie said.

"It's irr . . ."

"Yeah, I know," she said. "It's irrelevant. I'm starting to think I'm irrelevant."

Brent smiled.

Joan's computer buzzed another alarm. "Hold that thought," she said. She read the message and smiled. "We have him."

"Have who," everyone responded.

"The Pentagon traitor," Joan replied. "SIA has him and is transporting him now to headquarters."

"Maddie, you do what you have to do to find out everything you need to and we will work on things from our end," Brent said. "We make video contact again in three hours."

Everyone nodded.

"Oh, and Maddie?"

"Yes."

"Do whatever it takes to break him."

The transmission went black.

Inside the monastery, Brent continued to stare at the monitor.

"What are you thinking, Colonel?"

"I'm thinking we have a lot to do in three hours."

Brent and Tag sat with the brothers in the eating hall. This time, Brent was at the head of the table.

"I want to thank all of you for what you have done here. I have no words to express my gratitude." He wiped his hair from his face as he continued. "You went through a great deal over the past eight years and you did it all on faith. If you do nothing else, you can die knowing that you fulfilled your purpose."

"What will you do next, Chosen One?"

Brent looked at Brother Gregory. "Tag and I will be leaving in the morning."

"Where will you be going?"

Brent glanced at Tag and then back at Gregory. "We will be headed to Pakistan and then to our brothers' aid."

"We will accompany you."

"No," Brent said. "You destiny has been fulfilled."

"You were correct when you said that our purpose has been fulfilled. You were also correct when you said that if we die, we die having fulfilled our godly purpose. We will go."

As Brent thought about Gregory's words his phone chirped. He dropped his head to read the message. "It seems there are only a few knights in Pakistan. I will not risk the lives of those who have families. That leaves us with only a handful." He raised his head and looked out at the men who sat at the table. "I'll accept your offer, but you will journey only as far as Pakistan. That is where I will need you."

"We will do whatever the Chosen One asks," Brother Gregory said. "That is our destiny."

Brent and Tag spent the next two hours going over the drawing from the cave.

"During my last mission," Tag said, "there were over a thousand men there. Excuse me if I'm wrong, but I got the impression that Omar will want to present a united front. If the Brotherhood is there again with the same numbers, do you think it's smart for just the two of us to go in?"

A sly smile rose from Brent's lips. "If we pull this off the way I plan, I think it's the only way. Besides," he said, "they will think there is only one."

Tag looked at Brent and started to laugh. "You are certifiably insane."

CHAPTER 58

Video connection was made with HQ at the appointed time.

"The prisoner was very forthcoming," Maddie said. "He was an IT supervisor and was able to tap into Joan's conversations with her mole."

"That's not good," Brent said.

Maddie agreed. "The good news is that he wasn't able to break the encryption and he doesn't know where the messages originated from. He was only able to read the outgoing messages. Still, he was able to sell quite a lot of information."

"To who?"

"He sent everything to a man calling himself Falcon."

Falcon, Brent thought, *why is that familiar?*

Maddie's words broke his thought process. "The traitor will be spending the rest of his days at The Bay."

"Before you send him to Cuba," Brent said, "we have one more message for him to send."

A knowing expression flooded Maddie's face. "I thought you might, but do you think that's safe."

"Not if he was actually doing the sending. Joan, I need you to send the following message."

Joan sat at her laptop, fingers ready. "Go."

A few minutes later the message was sent.

"I'll be rendezvousing with you and I'm bringing reinforcements," Maddie said.

"No, I need you there, running SIA in case we run into trouble. Gather the agents and wait until you hear from me. If I don't contact you in three days, send in the cavalry."

"Do you think that's wise?"

Brent's expression went cold. He was a blank slate. "This is a squad mission and I will handle it. They will be expecting an army. We will send what they least expect."

"Which is?"

"Two men."

"What do I tell the knights?" Joan asked.

"Have them meet us at the coordinates I'm about to send you."

Maddie wiped her sweaty palms on her skirt. As the screen went black, she whispered, "God speed."

CHAPTER 59

Q landed the C-130 transport in Pakistan, forty miles south of Peshawar. Brent, Tag and the monks of Khor Virap all wore the traditional clothing of the monastery: robes and sandals. Brent and Tag lagged behind while Brother Gregory and the rest of the brothers disembarked the aircraft.

"I've never questioned you before, Colonel, but are you sure about this? A bunch of monks?"

Brent slapped Q on the back. "Don't judge what you can't see."

Tag shook his head. "Great, more riddles."

Q laughed. "That's how I'm sure he knows what he's doing."

"We will drop off the monks when we meet up with the knights and then Tag and I will backtrack," Brent said. "We will meet at the designated location at zero two hundred tomorrow. Be ready with the Black Hawk."

"Done," Q replied. And then, just like in every mission they had been involved in, Q proceeded to reiterate his portion of the plan back to Brent. "If you don't show up on time, I will proceed to the coordinates you gave me and hit them with everything I've got."

Brent nodded. "While we're gone, I need you to do me a couple of favors?"

"Anything, Colonel," Q said.

"Do you still have the tarp that you used to cover the B1-B in the Saudi oilfield?"

"Yes, sir."

Brent handed Q a monk's robe. "Cut me two pieces about this size and have them here when we get back."

Q smiled. He loved the way the colonel's mind worked.

"What's the other favor?" Q asked.

Brent handed him the guitar case which contained the Sword of Truth. "I need you to guard this with your life. If something happens, see that it gets to Bishop Jessop. He will know what to do with it."

Q was about to ask what was with the guitar case but thought better of it. He just took the case and nodded.

Brent turned to leave.

"Oh, by the way," Q said. "I like the clean shaven look. It's good to have you back, Colonel."

Brent placed a blacked out hood over his face, gave his friend a slight head nod and walked off the transport and into the morning sun. He felt the sun's heat on his face as he stood on the tarmac. *It's good to be back*, he thought.

By nightfall, Brent and his men had met up with the knights just below the ridgeline.

Brent knelt on one knee and spread out a map of the Hindu Kush Mountains. He isolated the portion that served as a boundary between Afghanistan and Pakistan and pointed at all of the places where someone could enter Pakistan. "We will have all other points blocked so this will be the only way the Brotherhood will have to escape."

"How do you intend to block all the other openings? There are many and there are only two of you."

Brent glanced up at the knight who asked the question. "We have reinforcements coming," he said.

Tag and Gregory eyed the men and then found each other's stare. Each knew that the colonel's words were deceptive; they just weren't sure why he found it necessary to lie to the knights.

As they searched for an explanation, Brent continued. "The enemy will have no choice but to walk through this pass. I need you to capture them and keep them here until help arrives." Brent stood and walked around the men. He was glad to see that they all appeared to be battle-tested soldiers. "This is not a kill mission. You are to capture and hold. Do not, I repeat, do not use lethal force unless your life is in danger." He put his hand on Brother Gregory's shoulder. "You are all to take your orders from this man."

They all acknowledged the orders.

Brent and Tag said their goodbyes and broke camp.

"Why the deception back there, Colonel?"

"In my experience with the Brotherhood of Gaza, I have found them to be extremely resourceful. They have infiltrated most governments. I'm not taking any chances on whether or not they have infiltrated the outer circle."

Tag quickened his step in order to keep up. "You think that's possible?"

Further from camp, Brent removed his hood. "Not probable, but anything is possible, Lieutenant."

Tag nodded and continued to walk beside Brent.

"We need to double time it back to the airstrip if we don't want Q dropping missiles on our boys," Brent said.

"Then, what are you waiting for? Get moving old man."

Brent smiled. "Shadow me."

At zero two hundred hours, Q had the helicopter warmed up and was ready for departure. He ran through a safety check and was about to take flight when he spotted Brent running toward him. He was confused because he expected two men. As Brent approached, suddenly he split in two. Q squeezed his eyes shut, thinking he was seeing an illusion.

Brent and Tag bordered the Black Hawk.

"You look confused," Brent said. "Is everything okay?"

"Yeah," Q replied, "just seeing things. I guess I'm just a little tired."

Brent looked over at Tag and back to Q. "Yeah, you must be," he said.

Three hours later, the two of them had donned their jumping gear and Q was ready to drop the chopper to seven hundred feet.

"When I drop this bird, you will have no lag time," Q said. "You need to jump without hesitation and you can't deploy until you reach three hundred feet."

Brent and Tag stared straight ahead.

"It's a death drop," Q said. "You won't have much time to slow your descent. Be ready for a hard landing."

He looked over at the two of them. They remained motionless.

Suddenly the helicopter dropped out of the early morning sky.

"Go, go, go," he yelled.

Q looked out the window and only saw one body dropping and only one chute open. He looked back to yell at whoever was still on board, but no one was there.

He shook his head. "I really need to get my eyes checked when this is over."

Brent and Tag dropped as planned. Tag had connected his jump suit to Brent's with a carabiner before they jumped. He was strapped to Brent's back. Tag deployed his chute at three hundred feet and readied himself for a hard landing. The chute was small for one person and definitely not built to take the weight of two men. Tag instinctively reached up and grabbed hold of the handles at the end of the toggle lines: The brakes on the chute. He pulled down as hard and as fast as he could and was able to slow their descent enough to relieve some of the impact. The landing was hard, but they were in one piece.

Once they buried their parachutes, they were ready to move out.

"Stay in my shadow until we reach point A," Brent ordered. "We can't risk being spotted. We will camp there until nightfall and then make our way to the party."

After they reached point A, both men grabbed some shuteye.

Brent woke before Tag. He had been unable to get much sleep because something Maddie had said was gnawing at him.

Falcon, he thought. *Why is that familiar?*

Brent dropped into a squat. As he relaxed, he went into a deep meditative state. He flashed back over the past few days. He saw nothing that threw up a red flag, so he drifted further back in his past. Back to Chloe's death and then back further. He retraced his life all the way back to his Phantom Squad training. He found himself standing at the base of the Grand Teton Mountains with the other trainees. He flashed through his days on the mountain.

Why am I here? He thought.

Suddenly he saw something that made his blood pressure start to rise. He slowed his breathing and maintained his meditative state.

His mind flashed forward and he saw the tape made by the captors. He concentrated on the stranger standing alongside Omar. *Son of a . . .*

Someone shook him from behind. Instinctively, he dropped his shoulder, grabbed the person's arm and flipped whoever was behind him. In blinding speed, he was sitting on top of the man with his knife pressed up against the person's jugular.

"Colonel, it's me," Tag yelled.

Brent stared down at him, muscles taut and blade ready.

"Colonel," he whispered as the knife pushed against his skin, pinching his flesh, "it's Tag."

Brent rolled off, sweat dripping from his skin and hair. With a quivering hand, he replaced his knife in its sheath. Hyperventilating, he said in a staccato voice, "Whenever you see me like that, don't . . . ever . . . touch . . . me. I'm not responsible for my actions."

Tag rubbed his neck. "Noted."

Brent stood and drank from his canteen.

"Where where you just then?" Tag asked.

Brent swallowed. "It's too hard to explain right now."

Tag pointed to his watch. "We're five minutes behind schedule."

Brent gathered himself and reached into his backpack and pulled out the pieces of tarp Q had acquired. He took his knife and cut a hole in the middle of both. "These are our new robes."

Tag took his and looked at it. It was sand colored camouflage. He laid it on the ground and saw that it blended in perfectly. "Nice."

Brent put his over his head and reached into his backpack and pulled out what looked like a piece of wood, about eighteen inches long and two inches in diameter. "It's time we put these into service."

Confused, Tag reached into his pack and took out an identical piece of wood. "What are these?"

"They are what I had the weapons department back at SIA develop for us," Brent answered.

They held their respective 'sticks' with one hand and depressed a hidden button. The eighteen-inch-long block of wood instantly became a six-foot-long staff—a carbon fiber staff.

Tag turned his staff in his one hand, spinning it like a baton. When he stopped, he held it in both hands. "I still can't believe how lightweight these are," he said. "Amazing."

"We will leave our other staffs here," Brent said. He then depressed another button on his staff and a six-inch blade sprung out of each end.

Tag smiled and did the same.

Brent had him push the button again causing the blades to become recessed in the staff.

Brent eyed Tag. "We act and fight like monks—until we can't."

Tag shook his head and laughed. "More riddles."

Brent allowed a slight smile to penetrate his demeanor. "You shadow me until we reach point B. We will bunk down once again until dark so we're not spotted and then we split up. We will meet back where the Brotherhood is keeping the president."

Tag's mind raced through their plan. He grabbed Brent's robe as he started to move. Brent stopped and looked back at Tag. "Are you sure of this plan, Colonel? I've been thinking that there has to be another way."

Brent shook his head. "They need to think they have won. It's the only way. We need them to let down their defenses. Once they are vulnerable, we show our hand."

Tag nodded.

"Let's move," Brent said.

CHAPTER 60

Omar stomped around the cave, kicking every rock in his path. "You said he would come!" he yelled.

Falcon eyed the prisoners and spit at the feet of the old man. "Do you really think the Americans will let their president die at the hands of terrorists?"

Omar stepped into Falcon and backhanded him across the face. "I told you before, never spit in my home."

Falcon drew his weapon and cocked the trigger. Before he could say anything, all of the men inside the cave drew on him.

"Did you really think the Brotherhood would follow you and not me?" Omar said.

Falcon released the trigger and holstered his weapon. "This isn't over," he growled.

"The message from your insider told us that no one was able to reach Colonel Venturi. He said that if we don't release the president and these men unharmed they would bomb us."

Falcon stepped in so that he was standing nose to nose with Omar. The old man's fetid breath pierced his nostrils as he spoke through gritted teeth. "He also said that the U.S. didn't know our exact location. They aren't going to send a massive air strike possibly killing thousands of civilians."

Omar stared back at Falcon.

A Mexican standoff.

"Get the camera setup," Falcon said. "I'm sending another message."

Omar waved for the task to be completed. "You better be right or you will die."

"I'm always right."

Falcon pulled Seven to his feet. "You are going to send a message to the United States." He handed him a piece of paper. On it was written hogwash about how the U.S. had killed civilians throughout Afghanistan and how President Dupree was personally responsible for their massacre.

Seven read the message silently, snarled and spit on the paper. "I ain't reading nothin'."

"If you won't read the message, I will get the message across another way." He called over one of the Brotherhood and told him to stand up the other prisoners and remove their blindfolds.

"I want them to see what happens when someone disobeys an order."

Without hesitation, Falcon began to beat Seven with his fists until his face was bloody and his eyes were just swollen slits. Seven lay on the ground in the fetal position, spitting blood and teeth.

"It's a shame to have ruined all that pretty dental work," Falcon laughed.

"You," he pointed at Jefferson, "You will read the message."

"Don't think so," Jefferson replied.

"You're just as stupid as you were fifteen years ago," Falcon said.

He then spun and side kicked Jefferson in the gut, causing the big man to drop to his knees. "I've been waiting a long time to take you apart, nigger."

"Screw you, Peck—"

Before he could get the word out, Falcon kicked the big man square in the mouth.

With an evil, satisfied smile, Falcon looked at the others. "Who's next? I'm just warming up."

Falcon eyed the rest of the prisoners. When he looked at Alana, she was staring back at him. He swung at her, pulling his fist back just before striking her face. She didn't flinch. Her eyes constricted and she scowled, matching his hatred with her own.

Falcon snarled. "What have we got here?" he drawled. He turned and kicked Seven in his injured shoulder causing him to moan. "How the mighty have fallen," he laughed. "It looks like the toughest member of your squad is a Bitch." He grabbed her by her hair and pulled her to her feet.

Her expression was stone cold as she continued to stare straight at him.

Falcon pulled out his knife and slid it down her cheek. "It would be a shame to mess up that pretty face."

Alana stiffened. A guttural growl came from her pursed lips. "There is nothing you could do to me that hasn't been done before."

Falcon grabbed a fist full of her hair and yanked her head back. "Wha'daya say, I try." His bile-filled breath made her flinch. With his free hand, he grabbed his knife and sliced open her front of her shirt exposing her bra.

"Maybe your friends back home would enjoy watching me screw you on film," he said.

Alana refused to show fear and swore at him in Hebrew.

Falcon's anger got the best of him and he cut her along the top of her bra line. Blood began to trickle down her left breast.

"Enough," yelled Omar.

Falcon snapped his head around as he stared into the old man's eyes.

"I think you've made your point."

As he turned to talk to Omar, Scarlet looked at her father. He mouthed for her not to let on that she was his daughter.

"I've got one more message to send the American government," Falcon said. "Roll the video."

With the video playing, Falcon grabbed President Dupree and made him stand front and center.

"As you can see," he said into the camera, "your elite squad is no match against me and the Brotherhood of Gaza." He pulled his semi-automatic pistol from his holster and placed it against the president's temple. "Find Venturi and get him here," he screamed. "You have twelve hours before I start taking lives." He flipped the gun in his hand and cold cocked the president with the butt of the pistol. The president slumped and fell to the ground. With the film still rolling, he kicked the president in the back with the steel toe of his boot. "This is not a game!" Falcon screamed. "If I don't see Venturi walk into this camp by zero two hundred hours tomorrow, I will kill each and every one of these scumbags." He pulled Alana towards him and roughly fondled her. "We will save the women for last." He kicked her in the back of her knees forcing her to drop in front of him. "These two," he pointed to Alana and Scarlet, "will be begging for death when my men finish using them."

He walked closer to the camera, so only his face could be seen in the camera. "That will be the next video I send." As the video ended, all you could hear was the laughter of the Brotherhood echoing off the walls of the cave.

Maddie, Bishop Jessop and Chloe sat silently as they watched the video feed.

Maddie couldn't take her eyes off of her husband. He was bloodied and unconscious. She was a mixture of anger and sadness. So torn up by what she witnessed that she had a hard time speaking.

"We can't just sit here and let this animal get away with this," Bishop Jessop said. "Can't we call in reinforcements?"

Maddie shook her head. "We don't even know their location."

The bishop went to say something else when Joan interrupted.

"Look at Seven's left hand," she said. "He's not unconscious and he's giving us a sign."

They all looked at the video again and watched Seven give a hand signal.

"He's telling us to stand down," Maddie said. Watching her husband signal them, gave her a bit of renewed strength. She stood and began to walk out of the control room. "We have to wait and hope that Brent knows what he is doing." As she turned to go into her office, Joan and Bishop Jessop could hear her say, "We do nothing unless the colonel sends us the distress signal."

CHAPTER 61

Brent and Tag went over the plan one more time as the sun set on the second day. Tag pulled out the rough drawing of the cave system and they reviewed the points of egress from the caves. Brent remained silent as he viewed the diagram.

"Once we set the explosives, we wait until the planned time."

He looked over at the lieutenant. "No matter what you see or hear, you stay black. At zero two hundred hours on the dot, you trigger the C4." He stared at Tag with the eyes of an assassin. "Then, we rain down holy hell on everyone in the Brotherhood."

Tag swallowed hard and nodded. "Damn right, we do."

At midnight, the two split, each dropping into the maze at different points. Tag set the first trap and was making his way to the next point when he heard two men speaking in Farsi. He hugged the wall, gripped his staff and waited. As the men turned the corner, he spun out of his hiding place and struck them as he had been taught by the brothers of Khor Virap. He struck with such speed that they didn't have time to react. As he stood over the unconscious men, Tag was surprised at how well the centuries-old method of fighting worked. He quickly bagged and tagged his prey and ran to his next destination.

Brent had dropped into the cave system at the other end and set his explosives in their designated spots. As he made his way from one location to the next, he couldn't help but marvel at how accurate Tag had been with his drawing.

The nearer he came to the room where the Brotherhood was keeping the president and his squad, the more voices he heard. He braced himself against a dark corner as the voices neared. Brent closed his eyes to block out his sight and try to heighten his sense of hearing. He was able to disseminate the sounds until he could clearly distinguish among three separate men.

Silently, Brent slid down the wall and closed his eyes. As he did, his sense of hearing amplified. He could tell from the sound of their footfalls that the largest man was in front and the other two were walking behind him in a side-by-side formation. He also heard the one in the front strike a lighter repeatedly. The man's voice rose in its inflection as his frustration grew at his malfunctioning lighter.

Brent rose to a standing position, eyes still closed. The sound of the enemy's footfalls became almost deafening as the men neared his position.

In one long second, Brent took a deep cleansing breath through his nose and exhaled through his mouth. He opened his eyes and depressed the button on his staff. He stepped out of his hiding place as it sprung to full length.

A cigarette hung from the man's mouth, his eyes wide with shock. Brent struck with such speed that the other two men had no time to react. Within seconds all three were out cold, lying on the hard stone of the cave floor.

Brent eyed his victims. The cigarette was smashed in the mouth of the one. Tobacco littered his bloody lips. Brent couldn't help but smile. "Didn't anyone ever tell you smoking was bad for your health," he muttered.

A vibration on his wrist brought Brent back into the moment. His watch's alarm. *Only thirty minutes until zero hour*, he thought. He looked again at the map and began to run to the other spots where he needed to set the charges.

Ten minutes before the designated time, Brent was close to where his friends were being kept. He lay on his belly and peered around a stone outcropping. What he saw made him catch his breath. All of his men were beaten and bloodied. Alana had been beaten and the front of her uniform had been torn. President Dupree lay unconscious. The only positive was that their gags had been removed and he could hear what they were saying.

"How much time we got left?" Jefferson mumbled through his busted lips.

"Not much," Seven answered. He spit blood from his mouth before continuing. "There has been a lot more activity in the last few minutes. They'll be back soon."

Brent watched as Fitzpatrick tried to open his swollen eyes. He could see that a couple of his teeth were cracked.

"The colonel?" he sputtered.

His ribs must be broken, Brent thought.

His voice strained as he tried to continue. "Do you think he got the message?"

Seven looked around at his beaten and tired men. "If I know Joan," he said, "he got the message."

Alana rolled toward him. "Let's just pray he got it in time."

Seven nodded.

Brent could see that Scarlet stayed out of the conversation. She hovered over her father protecting him.

Brent wanted to alert them, but he knew if he did they might change their disposition. He couldn't chance it. He had to wait and let the mission unfold as planned.

At o-one hundred hours and fifty-seven minutes, Brent's SAT phone vibrated. The go sign from Tag telling him all was ready on his end. Brent pushed the send button, letting him know that he too was ready. He thought of Seven and smiled. *Time to open a can of whoop-ass.*

Sliding his phone back into his pocket, he watched as two men walked back into the cave. One was old and wearing a throbe and a long grey beard covered his face. *Omar.* The other made Brent catch his breath. The man was older, but there was no denying who he was. Brent bit hard on his tongue, drawing blood as his anger percolated.

Brent wormed his way back into the dark corner where he had

been hiding and heard the first explosion at the far end of the cave system.

"What the hell was that?" Omar screamed.

"We've got visitors," Jensen smirked. "Get all your men here at once. That was Venturi's calling card."

Omar reached for his walkie-talkie as the next explosion knocked him sideways.

Anger encompassed his face. "I have no transmission," he snarled.

"Check all the frequencies."

Omar was ashen. He shook his head. "The radio is dead."

Before Falcon could speak, Omar ran out of the room as the next charge erupted. With this explosion, rock and dirt rained down on them.

Falcon reached for and grabbed the president and attempted to heft him over his shoulder. "I'm not leaving without leverage." He pulled President Dupree to his feet and began to heft the unconscious man over his shoulder when suddenly a Chinese steel star was embedded in his shoulder. He diverted his attention toward the piercing pain when a second found its way into his wrist. His hand went limp and he dropped the president to the ground.

His face was crimson with fury as he screamed. "Show yourself, Venturi." He snapped his head one way and then the other as spittle flew from his mouth.

The next blast filled the opening to the cave as Brent walked through like a spirit walking through a mist.

"Here I am, Private Jensen."

Falcon's complexion turned a hue of reddish-purple. He despised being called Private Jensen. His shoulders rose toward his ears as his rage escalated. He eyed Seven and kicked dirt in his eyes. "This piece of dung was no match for me." He jerked his head toward his shoulder eliciting a loud crack. He repeated the move to the other side. "How 'bout I whip your ass?"

Seven watched as Falcon grabbed his gun. He began to warn Brent when suddenly something knocked the gun from Falcon's hand. He swiveled his head and watched as a young man stood at the other opening with a long stick in his hands. *Lieutenant Achak,* Seven thought.

He looked back at Brent and saw a similar one in his hands.

"Want some help, Colonel?" Tag asked.

"What's our time?" Brent asked as Jensen began to circle him.

"Two minutes before this mountain comes down on us."

Brent didn't flinch at Tag's words. "Untie my men and get them out of here."

Jensen pulled a long knife from its sheath and eyed Brent. "You ain't leaving the party alive," he spat.

Brent took his staff and began to twirl it in front of him. The faster it spun the more of a whirling noise it made. "Do you think I would have come all this way not to dance?"

Tag untied the squad and lifted President Dupree over his shoulder in a fireman's carry position. "Thirty seconds, Colonel."

"Get moving. You know what you need to do."

Another explosion erupted and the cave began to fall apart like a deck of cards.

"But, Colonel . . ."

"Now, Lieutenant. That's an order!"

Seven grabbed Tag by the shoulder. "You need to lead us out of here or we all die. Let's move out. Now."

Tag dropped his head in defeat. He nodded and led the squad out of the cave.

Falcon smiled as rock continued to rain down into the cave. "It's just you and me."

Brent nodded. "The way you always wanted it. The way it had to be. Isn't that right, Private?"

Hearing Brent call him 'private' made his blood boil. He flipped the knife in his hand, held the blade and readied his aim. He cocked his arm back and just as he was about to let the knife fly toward Brent, the explosives closest to them blew. The cave collapsed, knocking them both down and pinning Brent under the rubble.

Jensen slithered out of the collapsing cave just as it all came down on top of Brent.

Brent looked up from his pinned position as the ceiling of the cave came down on top of him.

His world went black.

CHAPTER 62

Tag and the squad made it out of the mountain just as the final explosion caused the cave to implode on itself. When they emerged from the rubble, they saw the members of the Brotherhood who had made it out of the mountain before it collapsed. The terrorists lucky enough to escape were handcuffed, gagged and surrounded by a bunch of monks and a few Pakistanis.

Seven looked to Tag for an explanation. "Lieutenant Achak, who are these men?"

Tag, exhausted from the escape, laid President Dupree on the ground. Scarlet dropped next to her father and gently caressed his face.

Looking like a man who had seen too much death, Tag hung his head as he spoke. "These men are Brother Gregory and the brothers of the Khor Virap Monastery and the others are Pakistani knights: members of the Ambassador's outer circle."

Seven cocked his head to the side. "Khor Virap? The monastery at the base of Mount Ararat?"

Brother Gregory bowed in response.

Seven squinted through swollen and bruised eyes. "So that's what the colonel meant when he said he was going back to the beginning."

The brothers stood proud.

"I see you know of our existence," Gregory said.

"I know a bit of history, that's all," Seven replied. "I'm sure you will fill me in on the rest."

"It will be my pleasure," the older monk said. He scanned Seven with knowing eyes. "And you, you are the one who came before. The Enlightened One's first trainer."

Seven nodded.

As Brother Gregory spoke, he noticed for the first time that Brent was not among those who emerged from the mountain. "Where is The Ambassador?"

"He's not here."

They all turned to see Alana standing next to the caved in entrance. Tears ran down her cheeks. "He stayed in the cave so we could escape."

Confusion swept across Gregory's eyes. "Can we get to him?"

Silence.

Gregory was frustrated at the lack of a response. "There must be something we can do."

Everyone turned toward Tag for an answer.

Sadness and frailty finally broke through the young officer's demeanor as he lifted his head. "He ordered the charges set so that this would be the only way out." His eyes brightened with his next words. "But I tried to set them so that a part of the cave system wouldn't collapse completely—hopefully a backdoor exit." Before anyone could respond, he continued. "If Brent has any chance of escaping, it will be from within the mountain." Tag wiped a dirty sleeve across a dirtier mouth. "There is no way to get to him from the exterior without losing more lives."

Alana ran to him, pounded her fists on his chest, and screamed, "Don't you dare say '*more* lives.'"

With a forlorn expression, Tag opened his mouth to speak.

Before he could they all heard Scarlet yell, "He's awake. My father is awake!" She placed her fingers on his wrist. "His pulse is weak and thready."

Seven trained his thought on the situation at hand. "We need to evacuate the president and see to everyone's injuries. Then, Tag can tell us what the hell just happened in there."

By nightfall, Q had evacuated the squad and President Dupree to a U.S. military hospital in Saudi Arabia. The president was resting comfortably and everyone else's injuries had been attended to.

The squad walked into the room where Tag had been debriefed by the Secret Service. "I think it's time for you to tell us what happened," Seven said.

Tag pulled his long black hair away from his face. His eyes red and sunken from exhaustion. "Colonel Venturi and I mounted a two-man attack on the Brotherhood based on my recollection of the cave system."

Alana stepped forward. "What do you mean your recollection?"

"The Lieutenant had been there before," Seven said, never taking his eyes off of the Lieutenant. "That was the same place you had done recognizance on your last mission, isn't that right?"

"Yes, sir."

"Don't call me sir. My name is Seven and these soldiers standing behind me are . . ."

"The Phantom Squad, I know," Tag said. "I know everything. Brent told me—everything."

Seven took a seat by the young man and spoke in a softer tone. "If he trusted you with that information, then I, we trust you with our lives."

The squad nodded in unison.

"I know Brent better than anyone," Seven said. "He must have detailed his plan to you and told you what to do if he didn't make it out with the rest of us."

Tag took a sip of old coffee. "He never planned to make it out of the cave."

Alana, a ball of frayed nerves, clutched Tag's hair and yanked his head in her direction, forcing him to look into her eyes. "What do you mean he never planned to make it out?" she screamed.

Scarlet placed her hand on Alana's shoulder. "Let's let the lieutenant finish his story," she intimated.

Alana unclenched her fist, releasing Tag from her grip. Strands of Tag's torn hair still hung from her fingers.

Tag finger combed his hair. "The colonel's plan was for me to bring you out while he stayed behind to detain Jensen," he began.

"He knew Falcon was Jensen? How?" Seven asked.

Tag shook his head. "I don't know. The night before the attack, I watched him as he went into one of those trances of his. I sat there in the pitch of night and wondered how he could stay in that position for so long."

Seven swallowed. "How long was he under?"

"Hours," Tag replied.

Seven spit in his cup. "That's not good."

"Why?" Tag asked. "I saw him do it for even longer when we were in the monastery."

"His mind . . ."

"His mind . . ." everyone turned to see Brother Gregory standing in the doorway. They watched as he came forward and sat on the other side of Tag. "His mind—his consciousness—was expanded while he was at the monastery. I can assure you he was not in any danger while in his meditative state."

Seven packed his lip with tobacco in frustration. "You can't assure me of nothing, Padre." His mouth full, he grabbed a bedpan, spit and turned his attention back to Tag.

"When the colonel told me his plan," Tag said, "I asked, no I begged him to change it. I told him that there must be another way," Tag stared up into Alana's eyes, "but he assured me that his plan was the only way. He said his primary goal was to get President Dupree and his squad out alive." Alana's brown eyes, red and dilated, stared back at Tag. "He said that he had never left a comrade behind and he didn't plan on starting now."

Alana wept from despair. She swallowed her tears as she spoke. "What else did he say?"

"He gave explicit instructions for everyone, but said that were subject to any injuries sustained by the squad."

The squad stepped in closer to where Tag was sitting. As if distance would make a difference in what they heard.

Tag looked at each with respect and admiration and focused on Jefferson, Fitzpatrick and Scarlet before he continued. "He said that Jefferson, Fitz and Scarlet were to accompany President Dupree back to HQ and await further orders." He turned toward Brother Gregory. "He said to thank Brother Gregory and the brothers of Khor Virap and to tell them that without their help, he never would have made it back from the brink of self-destruction."

Brother Gregory closed his eyes as he listened. Hearing Brent's words, he stood tall and proud.

Tag stood as he continued to recall Brent's orders. "He ordered me to take Seven and Alana back to Alpha Camp and wait."

"Wait for what?" Alana asked.

Tag closed his eyes and slowly shook his head. "I don't know." He looked at Seven and Alana. "Brent said that you were to remember the Wailing Wall and do as you were ordered."

Seven stood, spit one last time, and addressed his men. "We have been given orders from our leader and we will do as we were told." He turned and walked out of the room. "Get some shuteye; we break camp at zero four hundred."

CHAPTER 63

It took all of Brent's strength to blink. As his vision cleared he surveyed his bleak surroundings. Dirt, fallen timbers and rock were all he saw.

He then turned his attention inward, taking stock of his injuries. He tied to contract various muscles to help figure out which bones were broken and which organs may have been injured. He quickly realized his right leg was broken. As he contracted his stomach muscles, sharp pain shot through him like a knife wound. To make it worse, he started to cough—his phlegm was bright red.

Brent knew he was about to lose consciousness as his vision began to fade. In those waning seconds, he looked toward God for assurance.

Father, I pray that all my men and the president made it out of the cave before it collapsed. I have completed all you have asked of me and I ask you to take me home.

At his weakest, a voice of strength spoke to him.

"You have done well my son, but your journey has just begun. You must find a way, a way deep within you, to carry on."

I cannot. I am begging you to take my soul and bring it home.

Brent faded back into unconsciousness and when he opened his eyes, he was once again standing on Mount Ararat.

It was once again a desolate landscape of ice and snow. The wind cut with more pain than any bullet or blade.

"Why am I here? Must I return to the beginning before I am welcomed into the house of the Lord?"

A shadow began to emerge through the mist of ice and snow. Brent expected to see the Light of heaven. As the figure moved closer, there was light, but it was not as bright as it had been in his past encounters. As the figure came closer, he could make out a feminine form. He opened his eyes wide when he realized it was Chloe, not the Almighty. He reached out for her, but his hands passed straight through. His momentum caused him to fall onto the frozen tundra. The pain of his injures amplified.

He staggered to his knees and stared at her bare feet. His guilt would not allow him to look into her eyes.

She reached out and was able to touch him. He felt her warm caress on his frozen flesh. Her touch brought a lessening of his pain. He tilted his head, leaning into her touch. He could smell her scent. For a moment, all was right in his world.

"Look at me," Chloe said.

He continued to look down.

"Look at me," she repeated.

With slow, awkward movements, Brent raised his head until he was looking into the eyes of his beloved. A fleeting smile flashed across his face, but quickly disappeared into the abyss of loneliness and despair.

With a glimmer of hope, he spoke. "Are you here to take me home?"

"I am here as a messenger of the Lord. I am here to tell you that you must stay in this world and fulfill your destiny." Confused, Brent opened his mouth to speak. Chloe slid a finger over his lips as she had done thousands of time before, to silence him. "I am here to remind you that you must stay to raise Faith and help her fulfill her destiny."

"What is her destiny?"

Chloe shook her head. "Only God knows of her destiny, but with all men that ultimately lies in her hands."

JM. LEDUC

Brent closed his eyes in thought. When he spoke, only two words emerged. "Free will."

Chloe nodded. "Free will. The moral character that you will instill in her, the love that you will shower upon her, the strength that she will learn from watching you, will forge in her the ability to choose the right decisions when her destiny begins to unfold." Chloe's eyes moistened with emotion. "Without you, the world's evil will have a strong pull on her. Satan will seek his revenge on you through her. You must stay here and help her resist his pull."

Brent swallowed hard. His saliva felt like shards of glass scraping his throat. He fought the pain in his lungs and inhaled deeply, breathing in her scent—receiving strength from the action. "I will do what is asked of me in remembrance of you."

Chloe bent down and kneeled in from of Brent. "I need you to understand that you are not at fault for my death. It was my time. My destiny, my journey was complete and that is why God called me home."

Brent cried into her hand.

Chloe spoke in whispered tones, the tones spoken between a man and wife. "Brent you must live your life to the fullest."

"I don't know how to do that without you in my life." His words cried out like a wounded animal.

"In time you will find love again."

Brent shook his head. "No, I won't. I don't want to. It would taint what we had."

"What we had was pure. What we had was what pumped the blood through my heart. What we had," she whispered, "you will not forget and you will make sure that Faith grows up knowing that her mother loved her."

Brent prostrated himself before her. His tears soaking her feet.

"But," Chloe continued, "you must live a life complete. A life with love and Chloe must know a mother's love. She needs that. We," she emphasized, "must ensure it."

"I don't know if I can do that."

"Through God all things are possible. Lean on Him when times are hard, look to Him for all answers, both big and small and you will know when the time is right."

Chloe once again cradled Brent's face in her hands. "Promise me you will stay with Faith and that you will try to love again."

Brent's words were broken by his grief. "I—promise—to—try." He squeezed his eyes shut and tried to regain his composure.

When he lifted his body from the frozen tundra, he saw Chloe walking back into the mist.

"I love you," he yelled.

"I love you more," she said as she disappeared into the heavenly light.

Brent opened his eyes, reached deep within himself, and began to claw dirt from around him. For the next day, he continued to dig himself out of his earthly tomb. He used his tattered clothing and a couple of busted support beams he found to form a splint for his broken right leg.

Not knowing how he was going brace his weight, he dragged his body through the rubble. With raw, bloody fingers, he removed one stone at a time from his path. His only source of direction was a faint light that shone through a small crack at the blown entrance of the cave. Sweat covered his flesh and clothing. He took that as a good sign. He knew when he stopped sweating, dehydration would begin to ravage his kidneys. Every few hours he took a sip from his canteen. A canteen that grew lighter with each sip. All other sustenance came from his promise to Chloe. He refused to give in to weakness.

Every time his eyes closed in exhaustion, Seven's words screamed at him like a mantra. "Sleep is a crutch! You need to learn to walk without leaning on this crutch. No one sleeps until the time is right. The time is never right if you are engaged in a mission." Seven would circle his exhausted men. "I wouldn't ask you to do anything I wouldn't do myself. We have all been awake for six days—one-hundred-and-forty-six hours and thirty-two seconds to be exact. If any of you fall asleep, we all die. I'll be damned if I'm gonna be responsible for any of your deaths and I will be even more ticked off if any of you cause my death."

Seven's words gave Brent the little burst of energy he needed to continue his dig. He reached forward to drag another rock out of his way and when he did, he felt something cylindrical. Something smooth in its structure. When he released it from the rubble, he looked and saw that he was grasping his staff.

He lay on his back and clutched it to his chest. A weak sound emanated from his throat. Laughter—painful laughter—the greatest laughter of his life.

With his new find, Brent dug at a speed he didn't know he had. He used the staff to leverage larger rocks out of the way. When he came to an area, nearer the light that seemed impassable, he pushed the recessed button on the staff and used the blade to dig through the wall of rock and debris.

Pulling himself through the hole he had dug, Brent was finally able to stand inside the cave. Leaning on his staff for support, he wondered if Tag had left this part of the cave intact on purpose.

Brent took the last swig of water from his canteen and moved with a confident limp towards the shimmer of daylight. Three hours later, he climbed out of an anthill. He stood on the Afghan side of the Hindu Kush Mountain range.

Brent leaned on his staff, scanned the horizon, and beamed at the glory of the barren, desolate landscape. He removed his knife from its sheath and unscrewed the end of the handle. Inside was a compass. Taking his bearings, he headed south toward his and Tag's first resting point. It was two days away. He looked up towards heaven and asked for the strength to make it to point A, to a place where they had hidden extra water and their weapons.

CHAPTER 64

In the two days that followed the squad's return to Palm cove, President Dupree made a remarkable recovery from his injuries. He was still in serious condition, but he was stable and improving. His concussion had begun to resolve itself and he began to speak of his forthcoming trip to National Arlington Cemetery.

Susan Collins, the administrator of the infirmary, the doctors and Scarlet tried to dissuade him from his trip, but there was no changing his mind. When anyone brought the subject up, he became increasingly agitated and his vital signs would spike. The only good news was that there was still time before the scheduled memorial service—time for the president's health to improve.

Maddie and the remaining squad members were in constant contact with Seven and Alana who had made it safely to Alpha Camp. Per Brent's orders, the camp was to stay vacant. No new soldiers were to be moved in and no military investigators were allowed to tour the facility. That job was left to the three who now resided at Alpha.

The one concession that Seven made to Brent's orders was the removal of the soldiers of Alpha Camp from their shallow makeshift grave. Military helicopters landed and the medical staff removed the men and women so they could be taken home for a hero's burial.

On the second night, they gathered around the radio and listened to Maddie tell them of the president's improvements.

"The squad is chomping at the bit," she said. "They hate being here doing nothing. They have asked repeatedly to join the three of you at Alpha."

"Negative," Seven replied. "We will follow the colonel's orders until we are told otherwise."

Maddie's next words stuck in her throat as she tried to speak. "What if you receive no word? What if Brent is . . ."

"He is not," Seven interjected.

"How do you know? How can you be so sure?"

Seven took a sip of bad coffee. "Do you remember when Brent disappeared after his fight with the Butcher? When that Blackhawk landed and scurried him and Chloe away?"

"Of course," Maddie replied.

"Do you remember what I told you while I prayed in the chapel?"

Maddie smiled. "You said that Brent told you not to believe with your eyes but with your heart and you knew deep in your heart that he was not dead. You said that it was the only thing keeping you going."

"That's right," Seven said.

Maddie leaned into the radio and softened her tone. "I can appreciate your faith, but how do you *know* he's alive?"

Seven shook his head. "I have no proof," he replied. "I only have the same feeling deep in my gut that he will return." He took a sip of coffee. "Tag said that we were to remember the time when he sent us to the Wailing Wall. That was the first time I saw Brent rise from the dead like a ghost and began to believe with my heart and not with my eyes. Until my gut and my heart tell me otherwise, we will wait here."

CHAPTER 65

Brent dragged himself toward the slight relief made by the dune in the sand. After two days, every dune looked alike. Over the past hours, his confidence became lax as each dune he came to was the wrong one. He stopped and for what seemed like the hundredth time consulted his compass. *I know this is the right way*, he thought, *I just pray I'm not hallucinating.*

He pulled his body over the top of the knoll and dropped into the rock-strewn rut on the other side. His vision was blurry from dehydration and he had to squint to try to clear his sight of its interminable haze. Hands burnt and blistered from the sun reached out and touched the etching in the rock. His fingers traced the signs of the Alpha and Omega which he had cut into the rock just days ago. Brent collapsed in an exhausted lump of satisfaction.

With an unsteady grip, he pulled his knife from its sheath and franticly dug below the rock ledge to find the two canteens buried beneath. He rolled onto his back and unscrewed the cap of one with his teeth. The water burned his bloodied lips as he drank with a ravenous thirst. It took all his will not to down the entire contents.

Brent spent the next few hours shielding his body from the scolding sun and taking small sips from one of the canteens. He knew if he drank too quick, his stomach would revolt and he would throw-up. By nightfall, the heat had diminished and his thirst was somewhat quenched. At least he began to sweat again.

He would give himself the luxury of two hours of sleep before making his final approach toward Alpha. He only hoped Tag got the squad out of the mountain on time and that someone would be waiting for him when he got there.

Two hours later, he woke to his internal alarm, took one final compass reading and trudged off, limping towards Alpha Camp. He had a full day of walking in front of him and wanted to make it there before dark once again fell over the desert.

As the hours passed, the pain in his busted leg became unbearable. Another of Seven's mantras played through his head: *Pain is weakness leaving the body.* This mantra played on a repeating loop through his mind as he limped toward his destination.

Six hours later, he saw the outline of the camp off in the distance. The sight of the camp invigorated him and he picked up his pace. Tag's story of his final approach after his last mission flashed through his mind. Brent stopped long enough to check his pistol. He removed his clip, made sure that sand hadn't become lodged in the trigger mechanism, snapped it back in place, pulled back the slide chambering a bullet, removed the safety and gripped it in his hand for his final approach.

Tag had drawn the night watch at camp and was keeping watch for anyone who might approach. In the last three days, his optimism for Brent's return had waned. He thought about Brent's orders to Seven and Alana and wondered about the story concerning the Wailing Wall. He had not asked about it and neither was forthright in giving information. What he did know was that Brent's words seemed to give them both promise that Brent would somehow make it out of the bombed out mountain and make it back to Alpha. Their optimism helped sustain him on these long watches.

Scanning the horizon with night goggles, he thought he saw a form off in the distance. Tag rubbed his dry, sand-scratched eyes. His eyesight had been playing tricks on him during the past couple of hours. Twice during the night he called to both Seven and Alana to tell them that he had spotted someone, only to have been wrong.

He put down the goggles and picked up his sniper rifle. He had more confidence in its sight than he did the infrared goggles. He dialed in the sight and continued to keep the image in his crosshairs. The image—now in sharper focus—brought a smile to his face. "I'll be," he mumbled. "Colonel, you never cease to amaze me." Supporting the gun on its tripod, he put his fingers to his lips and once again gave the warning whistle to the others.

Seven and Alana appeared at his side in less than a minute.

Alana approached yawning and rubbing her half-open eyes. "If you woke me again with false hope, I will take your gun and shoot you myself."

Tag looked over his shoulder at his friends and smiled from ear-to-ear. He handed over the goggles and said, "Take a look before you kill me."

She ripped them from his grip and looked to where he was pointing. She dropped them in the sand and began running toward the shuffling image.

Brent could see someone running toward him. Moments later, he could make out the long hair and shape of a woman. *Alana.* His heart rate quickened as he stood still and awaited her arrival. His heart filled with relief that she was alive.

Alana ran at full speed until she got close enough to see that Brent's leg was splinted. It took all of her composure not to jump into his arms. She wrapped her arms around him and felt his embrace in return. No words were spoken.

With her support, Brent lowered himself to the desert floor.

Alana lay on the sand so close to him that she was partially on top of him and finger combed his hair away from his face. Her sweat intermingled with his. Brent tried to wipe the moisture from his lips with his tongue, but it was so swollen from dehydration that it was an act of futility.

He pushed Alana's hair away from her face, looked into her dark brown, almond-shaped eyes and in a sand-scratched voice said, "Is this the way you greet all men?"

"Only those who have come back from the dead," she quipped.

As they stared and began to laugh, they heard another voice. "As soon as she pries herself off of your broken body, I just might do the same thing," Seven drawled.

Brent looked past Alana and looked at Seven and Tag. "If that's the case, I hope she stays right where she is."

Red with embarrassment, Alana rolled off of Brent and went to help him up.

"It might take more than one of you," Brent said. "I'm pretty busted up."

He wrapped his arms around both Alana and Seven while Tag braced his leg. The three of them lifted Brent into a standing position.

"Can you make it to camp?" Tag asked.

Brent's smile was still plastered on his face. A smile he wasn't sure would ever go away. "I've made it this far, I think I can make it the rest of the way."

When they let go, he wobbled and started to lose his balance. Seven quickly reach for him and steadied his friend and commanding officer. Leaning on his shoulder, Brent and his friends made their way to camp.

Inside the comfort of the camp, Tag triaged Brent's injuries, set his fracture and put on a proper splint. He then assessed the rest of his injuries. Seven and Alana walked in as he was finishing.

"Well?" Seven asked.

"He has multiple rib fractures, a broken fibula, a dislocated left shoulder, and some minor infection."

Seven spit in his cup and smiled. "So, he's fine."

"I'll be fine as soon as you reset my shoulder," Brent said.

Seven looked at Tag for an explanation.

"He wouldn't let me do it. He said you were the only one he trusted to pop it back."

"I know how much fun you have causing me pain," Brent said.

Seven shook his head and grabbed one the canteens. He held the strap for Brent to take. "Which way did you do it this time?"

"It popped out in the front," Tag answered.

Seven looked to Brent for affirmation. Brent nodded.

Brent bit down on the canvas canteen strap so he wouldn't break his teeth. Seven stood in front of his friend and told the others to stand behind Brent to brace him. With a gentle touch, he palpated the shoulder, tractioned his arm, and drove the palm of his hand into the humeral head. A loud pop could be heard as he closed the dislocated joint. Brent's only reaction was a slight grunt of pain.

Seven removed the strap from Brent's mouth and handed it to Alana. She was surprised by the depth of the marks left by his teeth.

"Wrap that shoulder so he can't even as much as scratch himself and then there are some people who would like to speak to him," Seven ordered.

Alana took the tape from Tag. "I'll do it."

The others walked from the room and left them alone. When she placed her hands on Brent's bare skin, she started to tremble. Brent covered her hands with his good one. His touch made her shake even more.

When he looked into her eyes, the same emotions he had had when they first saw each other back in her village outside of Jerusalem returned.

"I want to apologize for the way I treated you when you tried to contact me after Chloe's death."

"No apologies necessary." Her words were barely audible.

"When I heard that you had come to Palm Cove, it brought me hope," he said.

"How so?" she breathed as she began to tape his shoulder to his upper body.

"Knowing that you cared enough to come and the way I saw Faith respond to you helped me realize that there was another reason to live."

Alana stopped for a moment and sat beside him. She put the tape down and pushed his hair away from his eyes.

Thinking back to the way they 'communicated' at her home, he smiled. "Are we going to play that game again?"

She stared into his eyes with concern. "This is no game. What do you mean by another reason to live?"

Brent reciprocated and brushed her long, matted, dark hair from her face. "After everything that had happened, I shut down. My only thought was getting back at the Brotherhood. It was the only thing that kept me going."

"And, now?"

"Now," he said, "I have other reasons."

Alana wanted to push the conversation but she knew this was not the time. She finished taping his injury and stood. "You smell like a goat. I hope you don't plan on smelling that way forever."

Brent laughed at her comment. "Let's join the others and make that phone call."

Seven and Tag sat around a makeshift table and listened to a barrage of voices coming through the radio. They were unable to get a word in edgewise.

Seven saw Brent walk in and said, "If y'all will shut up for a second, I'll let him tell you."

Maddie took a deep startled breath. "Brent?" she squealed. "Are you there?"

"Where else would I be?"

"Don't be a wiseass, we've been sick waiting to hear from you."

Brent was helped to a chair. "I'm fine, a little busted up, but all right."

"Thank God," Maddie said.

"Brent?" a voice quivered.

Brent knew Joan's voice and it warmed his heart to hear it. "Hi, Sweetie."

Joan twisted her bottom lip and pulled on her lip ring to squelch her emotion. "It's a good thing you're alive or I would have had to find your body and kill you again."

Brent laughed. "Don't think for a minute that your promise of doing just that didn't help spur me on. Your wrath scares me more than any terrorist."

Laughter could be heard from everyone on both sides of the radio.

Brent spoke to his parents and told them he loved them and in the background he heard Faith coo. The sound of her voice took away all his pain.

"Can you place the radio next to Faith's ear for me?"

He whispered that he loved her and he began to sing the lullaby that he sang to her every night.

"Faith's asleep," Maddie whispered.

Brent closed his eyes. A feeling of warmth washed over him—a father's love.

"When should we expect you home?" Maddie asked.

Back in the moment, Brent looked around the table at the faces of his friends. His expression hardened. "We have some unfinished business to take care of and then we will be home."

Maddie stood up, put her hands on her hips, and forcefully tapped her well-healed shoe. "What unfinished business? As your superior, I order you to come home as soon as you are able."

"You're starting to break up. I couldn't hear your last statement. We will have to call back when we get a better satellite signal. Over."

Seven shook his head and spit. "You really know how to tick her off."

Brent's expression remained steadfast. "I'm going to take a shower and then I need a complete rundown of what happened back at the mountain."

Brent's movements were unstable as he turned to leave.

"I will help him," Alana said.

The boys all looked at each other and smirked like a couple of teenagers.

She rolled her eyes. "Don't worry, I won't look."

They laughed as she walked Brent from the room.

Tag smiled. "I bet she does."

Seven shook his head. "That's one bet I refuse to take."

"I heard that," yelled Alana from the across the camp.

Wide eyed, Tag looked at Seven.

Seven wrapped his arm around him and began to walk out of the office. "Did I forget to tell you about her sense of hearing?"

His laughter echoed throughout the camp.

CHAPTER 66

The four sat around the table as Seven and Alana recounted their ordeal. They told Brent of President Dupree's insistence on making the Mid-East trip and how they were ambushed at Alpha Camp.

"Did you know it was Jensen?" Brent asked Seven.

"As soon as I got a clear look at his pocked face," Seven answered. "But, it was too late. He's been well-trained."

"Trained by whom?" Brent asked.

"Joan's intel has found a long line of mercenary activity led by Falcon. He was trained *by* the jungles of South and Central America and the sands of Africa and the Mid-East."

Brent paused as Tag poured him another cup of coffee. "Your skills at brewing have improved since I've been gone."

Seven's face flushed.

"I was not about to let him make the coffee," Alana said. "My only stipulation before agreeing to join the Phantom Squad was that I was now in charge of that duty."

Brent took a sip. "My colon thanks you."

Smiles went around the table.

Addressing Tag, he said, "Was there any sign of Omar leaving the cave?"

"No, but I suspect . . ."

Brent shook his head. "He left before the major explosions

occurred. We have to assume he made it out alive." He looked around the table and answered their unasked question. "I saw Jensen leave before I blacked out."

"So we still have some cleaning up to do," Seven said.

"But where would we look? They could be anywhere," Tag said.

Brent shook his head. "When plans fall apart, or things don't go our way, we all go back to the beginning to regroup. That's where they went."

"I don't understand," Alana said. "You're talking in riddles."

Seven wore a broad grin. "What are you thinking, Colonel?"

Brent took a long sip of his coffee. "Jensen will retreat and try to band together another group of his mercenaries. He will want to meet them back where this all began for him. My gut tells me that will be where he was originally trained."

"Back at the Grand Tetons," Seven added.

Brent nodded.

"And Omar?" Alana asked.

"Back to the only place he has ever called home. The only place he feels safe."

"Gaza," Seven replied.

Again, Brent nodded.

"So what's our plan, Colonel?"

Brent looked at Seven and then the others. He sat back down and began to formulate a plan. "You and Tag will meet the rest of the squad and head to the Tetons. You know that area better than anyone. I'll let you formulate the attack."

"And you?" Seven asked.

"Alana and I will head to Gaza and deal with Omar." He took another sip of his coffee. "I want Q to take you and Tag out tomorrow. You will need to meet with the team back at HQ and go through the specifics. My gut tells me that Jensen has spent a lot of time on that mountain in the past fifteen years, so you will have to be ready for anything. Your knowledge of what makes him tick will be your advantage. All other bets are off."

"I will stay here until my leg heals. Q will fly in supplies when he comes to pick you up." Brent squeezed his leg and flinched. "The bone that's broken isn't weight-bearing so I figure I need two weeks before I can move out. We need to coordinate these missions." He stopped to think. "I wish we knew if Omar and Jensen were in contact with one another."

"Omar said repeatedly that he would kill Jensen if his planned failed," Seven said. "I'd bet, they haven't spoken."

Brent eyed the people around the table. "I'm not a betting man, so we take no chances. Fourteen days from now, we both attack at the same time. We stay in contact by Endowment encryption only."

Brent thought for a moment.

"Has there been any word on Red since he was sent to Dreamland?"

Tag put his hand up to stop the conversation. "Who the hell is Red and why would he be taken to Area 51?"

"Red was Omar's second in command. He was captured when the Brotherhood stormed HQ and," Brent said, "he was taken to '51' because there is a prison there."

Tag just stared, open mouthed.

"The most guarded, secretive prison in the world." Brent said.

"He has been debriefed using SIA standard protocol," Seven said. "It's my understanding that he has given up quite a bit of intel since his incarceration."

Brent nodded. "I'll have Joan send me everything. I need a complete layout of Omar's lair before we strike."

"I'm not going to tell Maddie what you have planned," Seven said. "I have to sleep in the same bed with the woman."

Brent laughed. "Let's get her and the rest of the directorate on the line. I'll break the news to her. I wouldn't want you to have to sleep with one eye open for the rest of your life."

"Hell, I do that already," Seven said. "I just want to know that I will be waking up each morning."

Brent laughed. "She can be a little hot headed."

"It's the redhead in her," Seven joked.

Brent smiled. "Take Tag and over the next few hours formulate a rough plan of attack. Teach him all you know about the Grand Tetons."

"In a few hours?"

"Trust me Seven, he's a fast learner and a new SIA operative."

He stared at Tag. "Isn't that right Lieutenant Achak?"

Tag's chest puffed up with pride. "Damn right, Colonel."

"I'll contact Joan," Brent added, "and get her moving on gathering all of Red's intel. We meet again at nineteen hundred hours. I'll arrange for Q to pick you up at zero seven hundred."

"How are we to get to Gaza?" Alana asked.

Brent thought of his friends in the Vatican. "Leave that to me. We will have some friends of mine pick us up at the allotted time."

At nineteen hundred hours, they again met in their makeshift headquarters.

"Well, how did your training go?" Brent asked.

"He learns faster than anyone I've met except for you. He even had some great ideas that we're going to implement when we get to our destination."

Brent looked at Tag.

"I'm going to teach the squad the art of shadowing," Tag said. "It should increase the surprise factor."

Brent smiled.

"And you? Was Joan able to gather any information on Omar's whereabouts?" Seven asked.

Brent nodded. "If my hunch is right, he went back to Khan Younis. She was able to get a detailed schematic of the layout of the catacombs under a structure called al-Qal."

Alana huffed. "Great, more caves."

Brent winked. "More caves."

"We better get Maddie on the line. I'm sure there is steam coming out of that pretty little redhead," Seven said.

"I arranged it with Joan. They should all be waiting for our call."

Minutes later a satellite connection was made to HQ in Palm Cove.

"Madame Director, it's Colonel Venturi and the others. Is everyone present?"

A voice came on the line, but it wasn't Maddie. "Everyone is here, Colonel." It was President Dupree and he wasn't happy. "What's the meaning of you disregarding a direct order from your superior?"

Brent had no time for bickering. "The last meeting I had with the directorate, I was fired from my position in the SIA and the squad, Mr. President. As per my release papers stated, these orders came directly from you and the Joint Chiefs. As of right now, I have no superiors and therefore I am not in violation of refusing any orders."

"And the others," President Dupree huffed, "are they complicit in this scheme?"

"They are being held against their will. They will do as they're told until I let them go or until you listen to what I have to say."

President Dupree's face flushed as his blood pressure skyrocketed. He took a moment to calm down.

"Let's cut the crap, Brent. We've been through too much together. What is it that you are planning?"

"What I am planning is to end this mission on a final note. I am under the impression that both of the men who planned your kidnapping have both escaped. I plan to bring them to justice."

"Bring them to justice or kill them?"

"I'm running this mission and I would not involve the lives of the squad or Lieutenant Achak for revenge. I will be running this mission, with your permission and with the permission of the Director of the SIA, as the leader of the Phantom Squad."

Applause could be heard coming through the sat phone.

"That's all I wanted to hear, Brent," President Dupree said. "There is a pretty blond nurse tugging at me and telling me to get back to bed, so I will leave you to discuss your plan with Maddie and the directorate."

"Thank you, Mr. President."

"Oh, and Brent."

"Yes, sir?"

"Thank you again, for everything."

"That's what friends do, John," Brent said. "Now you better get moving. You don't want to make Nurse Collins angry."

"Tell me about it." The president looked at Susan Collins and grinned. "She actually got me to change the date of my wife's memorial service. It's in sixteen days and I *don't* plan on changing it again. Do what has to be done and get back home. I expect to see you at Arlington National."

"I haven't missed that date yet, and I don't plan on missing it this year."

"Glad to know," the president said.

Brent and everyone at Alpha could hear the airlock snap shut as President Dupree left the conference room.

"Now that we got that out of the way, what is your status," Maddie asked.

"Our status is green, Maddie. I have arranged for Q to be here in the morning to pick up Seven and Lieutenant Achak and bring them back to the Cove. They will spend the next ten days getting the squad up to speed with all possible scenarios and then they will go Falcon hunting."

Joan stopped typing when she heard Tag would be coming back with Seven. She was momentarily distracted. The stoppage of her constant pecking on her keyboard drew everyone in the conference room's attention.

"Is everything all right, Joan?" Maddie asked.

"Hmm, oh, yes, everything is fine. Just a little glitch with the keyboard."

Scarlet giggled. Joan burned a look in her direction.

Maddie rolled her eyes and continued. "And you and Alana?"

"We will stay at Alpha for the next two weeks. I need time to heal and we need time to formulate our plan of attack on Omar."

"If Q will be with the squad, how will you get to Gaza?"

"I've contacted our friend, Cardinal Bullini, at the Vatican. The Swiss Guard will fly us to our destination by way of an unmarked Papal plane. All arrangements have been made."

"Well then, I guess there is nothing left to say except one thing."

"That is?" asked Brent.

"Speaking for everyone," Maddie said, "it's great to have you back, Colonel."

Brent smiled. "Thank you. It's good to be back."

"Oh, one more thing," Maddie said. "Lieutenant Achak."

"Yes, Madame Director."

"Welcome to the family."

"Thank you, I look forward to meeting you all in the next day or so."

"You have *no* idea, how much some of us are waiting to meet you," Scarlet said.

CHAPTER 67

Two weeks later, everyone was in place. The coordinated attacks on Jensen and Omar were to be synchronized down to the minute.

Three days earlier, Seven, Tag, and the squad were dropped on the Idaho side of Grand Tetons. That meant climbing to the summit and then back down to the Montana side to the place where Seven trained the original squad members. *The beginning.*

On the third day, the squad was in position to see Jensen and his men. Jensen was using the plane hangar as his headquarters. Seven came up behind Jefferson who was on night watch and handed him a cup of coffee. "What do you have for me, Sergeant?"

"Same as the night before," Jefferson said. "There are twelve men and Jensen. He doesn't sleep much and he's constantly berating his men. I saw him slap one and kick another for sitting while on guard duty."

"Same 'ole Jensen," Seven replied. "Treating everyone with the respect they deserve."

Jefferson's face contorted when he sipped his coffee. "It seems he's not the only one who can't break old habits."

Seven packed his lip with tobacco and smiled. "It's the way my mom taught me to make it, so drink it and shut up."

"No disrespect, but I think I know why your daddy died so young."

Seven spit and squatted next to Jefferson. "None taken, I suspect you might be right." He looked through his field glasses and said, "By the way his men act, they must be green. That's good and bad. It's hard to predict how untrained soldiers will act. We will have to be extra cautious when we make our move."

"Yes, sir. You still planning on attacking during daylight?"

"Yep, I want the sun cresting this mountain as we make our approach. The glare will blind them a bit and it's the time of day Jensen lets his guard down." He checked his watch. "You better go eat, we move out in three hours."

Seven kept checking his watch. It seemed five minutes wouldn't go by before he was rechecking. He heard one of his men approach.

"You a little anxious, sir?"

Seven glanced at Tag. "A little. I'm used to being in constant contact with the Brent. I don't like not knowing what's happening on his end."

"Excuse me for being out of line, but the little time I got to spend with him taught me that he always keeps his word."

Seven patted Tag on the back. "You're not out of line and thanks for reminding me. Now, if you call me sir one more time, I'm going to use an old Indian tradition and scalp you, got it?"

Tag pulled his hair back in a ponytail. "Got it."

Seven gathered the squad and went over the details one last time. "We make our approach straight down the fall line. We'll make it look like we are trying to stay hidden, but we will allow ourselves to be spotted." Seven spit. "I want to be able to pinpoint all of Jensen's men. Jefferson and I will take the lead. Fitz, you and Tag will shadow us. Scarlet, you will shadow Tag until we pass the large Oak tree two hundred yards from base camp. You climb the tree as soon as there is a diversion." He eyed Scarlet. "You are the only one who can shoot a bow from that distance with the accuracy we need. Jensen will think that there are only two of us coming for him. The idea is to lull him into a feeling of superiority. When we pass the last group of pines, we'll be out of sight for fifteen seconds. That's when we branch off." Seven used a stick to make a diagram in the dirt. "Tag, you and Fitz will stay behind the trees. When you see Jefferson and me run behind the rocks, the two of you climb as fast as you can into the pines."

Seven looked up from the dirt and eyed the squad. He looked more stone-like than human. Tag looked at the others and saw the same thing. *The mission was on.*

"Remember," Seven said, "this is a no kill mission. You are to use tranquilizer darts to stop Jensen's men. If you need to use live ammo, shoot to wound." He addressed Scarlet. "I'm counting on you to take out as many of the peripheral guards before the shooting begins."

She fingered the string on her compound bow. "I'm ready."

"One last thing," Seven added. "No one, I repeat no one takes out Jensen. He belongs to me."

"What do you have planned, Sev?" asked Fitz.

"He wants me man-to-man. That's what he's going to get. No one interferes, understood?"

They acknowledged his order.

Seven checked his watch one more time. "Let's move out."

From base camp, the sentry was scanning the hill just as he had been ordered. The glare of the sun was so bright, he had to keep lowering the binoculars to wipe his eyes. Looking through the glasses again he thought he saw two men walking straight down the middle of the mountain.

He lifted his radio to his mouth. "Sentry to Falcon, we have company."

Jensen came running out of the hangar and grabbed the glasses from his man. "I'll be damned," he said. "That little slime ball thinks he can just walk into my camp with that halfwit darky."

Jensen sounded the alarm and his men ran out of the hangar and took their designated positions. Two of them fell before they even reached their destination. Jensen heard their screams, but they were out of view and he had no idea what they were yelling about. The desperate tone of their screeching scared his other men and they started shooting at the two figures walking down the mountain.

"Hold your fire, you morons. They are out of range!" Jensen yelled.

Their fire gave Scarlet a good idea of where her targets were.

"Come on," she said to herself. "Someone poke your head out."

In her peripheral vision, she saw one run from the side of the hangar to try to get behind a hedge. He made it halfway before an arrow was embedded in his hamstring. He reached back for his sidearm when his wrist was pinned to the ground by another arrow. His cry had the desired effect and the others began shooting again.

Jensen was flush with emotion. He screamed at the top of his lungs, "The next one to shoot will find my bullet buried in his head!"

As Seven and Jefferson passed the last pine grove, they ran as fast as they could in opposite directions. Tag and Fitz were halfway up their prospective trees before their brothers took safety behind a couple of rock ledges.

Jensen smiled. "The idiots just pinned themselves in." He pointed to his men and then up the hill. "I want the three of you to go up the left flank." Pointing to three more, he said, "You three go up the right side. The rest of you follow me."

Seven radioed the squad. "No one shoots until they get close. I don't want our numbers given away until it's too late for them to retreat."

Jensen radioed his men as he made his approach up the mountain. "I want the flanks to keep shooting and don't stop. I want them pinned down. If either of them gets away, it's your own hide that will die on this hill."

Jensen's men ran and continued to shoot with abandon. They were so sure they had the enemy pinned down that they weren't worried about taking cover. The two in the front felt a sting in their neck as they ran. They dropped to the dirt before they knew what hit them.

Jensen heard someone from his left scream, "We've got a man down."

And then from his right another man yelled, "Same here."

Everything suddenly became quiet. Jensen was infuriated. No one was going to stop him from taking his revenge out on Seven. "Take cover and keep shooting," he said through his headset.

His men began shooting as fast as they could pull the trigger. Bullets sprayed everywhere along the hillside.

A stray shot hit the boulder in front of Jefferson, rock fragments struck and stung his leg. He ducked further down behind the rock. He radioed the squad. "They're getting closer."

"Let them come," Seven radioed back. "They still have no idea of our numbers. Wait until they are sure they have us pinned down, then I want all of them dropped except for Jensen."

The squad kept their position as Jensen's men climbed nearer. The closer they got, the better their aim became.

Scarlet could see their movements better than anyone. "They're swinging out wide and a couple of them are trying to make their way up the mountain to attack from the rear."

"Wait until they think they have us dead to rights and then take them out, Scarlet," Seven ordered.

Jensen radioed his men. "No matter what you hear me say, if you have a shot, shoot to kill." He stood up so he could be seen. "We have you surrounded," he yelled. "I don't care about Jefferson, I just want Seven." There was no response. "Venturi was no match for me and neither are you. Come out with your hands up and I'll let you live."

Again, no response.

Jensen's men used his words as a diversion to keep moving up the mountain. They were now almost even with the rock formations Jefferson and Seven were hiding behind.

"They're in place," Scarlet radioed. "It will be like shooting fish in a bowl."

Jefferson popped his head up from behind the rock and quickly dropped back down. Bullets flew all around him.

"I see you're still a man of your word," Seven yelled. "You were a cheating little peckerwood fifteen years ago and you haven't changed."

Jensen was crimson with rage. He began kicking the rocks and dirt all around him. No one was going to insult him, especially in front of his men.

"He's losing it," Scarlet radioed.

"Wait for his command and let them have it," Seven ordered.

Jensen thought he heard one of his men snicker in his earpiece.

"Kill the son of a—"

Before he finished his sentence, his men started dropping. When he saw them hit the dirt, his face turned ashen. Suddenly it was dead quiet.

"Pigeons are down," Scarlet radioed.

"I want an affirmative from everyone," Seven said.

"Everyone on the left is accounted for," Tag radioed.

"Same on the right flank," Fitz said.

"Jefferson and I will cause a diversion," Seven radioed. "When we do, I want everyone to drop from your perch, but stay hidden until I tell you to show yourself." He removed the dart clip from his gun and replaced the clip with one that contained live ammo. He pulled back the slide and chambered a round. "On my mark, Jefferson."

"I'm with you, Sev. Let's make him dance."

"Everyone in place?" Seven radioed.

"Affirmative."

"Now," Seven ordered.

Bullets rained all around Jensen. They struck the rocks and dirt by his feet and when he tried to run, they clipped at his boots. He fired wildly uphill, shooting out of frustration. Shots were fired over his head, one grazing his scalp. His firearm empty, he dropped to the dirt, covered his head with his arms and curled up in a ball waiting for the fatal shot.

Silence returned. When he had the courage to look, he thought he was seeing things. Five, not two stood fifteen feet in front of him, pointing their guns at his head.

"Keep your hands above your head and stand up, Private," Seven ordered.

Jensen was freaked out. He couldn't believe he had been out-maneuvered. Even in his fear, his bravado was still intact. He eyeballed Seven as he stood. "I knew you couldn't take me alone. You were always weak. Always hiding behind your men."

Seven remained unfazed. "Tag and Fitz, keep your guns on him. If he as much as blinks, shoot out his eyes. Jefferson, cuff and shackle him."

Jefferson reached into his pants pockets and produced two sets of cuffs. "My pleasure."

He grabbed Jensen by the arm and Jensen spit in his face. "You always were just a dumb ni . . ."

Jefferson cold-cocked him in the jaw before he could finish the word. Jensen lay face down in the dirt. "I know you said not to touch him, Sev, but he had it coming."

Seven smiled. "Yep, I guess he did."

He looked at his squad. "The rest of you, bag and tag the other men and drag them to the hangar. Work in pairs. We don't want to get sloppy now."

An hour later, everyone reconvened in the hangar. Jensen's men's injuries had been attended to and those who had been hit with the tranquilizer darts had come around. They were cuffed and shackled and sat along the side of the hangar.

Jensen was hanging in the middle of the room from a chain attached to the ceiling—his hands cuffed above his head.

Seven grabbed a chair, dragged it to the middle of the room, straddled it, and looked up at Jensen.

"It's good to be home, isn't it, Private?"

Jensen just sneered back at him. His eyes were full of hate. He smirked and said, "I bet that's what Venturi said when he reached the pearly gates."

"He's alive, you moron. Do you think you could actually kill the leader of the Black Militia?"

Seven's words made Jensen's face turn deep purple with rage. A guttural scream emanated from deep within and spewed from his throat.

Seven waited for his theatrics to calm down. "It seems the colonel was right," he said. "Everything ends as it began."

"What the hell is that supposed to mean?" Jensen spit.

"It means it ends here. You and me, the way you always wanted it," Seven drawled.

Seven's drawl brought out Jensen's southern roots. He poured it on like homemade syrup. Yanking at the chain above his head, he said, "It seems you got me at a little disadvantage. Is this the way you win all yer fights."

Seven stood and tossed the metal chair to the side. "Jefferson, toss me the keys."

Without taking his eyes off of Jensen, a set of keys landed right in the middle of his palm. Seven spit as he walked next to his prisoner. He reached up, unlocked one cuff, and then handed the keys to Jensen. The private removed the other cuff and then unlocked his ankle chains.

He circled Seven, rubbing his wrists where the cuffs had dug into his flesh. Jensen stretched his neck from one side to the other, causing a cracking sound. He started dancing around on his toes as he circled Seven. "I'm gonna enjoy this," he said. "I've been dreaming about this for a lot of years."

Seven stood rock still in the middle of the room, just watching Jensen's moves. Seven wondered if Jensen still gave away his actions with his eyes. He didn't wonder for long.

Jensen closed his hands tighter, white-knuckling his fists. Seven guessed the first flurry of punches was about to come, but he didn't move. Jensen danced right and then countered left, swinging for Seven's chin. With a slight head nod, Seven evaded the worst of the punch. Still, it hit him enough to cause his lip to bleed. The sight of Seven's blood had Jensen flushed with excitement, spittle flew from his mouth as he continued to attack.

Seven countered with a weak punch that Jensen blocked with ease.

Jensen laughed. "You were old fifteen years ago, now you're just pathetic."

Seven stood flat footed as Jensen came forward to attack. This time a kidney punch came from his left and Seven moved just enough to deflect most of the force. Seven dramatically doubled over and grabbed his side and let out a painful grunt.

Jensen's men, seeing their leader beating this man, started yelling for blood.

"Kill him, Falcon," one yelled.

"He ain't nothin'," another screamed.

Seven still holding his side, kept his eyes squarely on Jensen.

"What's he doing?" whispered Tag. "Should we help?"

Jefferson smiled a toothy grin. "Na, he's just bringing the pig to slaughter."

With Seven clutching his side and breathing hard, Jensen rushed him with a wide circling uppercut. Just before impact, Seven dropped to one knee and kicked Jensen with his other leg in a sweeping motion, taking out his opponent's right knee. The snap could be heard echoing off the cement walls.

Jensen fell in a lump at Seven's feet.

He finger pointed in Jensen's face. "Never underestimate an opponent."

He turned to walk away and Jensen moved his hand to his boot, sliding a small concealed semiautomatic from his leg. Seven turned, slid a knife from its sheath behind his back and threw it before Jensen had time to draw. The blade pierced his hand, pinning it to his calf.

Seven looked at Jensen, the defeated men, and then at his own squad. "Put a call into Q. Tell him we have a garbage pickup."

CHAPTER 68

Brent and Alana had spent the first ten days at Alpha Camp. Brent's leg had been placed in an air-cast provided by Q when he came to evacuate the others. They spent their down time getting reacquainted. They both agreed that time was needed and they would start fresh as friends. The past four days were spent in the Vatican meeting world religious leaders. A meeting no one thought possible— a meeting only the Ambassador could have organized.

Brent and Alana approached the entrance to al-Qal. Brent walked with a noticeable limp from his still healing leg.

"All your weapons have been checked?" Brent asked.

Alana rolled her eyes and adjusted the jacket she wore. Her weapons were hidden underneath. "You know they have. I've checked them, you've checked them, and I checked them again."

"I don't want to take any chances. This mission needs to be fast and without flaw."

"The only thing that can go wrong is if the authorities have not received the message from the Vatican," Alana said.

"They have," Brent assured her. "No one has seen Omar leave since he returned from the Hindu Kush Mountains. Intel tells us that he escaped with twenty of his best soldiers." He looked at Alana looking for signs of stress or anxiety; he saw none. "Our attack will be straight on, nothing deceptive. If we attack fast and with precision, they will have no time to mount a defense."

Alana shrugged her shoulders, adjusting her coat. "Let's go, I'm looking forward to getting rid of some of this excess weight."

Brent allowed himself a slight smile at her wit and then his expression turned to stone.

They walked side by side into the ancient structure and quickly made their way to an area blocked by a no admittance sign. Without hesitation, Brent moved the sign and led the way down a stone stairway. The stairs were hand chiseled, narrow, and built at uneven angles. As they made their way down the steps into the bowels of the Khan, they each drew their first gun.

Brent used his free hand to stop Alana as he heard footsteps fast approaching. They hid in the shadows of the stairwell until they were sure the men were close. He held up four fingers letting Alana know the number of men he heard.

She watched as Brent held his hand out, fingers splayed apart. He slowly closed one finger at a time until his hand was balled in a fist. The sign of attack.

As soon as his fist was made, they sprang out of the shadow and fired tranquilizer darts at the men. They hit the ground before they knew what happened. Without checking, they stepped over them and continued down the musty passageway. The catacombs under al-Qal continued to spiral deeper and deeper into the earth.

Brent suddenly pushed Alana against the wall as he heard footsteps approaching. On his mark, they pushed away from the wall and dropped five more of Omar's guards. They holstered their spent weapons and retrieved fresh ones from inside their coats.

Brent led Alana down another passage making their way closer to Omar's lair. As they were about to turn the next corner, shots were fired, clipping the stone wall in front of them. Brent and Alana dropped to the stomachs and inched their way behind a stone pillar. Brent pointed to the far upper right corner of the tunnel where a lone gunman was perched. They saw a red laser scan the ground around them. Brent signaled that he was going to cause a diversion. On his mark, he ran from the pillar to the far side of the tunnel, firing his weapon the entire time. The gunman reacted by adjusting his position. His movement signaled his demise. Alana rolled in the opposite direction, went to one knee and put a dart in his forehead. He struck the ground before he could get off a single shot.

Brent heard more footsteps and signaled Alana to stay where she was. Brent and Alana mowed them down before they could get within fifty feet.

Five more down. That left five if their intel was correct.

Brent figured Omar would be well guarded. The last of the Brotherhood would probably be with Omar, but he wasn't taking any chances. He and Alana snaked their way through the labyrinth of tunnels until they were just outside Omar's 'home.'

Darkness engulfed the area ahead of them. Brent signaled Alana to close her eyes and cover her ears as he reached for a concussion grenade. It wasn't loaded with explosives, it just caused a deafening sound and a blinding light when detonated. Without hesitation, he pulled the pin, counted to five and let it fly. It went off before it hit the ground. Screams of pain could be heard from inside the room. Brent and Alana ran to opposite sides of the entrance and fired at the blinded guards. For the first time since they entered the catacombs, Brent spoke.

"All of your men are down." He heard Omar scurry under his desk. "Is that how the leader of the Brotherhood acts, like a trapped mouse?"

Omar stood and wiped the dirt from his throbe. He had the look of someone who would die with dignity . . . until he saw Alana. "How dare you desecrate my home by bringing a woman here," he raged.

Alana stepped forward, waving her gun at him as she walked. "I'm more than just a woman," she said, "I'm a Jewish woman."

Omar shook with hate.

"But," she continued, "you can think of me as your executioner if that makes you feel better."

Brent moved a chair towards Omar. "Relax and take a seat. The two of us need to have a conversation."

"If the Ambassador can stand, so will I."

"Have it your way," Brent said.

Alana made her way around the room, cuffing the unconscious guards.

Defiance shown in the old man's eyes. He wanted to goad Brent. "What do you wish to talk about? The way my men killed your wife?"

Brent ignored the barb.

"Or maybe the way the Brotherhood infiltrated your precious organization?"

Again Brent did not respond.

Omar shook with rage. "Speak to me!" he screamed.

Brent wiped his hair back from his face and stared into Omar's eyes. "You have to pay for your crimes."

"I supposed you and your whore are going to make me pay?" Omar asked.

Alana lurched forward and backhanded Omar across the face. She yanked the old man's hair back, pulled a knife from her belt and placed it against his throat. "Call me that again," she seethed, "and I will cut out your tongue."

Brent slowly placed his hand on top of Alana's to calm her. As he felt her muscles start to relax, he slid the knife from her hand.

Beads of perspiration dripped from Omar's forehead as he tried to compose himself.

"My plan," Brent said, "is to bring you in front of a court of law and let them decide what the best punishment is."

"And what court would that be?" Omar asked. "The American system that is wrought with dishonesty?"

"Actually, I thought I would give you a choice," Brent said, "you can either be brought before an international court in Geneva and be tried for your crimes of terrorism, or you can stand in front of a court of your peers."

"My peers?"

"A court of religious leaders. Muslim, Jewish, Buddhist, and Christian. They would decide your fate."

Omar erupted in laughter. "I will take my chances before the religious council. The leaders you speak of are weak and can be twisted to my will."

Brent approached the man, cuffed him and said, "So it is spoken."

Outside al-Qal stood a regiment of the Swiss Guard. Omar began to scream when he saw them. He now knew his fate rested in the Vatican, a political and prison system, which was known for its harsh rulings. He looked back at Brent with a glint of defeat in his eyes.

"You will spend the rest of your life next to what you have fought for all your life," Brent said. "The Vatican prison is next to the some of the greatest religious treasures this world has. I have arranged for them to be placed in a glass room just outside the cell you will be in. You will be forced to look upon them without being able to touch them until your dying day."

With his final words, he delivered Omar to the Swiss Guard and he and Alana turned, walked away and didn't look back.

CHAPTER 69

Two days later, everyone stood around the mausoleum as President Dupree was about to speak. It had been thirteen years since his wife lost her battle with pancreatic cancer. As much as he missed her, he was glad she wasn't alive to witness the horrors brought about by the Omega Butcher, especially their own daughter's capture and fight for survival.

He looked at Scarlet, a woman now, a strong, resilient, patriotic woman. He then turned and smiled in Brent's direction. The man who saved his family more times than he could count. He knew that Brent had saved his daughter when he himself was powerless to do so.

A tear rolled down his cheek. A tear of gratitude, a tear of happiness, a tear of cleansing.

He thought about what Brent and I talked when he returned from his 'sabbatical.' He cleared his throat. "It's true," he said, "we must all go back to the beginning to find our way. We must go back to the beginning in order to understand our present and choose our future." With that introduction, he wiped his tears and began his speech. "We have come here to honor Sarah Stetson Dupree, a woman who was more than a wife and a mother," his eyes met Scarlet's, "she was our rock. It took something Brent said to help remind me of that fact and for that I will be eternally grateful."

He opened his Bible and read, "Isaiah 28:16. 'So this is what the Sovereign Lord says: See, I lay a stone in Zion, a tested stone, a precious cornerstone for a sure foundation; the one who relies on it will never be stricken with panic.' "

He closed the book and spoke of his wife and their life together for the next fifteen minutes. The president then thanked everyone for taking the time out of their lives to commemorate an important day in his life.

As everyone was leaving Arlington National Cemetery, Joan took Brent's free hand. His other was clutching a cane. "Will you go with me?" she asked.

"You know I will."

They broke off from the rest and walked toward where Joan's mother, Monica, was laid to rest.

"I haven't been here since she died," Joan said.

"I know," Brent answered.

"You know why?"

"Yes."

Joan was hoping for more from Brent, but he was short with his answers.

"Is that all you're going to say? No words of wisdom. No sage advice from the one President Dupree just called the cornerstone."

Brent smiled. "You caught that did you?"

Joan bumped him with her hip. "Nothing gets by me, you know that."

Brent stopped walking as they neared Monica's gravestone. "Then, you know why I am saying so little. This is between you and your mom. Only you have the words needed to make everything right," he touched her head and her chest, "in here and in here."

Joan took a deep breath and turned to look at her mother's stone, but she didn't move.

Brent took her face in his hands. "If you think she knew anything about what happened to you, let's turn and walk away." A tear rolled down Joan's cheek. With tenderness, Brent thumbed it away. "But, if you know in your heart that she was blind to it, that she knew nothing about it, then you owe it to her and to yourself to make this right."

Joan looked up at him and nodded.

"I'm going to visit Chloe's grave while you go talk to your mom," Brent said.

"Closure," Joan said.

"Something like that," Brent responded.

Joan walked to the gravesite and knelt in front of the stone.

When they came together again, Joan's eyes were red and puffy from crying, yet there was a radiance about her. She hugged Brent tighter than she had ever and called him 'Dad' for the first time.

"I will always love you as my daughter," he whispered. "Let's go home."

Joan looked and saw Alana holding Faith in the distance. She waved at them and looked at Brent. "A new beginning," she said.

He didn't answer. He just took her by the hand and went to join the others.

EPILOGUE

Two years later, Brent, Alana and Faith walked hand and hand as they crested a hill. In front of them stood a magnificent church. As they walked near, a group of priests stopped what they were doing and bowed in reverence. The clergy wore the garments more suited for rabbis than priests. St. Mary of Zion was steeped in Hebrew tradition. Although these religious men were followers of Christ, they still followed the laws of Moses.

The three walked through the church and out the back door where they laid eyes on a small stone building adorned with a small cross, the original St. Mary of Zion church. In front of the church was a small fenced-in courtyard in which an old priest sat. He was known as the Guardian. The one true keeper of the Ark of the Covenant.

The Guardian stood and opened the gate to the courtyard as Brent approached. The other priests began to mumble when they saw this gesture. No one but the Guardian was allowed inside the sacred courtyard. Brent stepped through the gate as Alana and Faith waited.

The two men embraced.

"No one since your great-great grandfather has been inside this grotto except the Guardians."

Brent nodded in reverence.

"But as it was for him and my grandfather, it is for you and me. Exceptions for the Ambassador are made." He looked around as if he was searching for something. "I hoped you would have brought the Ark home to rest, but you alone will know when it is time."

"My reason for coming," Brent said, "was to tell you that it is not time. Too many are still in search of the Ark for all the wrong reasons. I do not know who will return it or when it will be returned, but I wanted to tell you personally."

Brent expected to see sadness in the man's eyes, but instead, he saw joy. The Guardian was looking past Brent and his vision was locked on to Faith's.

She waved.

He squatted down and asked her to come to him. She looked up at Alana who told her it was all right. Faith walked inside the gate and took her father's hand.

The Guardian used a soft hand and brushed her hair away from her face. "And the child shall be called Faith," he whispered.

Brent squatted next to him. "How did you know my daughter's name?"

The Guardian smiled. "She looks just like your great-great grandmother and her name was Faith."

Brent was surprised. He had never known his great-great grandmother's name nor had he ever seen her picture. Brent squatted next to the two of them. "But that's not all, is it?" he said.

The Guardian wiped Faith's hair from her face once more. Along her hairline was a small red mark, a five-pointed star. "She wears the mark."

"The mark?" Brent said.

The monk nodded. His words became breathy. "The mark of the one who will change the world." He stared into the eyes of Brent. "The mark of the one who will usher in a new beginning, the mark of the Cornerstone."

COMING WINTER 2013

SIN

THE SINCLAIR O'MALLEY SERIES

BOOK ONE

J.M. LEDUC

CHAPTER ONE

The smells of the fish pier permeated Alex Bell's olfactory senses as he stepped out of the black sedan: salt, suntan oil, diesel fuel and the fresh catch of the day. If he inhaled deep enough, he could smell something else—death. His eyes darted back and forth, quick to survey his surroundings. He walked toward the beach and could hear the sound of the sand crunch under his black wingtips. The seagulls and palm trees gave the perception of tranquility. Everything he smelled, heard and saw should have brought back fond memories of his childhood, but they didn't. Approaching the yellow crime scene tape, he knew his memories of the Florida Keys had been washed away for good—washed away by the death of three of his best agents and two Coast Guard officers.

The local police chief, Ezekiel Miller stood just on the other side of the crime tape. Alex pulled his credentials out of the inner pocket of his suit coat and flashed them toward Miller. The chief briefly glanced at the badge, took the well-chewed toothpick out of his mouth, and slid his mirror-lensed imitation Ray Bans down his reddened, bulbous nose.

"Federal Bureau of Investee-gation, huh?" He looked around at the small town fishing pier. "You boys must be slow. Guess you must of caught all them bathrobe wearin' sand niggers that bombed the good ole U.S. of A.?"

Internally, the police chief's language or lack of it scratched Alex's conscience like nails on a chalkboard. Externally, his appearance didn't change one iota. He slipped his badge back inside his jacket and continued to stare at the pear-shaped, potty-mouthed, star-wearing inbred.

Alex lifted the crime tape and stood close enough to the sheriff to tell what shade of gray his 'white' tee-shirt was. "One of the things we're taught during our training is to multitask," he said.

Chief Miller cocked his head to the side like a confused hound dog.

"You know," Alex continued, "like being able to eat fried foods and smoke cigarettes at the same time. That sort of thing."

Miller tossed the toothpick on the ground and popped a new one in his mouth. He poked Alex in the chest with his finger. "You makin' fun of me?"

Alex glanced down at the sheriff's finger and back up to his sunburned face. "Before things get out of hand, let's get three things straight." He held up one finger. "I want to be here as much as you want me here, so the sooner you can answer my questions, the sooner we can end this 'friendship.' Two," another finger went up, "I'm here because five men have washed up on the shore of your little hamlet. All dead and . . ."

"We can't help it when tourists try to go fishin' in bad weather and capsize their boat."

Still holding up his two fingers, Alex was beginning to lose his cool. "They didn't drown, asshole; they had been drugged and shot in the back of their heads from close range."

Miller moved the toothpick from the left side of his mouth to the right using his tongue. "Them bodies just washed up yesterday, how you know all that?"

"It's called forensics. Now, what I would really like is for you to show me exactly where you found the bodies and then I want you to take me to where their boat was impounded."

"Wait," Miller smirked, holding up two of his own fingers, "that's only two, what's number three or did you miscount?"

Alex removed his sunglasses and snarled at the sheriff. "Three, you ever poke me again or touch me in any fashion, I will rip your finger off and shove it so far up your ass, it will take you a month to shit it back out."

He didn't wait for a response, just turned toward the water and walked towards the CSI officers.

CHAPTER TWO

The funeral service was well underway when the minister was interrupted by the deep rumbling of a motorcycle's exhaust. As it neared the gravesite, a few mourners shook their heads, and a few others stifled a grin.

Frank Graham, the director of the Federal Bureau of Investigation kept his head down, but peered over his shades at the rider as she killed the engine of her 1952 Harley Davidson Panhead. The late morning sun reflected off of the bike's white pearlescent paint and onto her mirror-lensed sunglasses as she swung her leg off the saddle. She stood next to her bike, removed her helmet, and shook out her long, dirty-blond hair. Arching her back to stretch, her curves caught everyone's eyes.

A voice chirped in his earpiece. "She's headed your way."

The preacher looked back down at the *good book* and finished reading from Psalms 23. Finished, he closed the Bible and looked around at the hundreds of people who were gathered. "Even though Alex didn't have any living blood relatives, I would be remiss by saying he had no family." He spread his arms at the sea of humanity. "His family is here paying tribute to his life and mourning his passing."

When the service was over, the blond biker walked toward the casket, removed the black glove from her right hand and with a tenderness that was antithetical to her demeanor, placed a white rose on the mahogany coffer.

She stood and turned from the gravesite and faced her past.

"I'm surprised to see you here, Agent O'Malley."

She removed her sunglasses and eyed the man from top to bottom and back again. "Nice suit. Did 'Men In Black' have a wardrobe giveaway?"

She replaced her glasses and attempted to leave. She didn't get ten feet before 'clones' of the first blocked her path.

"Is this the game we're gonna play, Frank?" she asked.

"This isn't a game, Agent. I need you to come in and I'm willing to do what is necessary to make that happen."

Sinclair O'Malley stood eye-to-eye with Frank Graham, ripped her glasses off and burned a death-stare into his flesh. "I'm no longer an employee of the bureau or the United States, so cut the bull with the agent crap."

Graham didn't blink, he just smirked. "You left us no choice, Sin. You broke every directive you were given. You went so far outside the system, you're lucky you weren't brought up on charges."

Her jade green eyes pierced Graham's shell. "What's with the 'us' shit? It was your testimony that put the nail in my coffin." She snapped her head toward the other agents. "In fact, Alex Bell was the only man with enough balls to stand by me. The rest of you empty-sack bastards can go to hell." She again addressed Frank Graham. "I came to pay my respects to the only man worthy of them. Now if you will excuse me, I'll be on my way."

"It's not that easy, O'Malley," Graham said. "We have unfinished business and I need to take you in."

Sin took a step toward her bike. Again the agents moved in, each with their hand on the grip of their holstered weapons.

"That's not a card you want to play, Frank," she said. "Do you think I would just show up alone?"

Graham snickered as he stepped closer to Sin. "We have this cemetery surrounded. You have nobody."

The left side of Sin's full lips turned upward as she returned the snicker. "You want to roll the dice on that one?"

Graham pushed a button on his jacket. "Any sign of hostiles?"

"Negative," came the voice in his earpiece.

Sin stepped toward her ex-boss.

He could smell her perfume mixed with sweat. The aroma, seductive and evil, drained the color from his face. He closed his eyes, scrunched his nose, and exhaled through his nostrils.

"We can both piss into the wind," Sin said, "you can let me walk out of here, or you can tell me what this little *show* is really about . . ." Frank opened his mouth to speak, but Sin continued, "because we both know you have nothing on me."

Sin shouldered her way past the other agents and began to straddle her bike. Graham stood, wide-stanced, and placed his hands on the handlebars. Sin settled into her seat, crossed her arms across her chest and waited. Her eyebrows went up and her head cocked to the side.

Frank dropped his head and shook it from side to side. "I want you to come back in," he mumbled.

Sin pulled on her earlobe with a well-manicured painted nail. "What was that? I don't think I heard you correctly."

He looked straight at her. "You heard me."

Sin leaned forward and kick-started her Harley.

"Damn you, Sin!" Frank yelled over the growl of the bike. "Turn that fucking thing off."

She tapped her gearshift with the toe of her left boot and began to let out the clutch.

"I said I want you back," he screamed.

Sin squeezed the brake and stopped her bike. "You see, that wasn't so hard, was it."

Frank bit his tongue. He wasn't about to give her any more ammunition.

"Follow me to headquarters and I'll fill you in."

"Why?"

"Why, what?"

"Why do you want me back?"

He looked around and eyed the other agents who were still loitering about. "I prefer to talk in private. Please—for Alex."

Sin nodded. "That's all you had to say."

ABOUT THE AUTHOR

Mark Adduci, writing as J. M. Leduc, is a native Bostonian, who transplanted to South Florida in 1985. He shares his love and life with his wife, Sherri and his daughter, Chelsea.

Blessed to have had a mother who loved the written word, her passion was passed on to him. It is in her maiden name he writes. When he is not crafting the plot of his next thriller, his alter ego is busy working as a professor at The Academy of Nursing and Health Occupations, a nursing college in West Palm Beach, Florida.

J.M. Leduc's first novel, "Cursed Blessing," won a *Royal Palm Literary Award* in 2008 as an unpublished manuscript in the thriller category. It was published in 2010. He has subsequently written "Cursed Presence" and "Cursed Days, books two and three of the *Trilogy of The Chosen*, as well as a novella, "Phantom Squad." He is a proud member of the Florida Writers Association (FWA) and the prestigious International Thriller Writers (ITW).

He loves to interact with his fans and can be reached at jm_ leduc@yahoo.com and on Facebook.